WATERFALLS — HAWAII

KELEA:
The Surf-Rider

A Romance of Pagan Hawaii

By
Alexander Stevenson Twombly

Author of "Hawaii and its People,"
"Masterpieces of Michael Angelo and Milton,"
Etc., Etc.

Fredonia Books
Amsterdam, The Netherlands

Kelea: The Surf-Rider A Romance of Pagan
Hawaii

by
Alexander Stevenson Twombly

ISBN: 1-58963-473-X

Reprinted from the 1900 edition

Fredonia Books
Amsterdam, The Netherlands
http://www.fredoniabooks.com

In order to make original editions of historical works
available to scholars at an economical price, this
facsimile of the original edition of 1900 is
reproduced from the best available copy and has
been digitally enhanced to improve legibility, but the
text remains unaltered to retain historical
authenticity.

To the

HAWAIIAN FRIENDS

who welcomed the author to their homes

in 1894,

and to all the SCHOLARS, native and foreign,
whose researches among the Traditions and Folk-lore
of the Islanders have made it possible to write
this story of their ancient manners and cus-
toms, this work is gratefully inscribed.

CONTENTS.

ILLUSTRATIONS.

KELEA:

THE SURF-RIDER OF MAUI.

CHAPTER I.

PU' ALOHA, THE FLOWER OF LOVE.

THE name *Pu' Aloha*, "Flower of Love," brings to us the vision of a beautiful girl, who, before the white man came, or the Hawaiian islanders flung their idols to the flames, became the idol of Hookama, the chief bird-catcher of Oahu.

The maiden, in all the unveiled charms of sixteen summers, stood looking seaward, her hand to her eyes, as if watching for signs on the sea toward the south. Although she lived in the family of Numuku, one of the high chiefs of Oahu, she was not his daughter, but a part of the spoils of one of his forays into a neighboring island.

Hardly able to walk when brought to the chief's household, she was a pretty child, with something in her blood unlike other Hawaiian infants—a strain perhaps of a forgotten foreign

ancestry. Numuku was attracted by her and
intended to rear her for a wife, when she
should become of marriageable age.

She was brought up in the chief's enclosure,
which contained his large grass house and the
smaller houses of his women and servants.
These habitations stood on an eminence about
a mile and a half from what is now the harbor
of Honolulu. A picturesque ravine bounded
the enclosure on the south, and even to-day
defies the transforming hand of civilization,
the one spot near the modern city that has
marks of its primitive beauty and simplicity.

Hedges of prickly pear in blossom still line
the zig-zag path from the plateau above. A
short turn leads under a mass of rock, Titan-
piled, dark in the shadows and covered with
trailing vines. It is the sweetest dell in all
the region. Wild roses dispute possession of
the soil with the brilliant *lantana*. Broad
leaves wave over bunches of ripe bananas.
Two grass houses, gray with age, stand on
either side of a stream that rushes noisily over
the stones. A solitary palm, rooted in the
rocks, sentinels a pool a little higher up the
stream ; it is the last remnant of a grove
which hung over sparkling Kapena, a bathing
place and reservoir of prolific springs on the
heights.

It is a place for dreams—dreams of the past, with fascinating flashes of bright color, mysterious valleys and beautiful traditions. Clouds overhang the hilltops or send atomizing showers to cool the vales. All Hawaiian myths and legends are whispered to the dreamer in this spot, secure from intrusion amid the hum of insects and the sweet odors of a semi-tropical afternoon.

A little more than a century ago, Numuku's possessions included this enchanting ravine and extended to the mountain top from the coast below. From the eminence on which his spacious, thatched house was placed, the eye, overlooking valley and plain, caught glimpses of the blue sea to the horizon, while near the shore a fringe of white foam, breaking over the reef, bounded his domain.

Within this range, he was almost absolute master. The life and death of his dependants were in his hands. He owed a sort of feudal allegiance to the king of Oahu, but that was all. Beyond the reef the open sea was common ground. Kuula, the fisherman's god, was above all chiefs and the king himself, in the wide ocean.

Dazzling indeed was Pu' Aloha in the sunlight, for the shining orb had often kissed her half-clad beauty, giving it a rosy hue. A child

of nature, always in the open air, full of the
exuberance of health, graceful in pose and
movement, unconscious of her own loveliness
and filled with the joy of all things about her,
she had grown like the flowers. Not a care
or a cloud had ever cast a shadow until this
hour over the brightness of her life.

She was brought up with an adopted son of
Numuku, the boy Hookama, six years her
senior, who was from her infancy her only
playmate. Together they enjoyed sliding
down the sides of the ravine, his arms around
her on the same sledge while his foot guided
their course. Together they wove garlands
of the dainty *lehua*, growing profusely in the
valley. Like a foster-brother Hookama carved
charms of bone for the maiden's neck and
made bracelets and anklets of glittering shells
for her limbs. Gradually her playfellow became a large part of her life ; the mystery of
young womanhood, breaking into her consciousness, revealed the beginning of a passion, undefined yet resistless, and as natural to her being
as the opening of a flower to the sun or the
cooing of a dove to its mate.

She had a house of her own, over which the
convolvulus clambered, and the few *wahines*
(girls) who served her were strictly charged
to talk with her only on household matters.

She was not haughty or unkind to them, but
they were her menials. The wrinkled crone,
who taught her to cook simple viands, to strip
the cocoanut and to stamp rude figures on *tapa*
(native cloth) was a genial soul with a pleasant
word for her *pua* (blossom), but beyond her
sphere as an instructor she was told to hold
her tongue.

Up to the time of our story, the girl knew
nothing of the disagreeable native world outside
her home. She might espy, when the atmosphere was clear, some of the hideous images,
gods guarding the wall of a temple on the hill,
but she thought of them as she regarded the
beetling crags to the north, in a sphere wholly
apart from her own.

Once in a while, some hard-visaged men, the
kahunas, medicine-men of the tribe, were
admitted to the chief's presence, but their
cruel functions were never mentioned in her
presence. When she passed any of these
creatures it was without fear or curiosity.
She turned her face away because she did not
like their looks.

She did not even know that there were
human sacrifices offered in the temples. All
the world outside the enclosure, except
glimpses of little villages and the sea, was an
unknown country. She had her pretty flowers,

her beloved ravine and her playmate ; why
should she concern herself about what lay
beyond ? She grew into an altogether bewitching princess, out of place perhaps among
pagans, but, like a certain flower found in
crevices of black lava, quite as choice and fragrant as many flowers planted in a more congenial soil.

One other of her attendants should be
mentioned ; a queer dwarf who lay at night
outside her grass house to guard it. She called
him Menehune*(brownie)and half believed that
he belonged to the good little people that she
had been told made gourds grow in a single
night and danced in the moonlight on the
mountains. He was a frolicsome fellow, and
true as steel to his young mistress. Pu' Aloha
was never at a loss for amusement when he
was at hand. He had slits in his ears and could
put his thumbs through them, letting his large,
uncouth hands hang down in front. His face
was embellished with several lines across the
nose and the cheeks, which he said he got in

---

* The Hawaiian language is most musical ; but, in order
to realize this, it must be borne in mind that, in representing
the words and names in our roman letters, the vowels take
the European sounds (a being *ah ;* e, *a ;* i, *ee ;* o, *o ;* and u, *oo.*)
Moreover, there are, as in Italian, no silent letters, each
vowel being pronounced. Thus, the word *wahine* is *wa-hi-
ne* : the name Menehune. is *Me-ne-hu-ne* ; etc.

the wars. His language was in monosyllables and signs, but for purposes of his own he really feigned to be more of a fool than he was.

Hookama, the playmate of Pu' Aloha, was a full-blooded native, adopted, as his name implied, by the chief Numuku. He had never been told who his parents were, nor did he care much to know. He was treated as the chief's son, and was full of life and vigor. He could beat many other chiefs' sons in throwing the spear and swimming in the surf. His physical proportions made him a marked figure among the higher retainers of the chief. He could climb precipices, leap chasms, and, because of his accomplishments in this line, Numuku made him his head bird-catcher, a pursuit requiring great daring and adroitness. He could cling to a reef while a dozen heavy seas swept over it, and in warlike prowess had already distinguished himself. In the last battle with a neighboring tribe, by his boldness and sagacity as a scout he enabled his chief to surprise in a rocky defile and cut off a hostile band, double the number of the chief's followers. He accepted of course the gods and traditions of his race. He liked best to listen when the old prophetess, one of the chief's household, chanted a *mele*, filled with the romance and myths which constituted a large part of the knowledge of the Hawaiians. Many of these fanciful and poetic stories he learned by heart, and often beguiled an hour of idleness with Pu' Aloha, by relating them to her. In these myths, he chose exceptional passages which tell of noble conduct and faithful attachment, in the midst of much that is cruel, false and vile. By an instinctive feeling, the grosser allusions and tales he kept from the maiden, as he would shield her from nettles and prickly shrubs in her play.

He fell in with most of the customs of the people, some of which need not be narrated; but there was one thing he abhorred. It was the manner in which the chiefs and priests obtained victims for sacrifice to the gods. The *mu* (assassin) stole up behind a feeble or defenceless native and clutching him by the neck or arms carried him off to death by strangulation.

This Hookama considered a most cowardly act. To stand one's ground and take the chances in a fair fight and then, if conquered, to meet even a horrible death in the *heiau* (temple) was a part of the savage's religion, but to take a man at unawares and throttle him, as a gift to the gods, seemed meaner than cowardice.

To such a playmate and companion Pu'Aloha
became a sort of divinity to be served and
honored. He was her vassal. He never
dreamed that she was like other maidens, to
be wooed and won by him.

Several weeks before the day when Pu' Aloha
stood looking seaward, Hookama had been
sent by his chief to Hawaii, the largest and
most southern island of the group, about two
hundred miles away. Ostensibly his mission
was to obtain some rare feathers of birds, not
found on the other islands.

The expedition was fraught with peculiar
danger because the king of Hawaii was
hostile to the king of Oahu, who was at this
very time fighting on the side of the king of
Maui against him. If a bird-catcher or any
other native from Oahu was caught on the
island of Hawaii he would certainly be sacrificed to the gods. Numuku knew this peril,
and for that very reason sent Hookama to meet
it. One of the chief's retainers, Paao by name,
had for a long time entertained a passion for
Pu' Aloha and kept an espionage over her,
becoming extremely jealous of her growing
intimacy with Hookama. Paao lived in a grass
house outside of the enclosure, and behind a
thick growth of cactus could act the spy. He
was keeper of the chief's mantles, and used

every pretext to present himself at the door of the big house.   Once he accosted the maiden, as she was seated under the *hao* tree near her house, weaving wreaths, but she merely looked up and replied carelessly to his flattery.   It was not long before his obtrusive attentions provoked her to repel him with an indignant answer.   After that, she conceived the utmost aversion toward him and avoided him whenever he approached.   He was a person of some hereditary pretension, tracing back his pedigree to a priest of the same name who migrated to the island in the eleventh century.   The maintenance of records of lineage among the chiefs and higher classes of the Hawaiian Islanders, is an incidental evidence of their intellectual superiority to other Polynesians, although it does not seem to have carried with it any pride of moral quality.   If indeed Paao was descended from this ancient priest, he inherited an unenviable legacy with the name, for not only was this distant ancestor well versed in sorcery but was of a most cruel and unscrupulous nature.

Pu' Aloha, wholly unsuspicious of evil, openly showed her partiality for the chief's bird-catcher, and Paao took advantage of this to poison the chief's mind against Hookama. Under the impulse of jealousy, Numuku determined to get rid of the young man. Hookama himself was greatly elated by the prospect of launching his boat at the chief's command to do a daring deed. He knew the danger but was eager to encounter it.

His canoe, hollowed out by his own hand from the trunk of a *koa* tree was staunch and sea-worthy. He had tested it in many a storm and amid the breakers. The sail was of stout matting, of a tri-form shape, and from the mast fluttered a colored streamer, suggestive of his rank. A rude image which he had roughly hewn from wood and which resembled neither god nor man—a kind of "totem," with a queer head and a human body—was lashed in the bow of the canoe. It was a fancy of his to ask oracles of it and give imaginary answers. The monster was the result of a sportive freak and afforded him amusement rather than any serious concern. He knew that only the highest chiefs could carry real images of the gods with them on their expeditions.

He loaded his boat with a few necessary supplies; calabashes of food, fishhooks, and lines of cocoanut fibre, a bird-catcher's outfit, his weapons, and a small mantle of yellow feathers, which he had secretly made for himself. He had some bright *malos* (girdles) and a roll of *tapa*.

Springing into the canoe, he pushed it into deep water with a light and brave heart, waving his paddle to the crowd of idle natives on the beach. Among them was Paao, who affected a great friendship for him and gave him a dagger made of a shark's tooth, valuable both for use and ornament. It had a poisoned tip, although Hookama was not aware of it. A light wind was blowing off shore, and, setting his mast and sail, the youth steered his craft through the single opening in the reef. Like a bird on the wing, lightly skimming the wave, the boat passed into the open sea.

Then Hookama climbed out and stood on the outrigger, and with dextrous motions, flourished his dripping paddle blade above his head, tossed it high and caught it in its descent. It was the signal of farewell that he had agreed to give Pu' Aloha, who was watching him from her perch in a tall *koa* tree, where he had made for her a rude resting place, with a netting which secured her from falling. She waved her bright red mantle as she saw each movement of his play in the clear atmosphere. Proudly she looked at his form and wondered at his skill. Then lying back in her nest she lost herself in a delicious languor of love and dreams.

But the glance which Hookama had given

to the bright red spot on the cliff was not lost
by Paao, who took his way sullenly along the
beach, muttering curses on his rival and striking with his stick every cowering native that
crossed his path. He was hated as much as
Hookama was liked by the common people.

Passing what is now called Koko Head,
Hookama lowered his sail to meet the seething waters of the Kaiwi channel between
Oahu and Molokai, where the currents and the
trade winds clash and keep the waves in violent cómmotion. Thrusting his paddle into
the contending billows he battled with them
as if revelling demons threatened to engulf
him.

The wind-god put him on his mettle under
the giant cliffs of Molokai. Ghouls and goblins of the dark caverns seemed to haunt the
shadows of overhanging rocks. Nothing
daunted, late at night on the second day of
his venturesome voyage, he reached the island
of Maui and landed at Waihee, once the lovely
inheritance of Namahana, daughter of the most
renowned king of Maui's long line of warrior
chiefs.

CHAPTER II.

KELEA, THE SURF-RIDER OF MAUI.

THE white sand of the beach was luminous in the full tropical moonlight, as our stalwart young savage strode up from the sea towards a line of lofty cocoa-nut palms. Beyond was a village of thatched huts, nestling in the midst of luxuriant foliage. He had drawn his canoe above the reach of the incoming tide and now sought a resting place for the night.

He was weary after his toilsome journey of many a score of leagues through the boisterous channels between his home on the island of Oahu and the island of Maui which he had never visited before. But there was an air of bravado in his swinging gait, for he was on a quest from his chief, which meant great honor if he succeeded, disgrace and perhaps death if he failed.

His brawny muscles were wet with the spray

HAWAIIAN GRASS HOUSE

of the breakers and his graceful form was un-
encumbered by any clothing save a *malo,* or
breech-cloth, around his loins. His face was
fine and prepossessing, for he was of royal
blood. His name, Hookama, the Adopted
One, gave no hint of his rank, but every
islander of the Hawaiian group would know at
a glance that he was no ordinary personage.

Approaching a large grass house, overrun
with vines, he was surprised to find the entrance open, no occupant within, and the remnants of recent feasting spread out on the
floor. Calabashes partially filled with food,
garments of *tapa* cloth and mats, heaped in
confusion, told of the hasty departure of the
owners of the house.

From the village of Waihee where he acci-
dentally landed, the famous queen Namahana,
with her husband, a warlike chief, had been
driven out by her half-brother, now king over
a large part of the island. She had lived here
in princely style; her gardens, taro patches
and palm groves were extraordinary in size
and luxuriance. Her possessions had passed
to a favorite chief of the usurper and were still
maintained in a royal way.

The youth Hookama was in too great need
of sleep to seek the cause of the disorder in
the house, which was evidently that of a chief-

tain : hastily partaking of the food, he flung himself on an irregular pile of mats and dropped into a deep slumber.

How long he slept he did not know, but when he awoke it was to find himself surrounded by a bevy of laughing damsels, profusely adorned with flowers and apparently enjoying themselves at his expense. The morning sun shone brightly through the doorway. The young stranger lay stretched on the mats and, as he awoke with a sudden movement and sat upright, the girls drew back and fell over one another in their effort to get beyond his reach. Their hurried movements showed that they had been too inquisitive in investigating the tattoo marks on his shoulders and breast in their curiosity to discover his rank.

A courtly salutation from the object of their scrutiny allayed their fears and gave them ample opportunity to recover their composure. They were a merry group, obviously from the better class of natives. One seemed superior to the rest and was the leader in their frolic. With well-rounded forms, clothed in the *pau*, the customary short skirt of the women of Hawaii, and some of them wearing bracelets on the wrists, they made a pretty picture as the youth gazed inquiringly into their faces and watched their graceful postures.

Their hair was short above the forehead ; long wavy locks fell over their shoulders, and there was a simplicity in their looks and actions which the life of high caste native women naturally produced. One or two might be the belles of the village. They were all of large frames, well proportioned. When they stood erect their figures had considerable style and beauty of outline. They were too large and plump for nymphs or fairies of civilized legends, but, judged by Hawaiian standards, were an attractive group.

Some of the younger girls began to giggle when the silence became embarrassing, neither party being prepared to begin a conversation. A few sidled towards the opening. They had no right to be prying about in a house belonging to the men, especially when a man was in it. When then a few of the more timid made a movement towards the door the whole bevy rushed out, and Hookama, following, saw them fleeing to the beach, where most of them plunged into the water like a flock of sea-birds and began to sport in the surf.

A part seized their surf-boards, pushed them through the nearer breakers, and then, lying down upon them, rode back to the shore. These boards were made by stone axes from hard *koa* wood, slightly hollowed and polished, broad enough to carry the body and from six to eight feet in length.

On these floats some even stood erect and balanced themselves as they were carried along by the smaller rollers. Their audacious struggles with the waves, their loud shouts when a big roller tumbled them over, and their comely shoulders rising from the sea, made the scene a lively one. The spray they tossed with their arms sparkled in the sunbeams, completing the beauty of the sight.

A few of these water-sprites, more daring than the rest, swam out beyond the combing breakers and disported themselves in deeper water. One or two chanced to find Hookama's canoe which he had left on the shore, and were examining its contents, carelessly left in the boat in spite of the fact that the people of Maui were known to be arrant thieves.

But these inquisitive damsels, happening to look back, saw Hookama coming from the chief's house and sprang away, leaping into the surf to join their companions in the morning bath. They, however, had found out by the scarlet cloak in the canoe that the stranger was a chief of high degree.

Hookama, accustomed to the merry games of water nymphs at Waikiki, a village on one

of the beaches of Oahu, needed no second impulse to run towards the group of mermaids
and soon was among them battling with the
breakers.

The girl he had noticed at the house as the
comeliest and the strongest, oblivious of everything but the joy of buffeting the waves,
suddenly found herself far away from the
others and looking out ahead was horrified to
see the back fin of a large shark cutting the
water and coming in her direction. With a
scream of terror she turned to the shore and
a huge wave, combing at that instant, enabled
her by vigorous swimming to increase the distance between her and her pursuer. She had
never known a shark to venture so near the
beach.

Then began a desperate race for life. The
girl was in deep water where a shark can
easily take its prey, and she knew that her
only chance to escape was to reach a sand-bar
which jutted out from the shore, although
quite a distance from where she was. Her
swimming was the admiration and envy of all
her companions on the island. Her courage
in the breakers was phenomenal; but now
her fright prevented her from using her
strength and skill. Her shrieks rent the air
and reached the ears of Hookama and the

wahines who cried out in terror when they saw the perilous situation.

Hookama, with no thought but to rescue the girl from the jaws of *Noa-alii*, the shark-god, plunged into the deep sea. The danger of the maiden inspired him with almost incredible strength. She was swimming in a direction parallel with the beach, and Hookama took a course nearly at a right angle to intercept the shark before it could snatch its prey. The shark was gaining rapidly in the race, but had some distance yet to compass. The approach of a new person diverted its attention only for a moment, and then it kept on, preferring, as sharks do, the lighter victim to the darker one.

The girl saw Hookama coming to her rescue. She counted the strokes of his arms as he swam. He called to her as loud as he could to keep up her courage. He had some experience in hunting sharks for sport, and knew their habits, but so great was the emergency that he could almost see in his mind's eye the awful jaws of the monster crunching the girl's flesh.

Moments passed which seemed hours, and the shark was lessening the space between it and the girl, who must yet go a considerable space to reach shallow water. To Hookama's relief, the fish suddenly turned and made for him. There was no fear or hesitation in Hookama's mind. He had never known what fear is, and, a shark—god or fish—mattered nothing to him so long as that girl's face, looking over her shoulder, was before his mind. She at least was saved from a horrible death.

Taking his shark's tooth dagger in his teeth —it had been fastened in his waist-cloth—he coolly awaited the monster's approach. The situation was a desperate one. Could he meet it at such odds? Removing the dagger from his mouth, he drew two deep breaths, treading water till he saw the shark, now close upon him, sink down in order to turn belly-upwards to enable his short under jaw to seize the legs of his prey.

There was a white flash under the clear water just where the shark disappeared. Hookama knew what it meant. Gleaming beneath the waves, a few feet below the surface, the terrific creature moved in a curve which would bring it up in a few seconds for its attack.

The water became troubled and foamy. It was difficult to estimate exactly the movements of the shark, but the youth, taking the only chance left to him, quick as lightning and by a muscular effort of which few athletes are capable, dove and swam under water—the dagger now in his right hand, and his eyes wide open—trying to gain a lower depth than the shark.

Fortunately, the shark did not turn wholly over, and the sudden dive of Hookama disconcerted the huge fish, so that when it passed the youth, it presented the belly side-wise, affording a wide surface for a thrust.

Instantly, Hookama jerked the dagger desperately through the soft flesh, and the rapidity of the shark's motion swept the sharp blade along, making a deep, lengthy gash. The young man rose to the surface some yards away and knew, by the splashing of the shark's tail above the waves and the bloody foam floating around it, that the contest was over.

With the reflection that it was a good thing to have a dagger at hand, since nobody can tell when it may be needed, Hookama swam by easy strokes to the sand-bank, to see how it fared with the girl. Looking back, he saw the shark still lashing the sea in convulsive throes, but its spasms gradually decreased until it lay lifeless on the surface, its huge bulk motionless except as rocked by the waves.

The rescued maiden reclined upon the edge of the sand-bar, where the ripples touched her feet. She was almost exhausted and but partially recovered from her fright. As Hookama approached, she raised herself on her elbow and shaded her eyes with her hand, as if from the glare of the sun, but in reality after the coquettish manner of a maid, who finds herself for the first time alone with a man towards whom she feels the awakening of a new sentiment.

When she tried to express her thanks, the youth laughed merrily and said : " It wasn't much of a shark after all. The shark-king must have sent one of his clowns in search of sport ; " but both he and the girl were glad that the " sport " had terminated without more mischief in it, so far as they were concerned.

Hookama could not take his eyes from the attractive maiden, who, on her part, was equally his captive. It was not so much the girl's fresh and rather handsome face that attracted the youth, as the pluck she had shown and the muscular proportions of her form. The eye of a savage cares less for fine curves and delicate lines in a woman, than for the robust contour which betokens strength of body and sturdy endurance. The two then swam leisurely towards the beach, and while Hookama praised her swimming, she, on her part, was wondering whether or not a shark-god, or any god, could compare in beauty and vigor with the hero who had saved her from the

tragic fate of a visit to the coral shades
below.

When they reached the shore she disen-
tangled the seaweed which clung to her dishevelled locks, and turning towards the ocean,
shook the glutinous mass and vowed an offering to *Kane-huli-koa* (god of the sea,) as she
laughingly said to Hookama, " Because the
deity had sent such a noble messenger to the
rescue."

The *wahines*, who in terror had watched
the exciting contest from the shore, were over-
joyed at the result.   They clustered about the
maiden, threw a *tapa* mantle over her shoulders,
and insisted that Hookama should return with
them to a house, which they pointed out as
the home of Kelea.   This was the rescued
girl's name; she was the daughter of the chief
of *Waihee*, and a descendant of the famous
Kelea, the surf-rider of Maui, celebrated in
the myths and legends of Hawaii.

When the party reached a large grass house,
the girls, drawing back a curtain of richly
stained *tapa* cloth from the opening, disclosed
an apartment of unusual size and decorated
with shells festooned from the rafters.   Other
evidences of feminine taste showed that its
owner was of the highest rank.

A wide couch of fine mats filled a corner of

the room. On this, the *wahines* asked
Hookama to lie down, that they might apply
to him the *lomi-lomi* process, by which the
muscles are made soft and supple and the
circulation of the blood quickened.

The girls annointed his body with fragrant
oils ; then they applied their strong hands to
the flesh, working the joints and manipulating
the muscles, all the while murmuring a chant
as their bodies swayed to and fro in their work.
The theme of their improvised measure was
the shark-god, *Kamoho-alii*, who could take on
a human form at will, and frequented the
waters around Maui; they assumed that
Hookama was this god and that he sent away
the shark that pursued Kelea, by his superior
authority.

When Hookama was rubbed and polished
to his supreme refreshment and content, Kelea
took his place for the same enjoyable ministrations, and he went out to take a good look
at Waihee and its surroundings.

Waihee Valley! How can it be described?
a paradise of verdure, with a ravine carpeted
in moss and decked with wild begonia; trailing vines and towering ferns, with the scarlet
blossoms of the *lehua* tree on every side;
picturesque, tropical, overshadowed by a lofty
mountain, and the ocean lapping its shores.

Few places, even in Hawaii, equal it in its variety and beauty of scenery.

There were numerous grass houses; the best of them for the chief and his attendants, and a hundred inferior huts for the natives. It puzzled the young *alii* (chief) that there were no canoes on the shore, no men lounging about and no women in the *taro* patches.

To be sure, it was early in the day, but not too early for village life. It was not long, however, before Hookama saw the bent form of an old man, with grisly beard, and a stick in his hand, emerging from one of the better class of the grass houses.

It proved to be a priest, left in charge of the *heiau*, or sacrificial temple. From him Hookama learned that the apparent desertion of the village was caused by the news of an impending battle, twelve or fifteen miles to the south. Kahekili, the king of this island of Maui, was awaiting an attack from the King of Hawaii, whose movements had been made known to him only a few days before.

"Even now," said the old man, "the canoes of the feather-war-capes are mirrored in the waves, and," covering his eyes with his shaky hand, "I see a bloody field and the *heiau* altars piled with victims."

Further conversation made Hookama acquainted with the expected arrival of his own king, Kahahana, the young *moi* of Oahu, who, as he knew, had left his own island the previous week, with a large reinforcement of warriors, to aid Kahekili, King of Maui, his wife's half-brother.

The aged priest pointed to a small *heiau*, and said he must go and pray for success to the arms of his chief; he also informed the youth that the chief to whom the King of Maui had given this beauitful estate of Waihee, hastily departed with all his men, his wives and servants, the day before. The infirm and some women and children had been sent with a guard to the hills. His daughter, Kelea, and the younger daughters of the lesser chiefs of the settlement remained.

"What," asked Hookama, "with you alone for a guard? As well leave tender fowls in charge of a toothless dog!"

"Ah!" answered the priest, "well enough may the soft plumaged birds stay with an old dog like me, unless a bird-catcher chances to set his wily snares for their capture;" and he looked at Hookama with a glance full of meaning, the word "bird-catcher," spoken at a venture, having brought a flush to the young man's cheek. By that word, the youth was sure that the old man was a *Kehuna-nui*, a diviner and sorcerer.

But the news of an imminent battle and of his *moi's* expected arrival on the scene, a few hours' march away, changed the whole current of his thoughts and plans. Hastily bidding the old priest "Beware of bird-catchers, and look well to the *alae* (sacred birds) and especially to the *uau* (a bird living near the water)," he hurried back to the house where he had left Kelea. Entering hastily he beheld her braiding her luxuriant tresses with bright flowers and displaying charms which he had but partially seen before. The delicate tint of her cheeks was heightened by the *lomi-lomi* process, and the softness of her eyes increased the young man's admiration as she met his gaze with an answering look of gratitude and constraint.

Hookama broke the silence when Kelea arose from the couch, as Hawaiian women always did in presence of their lords, by saying :—

"Yonder mountains are bright with the splendor of a victory ; Hookama is no slave even to the *uau* with soft plumage, that he should not serve her king and his own. Kelea is a pleasant name : it is like the ripple of the sea on the sands, but shall the spear be buried under the foam-crests because the bird-note casts a spell over the young warrior's heart ? "

The maiden saw in an instant what he meant, and that, though she fascinated him, he intended to tear himself away from her to do battle for his king. But it was not in her nature to repress the passions of her soul, for was she not the favorite and spoiled daughter of a great chief, and had not this handsome youth saved her from the awful shark-god, who would have carried her to the coral groves, his victim and his bride! Prompted by some quick intelligence of an easy conquest, the girl, with the right which Hawaiian women had to woo a backward lover for themselves, impetuously flung herself upon the half-abashed Hookama, and, before he could avoid her swift caress, he found himself a captive, the eyes of Kelea gazing fondly into his own, her rosy fingers clasping him and her wavy hair falling over his shoulders, as she laid her head on his breast and defied him to leave her.

She had already sent away the girls who attended her and when Hookama had returned, there was no one to intrude upon the scene.

For an instant he hesitated and the girl might have claimed him as her own by further advances, had not the passionate words springing to his lips been interrupted by a rush of footsteps and a hum of voices, as the whole party of *wahines* flocked pell-mell into the

house, clamoring for Kelea to come out and
command the old priest to promise not to tell
the chief that a young man had spent the day
with them.

"The old *kehuna*," they cried, "will do
what his royal mistress bids him ; or if he
won't, she can make this *alii* from Oahu kill
him, and we'll feed him to the sharks. Come,
come, Kelea, come quickly, and save us from
the miserable informer !"

But the baffled girl, her eyes blazing and her
breast heaving like a tempest ; abashed, too,
at being discovered with her arms about the
stranger, called out in shrill tones, "Away,
away ! Save you from the *tabu !* no, no !
The *kehuna* will keep his clutch on me, for he
has an old grudge against me already. If he
can hurt me through you, he will be satisfied.
Away with you all ! What is a score of
wahines like you to a *moi's* daughter like me !"
She hardly knew what she was saying, so violent was her anger.

Then she drew herself up to her full stature,
which gave her the dignity of an outraged
queen ; the maidens fled before her and in the
seclusion of a neighboring grove continued
their wailing cries. The old priest, meanwhile,
ascended to the *heiau*, muttering maledictions
on man or woman who defied the *tabu*.

This new attitude of Kelea not only re-
strained Hookama from further dalliance but
revealed to him the need of caution. Could
he enter into any intimate relations with a
woman who showed such supreme temper and
malignity in her nature towards those who
opposed her will?

"How different she is," he thought, as the
vision of one whom he had left behind flashed
across his memory, "from my 'Flower of Love'
in far off Oahu!"

It was therefore with something like a
repellant feeling that he looked at Kelea, as
his apprehensions deepened with the girl's increasing wrath. His great desire now was to
break away from the passionate creature who
had revealed to him the darker side of her
nature. While he could not help admiring her
magnificent manner, her violence quenched the
transient fascination which had cast its spell
over him. But he craftily spoke honeyed words;
bade her wait for his return, when as a victorious warrior he might lay his trophies at her
feet. He vowed most solemnly by the god of
war and a thousand deities besides, that he
would come back and be her captive, if she
would let him go to join her father and his own
king, the *moi* of Oahu. "No warrior," he said,
"will turn to love when the battle calls him."

"What do you give me in pledge of your promise?" asked the excited girl.

He had nothing except the shark's tooth dagger, but this he yielded readily and Kelea hid it away in the thatch of the wall, close by her couch.

"Remember," she said, as she touched noses with him for the last time and reluctantly released him from further embraces, "remember that Kelea will claim half your name (the bride-token), even if you flee from her to the farthest island towards the setting sun."

Hookama, glad to be released on any terms, hurried to the beach, replaced the mast, the calabash and other effects which the *wahines* had scattered around the canoe, and, setting the sail, after a last wave of his hand to Kelea, bade adieu, as he hoped forever, to the sweet valley of Waihee, where he had met with such unexpected and surprising adventures.

CHAPTER III.

NUMUKU, A CHIEF OF OAHU.

UNTIL very recently, the foster father of Pu' Aloha, if we may call by that name one who was meditating marriage with the maiden, had given no thought to the companionship that existed between her and the bird-catcher. His mind being now warped by the hints thrown out by Paao, he watched the girl in the absence of Hookama and vowed a rich *malo* for the loins of his god if the youth did not come back alive.

He was too shrewd to give the least hint to Pu' Aloha of his displeasure ; on the contrary he showed her special favor. He sent a bracelet of priceless shells to her house and planted a *tabu* pole in front of her door, as a mark of unusual attention. By this carved stake, ornamented at the top with a small streamer of white *tapa*, the house was *tabu* (forbidden)

to any one but himself. Whoever intruded
was liable to suffer death, and the pole could
be removed only by his own hand.

The girl was pleased at this mark of regard and
wove a special wreath of *lehua* blossoms with
which to receive him.   The uncouth, bronzed
bulk of the old savage contrasted strangely
with the lovely figure of the maiden, as she
rose at his coming and placed the chaplet over
the chief's neck.   There was a trace of nobility
under the rude lines of the man's face, and, as
he looked into the frank eyes of the girl, the
suspicion he had harbored almost disappeared
from his mind.

Something in her beauty overawed his
nature, accustomed as he was to the coarse
surroundings of his life. Were it not that
two of his front teeth were gone, knocked out
years before during the funeral obsequies of
his predecessor, his smile might have been
attractive as he recognized that his captive
had grown into a young woman of surpassing
loveliness.   Even a savage may be conscious
of a certain kind of inferiority in presence of
so fair a creature.

He felt a thrill through his pagan soul and
wondered if somehow a goddess were not
imprisoned in this beautiful body. He had
heard of such transformations, and for the
moment was overcome by a feeling of awe.

Seeing his peculiar expression, Pu' Aloha conceived the idea that she had a power over her master which he could not resist. She had a consciousness that she might control his actions, and it at first gave her the momentary enjoyment of a sense of undefined authority, without the least desire to exercise it. An instant later, she determined to use her power to make her union with Hookama sure.

Like a flash of dazzling light she sprang forward, seized a yellow mantle from the swinging line of twisted cocoa fibre above her head, and with a gesture of feigned deference, put it about the naked shoulders of the chief. Then drawing back, she bent a knee and saluted him as she had seen his retainers bow when he passed by.

A perplexed look came into his eyes as he sat down on a heap of mats. The maiden seated herself beside him, as she had often done, and playfully clasped her arms about the savage, fixing her eyes steadfastly on his. Nestling closely—for had he not always been kind to her?—she told him all the story of her new feeling for Hookama. It was the artless talk of a child who did not dream that it was wrong or contrary to his wishes for her to love the playmate of her youth; and yet there was a shyness in her manner which

made her speech rather hesitating and broken ;
a sort of natural modesty that added depth to
her words. While she continued her confidences she hid her face in a fold of the soft
mantle, so that she did not see the storm
gathering on Numuku's forehead.

She had no time to finish her story with
the request that she might have the young
bird-catcher for her own. She felt the thump-
ing of the massive chief's heart, and his body
swayed under her clasp, while an impatient
grunt issued from his lips, as if a latent evil
spirit worked within him.

Perceiving this unexpected change, and
dreading what it might portend, she faltered
in her speech for a moment and the next was
at his feet, embracing his knees. Shaking her
off, the chief arose to his full height ; the *tabu*
stick which he had brought in his hand fell to
the ground ; the mantle dropped and the tall
figure towered above the prostrate girl.

Terrified beyond measure, Pu' Aloha cowered
upon the floor, not daring to raise her eyes to
the face of the displeased chief. Why he was
angry with her she did not know. It was the
shrinking away from the gaze of its master of
a dog that has received a blow without under-
standing why it was given.

But when Numuku made an angry gesture,

leaning toward her with a manner full of warning, she leaped to her feet, and, regaining her self-command, drew herself up with the air of a queen and disdainfully confronted him. She looked at him with superb scorn, as much as to say: "Touch me as you would touch a goddess."

Then softening, and remembering that her power lay in her fascination, she asked in soothing tones: "Why look thus terribly on me, thy flower of love (*pua aloha*)? What has the tender blossom done to cause the storm to burst upon it?"

The chief, in sputtering gutturals, too angry to speak clearly, replied in a single word which he spit at her; it was the name of him she loved—Hookama! But the way he uttered it, as if he loathed the man who loved the flower to which he had no claim, nerved the heart of the girl. Realizing the true object of his wrath, the courage of her now fully-blossomed love enabled her to confront the savage without a tremor or a fear:

"Deny me, O Numuku, and I defy you!"

She snatched a shark's tooth dagger from the thatched wall where its handle protruded, and held its point to her breast, as she retreated with her eye on the chief.

Amazed at her intrepid spirit, with the cunning of his race the strong man assumed the manner that was usual with him in her presence and burst into a loud laugh—a guffaw it might better be called—and, quietly settling down again upon the mats, shook his sides as if trying to suppress his mirth.

" It was my jest with you, child! To see what stuff was in you. My little flower, think you the lightning strikes a leaf when it can rend a pandanus tree? I would defend you even against the great god Lono. Hookama is my adopted, just as you are."

Then drawing her to him, leaving the sharp dagger in her hand as if it were a plaything which it did not concern him to notice, he laid his large, hard hand, which had wielded many a weapon, soothingly on her fair head.

" The man that harms thee is doomed to the ' breaking of bones ' before the sun goes down."

Seeing that she was reassured by his words and manner, he proceeded to tell her of a custom in the land which allowed a woman two protectors; one, to be like the personal attendant of a chiefess; the other, a lover to whom the woman is consecrated by a ceremony. Both are equal in a sense, but with unequal privileges unless the woman wills otherwise.

" Trust me, my Aloha!" concluded the old

deceiver, making a grimace under his mask of smiles, but unperceived by the girl whose face was hidden in her hands : " I will be your protector. Hookama shall be your servant—your bamboo flute, to play on as you list—your lover if you will—while I defend you both against all ill."

The gutturals and croaks of the old man were as music to the ears of Pu' Aloha, for they told her that Hookama would be hers. The custom of the land made no difference to her and awakened no repelling emotion, since she hardly thought of it in her ecstasy of hope.

Springing again to her feet, she gracefully twisted her body as if to inaudible music, in token of her desire to please the old man who sprawled on the mats. Then roguishly eyeing him, she took the wreath from his neck and scattered the thousand fragrant petals over the room, finally tripping from the house to sit down under the spreading branches of her favorite *hao* tree and think over the blissful future. She had quite forgotten even the existence of Numuku.

As for him, no sooner had her form faded into the evening twilight than he gathered himself up, pulled his great ears and went to his own house.

Once inside and the *tapa* across the doorway, he clutched a two-handed club, swung it around his head in a frenzy of fury, as if slaying an imaginary foe. The contortions of his face showed that wrath overmastered for the time any tender feeling towards his adopted child, who up to this hour had been as the apple of his eye.

At last, regaining a measure of composure, with a scowl which by no means heightened the beauty of his countenance, he muttered to himself: " Priceless feathers in the helmet of my god, when Hookama's heart is torn out by the roots and laid on the altar!" With that he tumbled in a heap, and the guard who had come to the door knew by the accustomed sounds that the chief had departed to the land of unquiet dreams. The souls of sleepers were supposed to leave their bodies, to wander in realms remote and sometimes not the most agreeable.

This time, Numuku's soul went forth into the night, attended by sounds as harmonious as the blare of the conch shell, calling warriors to the battle.

The old fellow had his moods. Unless angry, he was good natured. By no means was he as cruel as many of the chiefs. He had also considerable self-control when he could gain his

ends by holding in his wrath. Usually indo-
lent, apparently indifferent, he ruled his sub-
jects leniently enough, provided they brought
him the regular supply of food and drink.

ends by blotting out twenty. Visually indistinct, apparently indifferent, he takes his sub-jects and they one day provided that, brought him out on plan, a supply of literal and what

CHAPTER IV.

THE BATTLE OF THE SAND HILLS.

HOOKAMA, having started from Waihee in the morning and having less than ten miles to sail in a southeasterly direction, arrived before the sun was high, in the offing outside Kahului Bay.

Here an exciting scene presented itself. Hundreds of war-canoes, double and single, some with triangular sails set and pennons flying, some propelled by a score of warriors, were hurrying towards the beach, their pace accelerated by a fresh wind from the north. The sea was covered with white caps and the billows rolled high, their crests often enveloping in foam the frail crafts that battled with them for the mastery.

Bronze figures, with red and yellow feather helmets, stood erect in their canoes, steering with paddles and apparently oblivious of the spray dashing over them, intent only on distancing their competitors in the race and eager to arrive first at the only opening through the breakers, which was so narrow that only one double canoe could enter with safety.

Tying a red streamer to his mast, in token of his rank, Hookama, whose craft was the only canoe with one occupant, steered boldly among the competing boats, and making better time than the rest, reached the entrance in advance of many whom he passed in the race.

One burly chief, with tattoo marks all over his body, called out, banteringly, "What shell of an egg are you riding, my *apapani* (little song-bird)?   Better straddle a *honu* (turtle) and try a race with your *kahu* (nurse)!"   But when Hookama passed him, with the twenty paddlers vainly trying to forge ahead, and called out in reply, "Ha, ha! my *hoko-lele* (meteor); ask the women to put on your *malo* for you, the next time you risk a sea-voyage." The chief scowled at him and flung a javelin which passed harmlessly over his head and was caught by Hookama's left hand on the other side.   Calmly placing the trophy in the bottom of his canoe, the young sailor bounded over the waves, reached the entrance and had beached his canoe and stowed away the mast, long before the irate and discomfited chief had crossed the outlying breakers.

A multitude of war-canoes, and canoes laden with provisions, calabashes, live pigs and bananas, were drawn up on the beach, and thousands of warriors from the northern coast of Maui, assembling at the command of the king of Maui, were hurrying to and fro, adjusting their *malos* and weapons, gesticulating and singing rude songs, pushing each other angrily or playfully, and gathering into squads under their respective leaders. It was a mighty surge of dusky tribesmen from the most turbulent island of the group, Maui being noted for its independent *aliis* (chiefs) and its irrepressible tumults.

Awaiting the arrival of the chief who had hurled his javelin at him, Hookama at his approach calmly held out the weapon by its point and politely begged the owner to try his luck again, assuming an attitude a few paces off with his arms folded and with right leg advanced. The *alii*, who had evidently imbibed too much *awa* on the voyage, eagerly grasped the weapon by the handle, as offered by Hookama, and with a fierce imprecation launched it at his sneering foe. Hookama caught it in a twinkling with his left hand, flung it back with his right, and the red feathered helmet on the warrior's head was pierced through in its upper part, too high to wound its wearer, but with a force which un-settled the tipsy warrior's gravity and caused him to totter on his feet.

Just then, as luck would have it, a porker, which had been landed from a canoe near by, ran headlong beneath the chief's legs and fin-ished the incomplete result by sending the huge bulk of the *alii* sprawling on the beach. Then the warriors, who had come in the double canoe with the chief, and who had hardly taken in the situation, so quickly was the affair over, poised their spears and would have hurled them at the audacious youth, had not a score of other warriors immediately sur-rounded Hookama and called on the *alii's* retainers to hold their hands.

The crowd laughed heartily and called out, "Sharpen their fingernails and let them fight it out. The young one is an *alii* too, and no fool." This turned the tide in Hookama's favor, although the outraged chief, regaining his feet, insisted on a swift retribution by his men. Finally, however, he called off his war-riors and was led away by two of them, every now and then turning back to curse the "dog of a pig" that had served him such a trick.

As the king of Oahu, Kahahana, had not yet arrived from Molokai, where he stopped on his way to quell an insurrection, Hook-

ama left his canoe in charge of one of the keep-
ers of the war-canoes on the beach, and, taking
his weapons and effects, set out for the high
land where, he was told, a camping ground
had been selected for the expected warriors
from Oahu.

On reaching the plateau west of the village
of Waikapu, about a mile and a half from the
shore, the youth's eye roamed ever a marvellous extent of country. He noted mainly the
military advantages of the situation. His
heart was swelling with a proud ambition to
partake of the glory of the coming fight.

He learned from one of the warriors of Maui
that an old, restless and bloody chief from the
neighboring island of Hawaii had already
landed at Maalaea Bay, which is situated between East and West Maui, on the southern
shore. The island of Maui has, on the map,
something of the shape of a trowel, the handle
being the smaller western end and the blade
the larger eastern part. Between the handle
and blade, so to speak, is an isthmus, about
twelve miles across from Maalaea Bay to the
Bay of Kahului, where Hookama landed when
he arrived from Waihee.

The isthmus is a mile or two of varying
width, between fertile plains and lofty mountains on the east, and less lofty but equally

romantic ranges on the west. It is an uneven, sandy plain, swept by strong winds.

The next day opened in peerless beauty. Winds from the northwest lifted the light sands of the plain and fretted the fronds of the palms, but not a cloud appeared in the sky. There was the bustle of forces marshalling in the camp of the king of Maui, though not a single warrior appeared in the plains. The army, hearing that the Hawaiian enemy had started from Maalaea Bay, was lying in ambush among the sand dunes in the form of a semicircle. Now and then, a scout stole along the edge of the valley, or through the salt marshes and jungles.

The king of Hawaii sent this day only eight hundred of his bravest warriors to cross the sandy isthmus, intending to follow on the next day with his whole army. These doughty Hawaiian braves were a picked body, called the *Alapa*, the flower of the army, all equal in height and with spears equal in length. They grimly jested as they set out on the wearisome march, and expected to return with many prisoners for sacrifice to the gods.

At the other end of the isthmus the army of Maui was equally confident. Hookama, as his king had not yet arrived, was stationed with a band of Mauians in the reserve. The king of

Maui stood on one of the highest sand hills,
where, hidden from those coming from the
south, he could be seen by his own men, and
also obtain a good view down the valley.

As the Hawaiian *Alapa* struggled forward
through the sand, which the sun's heat made
oppressive, even these stout warriors became
somewhat weary, but not one lagged behind.
Occasionally, the whole phalanx broke out
in war-songs to cheer their toilsome way.
Towards noon, Hookama, straining his eyes
southward, saw a faint cloud of dust rising in
the distance. Soon, as the solid ranks came
in sight, moving with quicker step, the am-
bushed warriors of Maui could hardly repress
their admiration at the magnificent sight.

"These are no dogs of foeman," said Hookama, to a chief near by. "They are sons of
gods." Usually, before a battle, leading chiefs
stood forth, bandying taunts, and finally hurling spears at each other, as a signal to begin
the fight. But no challenge came from
either side, because the advancing company of
grim warriors saw no army in array against
them. They heard no sound and saw no
spear.

It was a grand spectacle, as the *Alapa* halted
for a moment, looking around them for an
enemy to attack. A few of the leaders wore

helmets, and brilliant *malos* around their loins, but the rank and file were naked, free, adorned only with their spears, war-clubs and daggers.

Suddenly, from the summit of a low sand hill, abreast of which the main body of the Hawaiian *Alapa* had come, uprose a mighty form, black as night save for the crimson helmet on his head, and holding a ponderous spear, twenty feet in length, in his right hand. With a voice like the roar of a cataract, the huge warrior shouted to the astonished hostile phalanx, which halted by a common impulse: "Fly, thieves, plunderers! fly to your miserable *moi*, and tell him that he sneaks in his canoe with the *wahines*, and dare not lead his men to meet the wild boars of Maui! Begone, or let the sand be your graves, and the *heiau* yonder drink your blood!"

Then, as Kahekili lifted his spear and flourished it above his head, from out their coverts sprang a thousand spearmen, with but a few hundred yards between them and the advance-ranks of their mighty adversaries.

With admirable coolness, the *Alapa* formed in serried lines to meet the onset. Before the warriors of Maui came near enough to hurl their spears, a shower of javelins fell upon them, flinging the foremost in great numbers to the ground and causing those behind to fall over them, so fierce and headlong was the attack.

Then in savage fashion, man to man and foe to foe, in grapple and in dagger-thrust, the braves of Hawaii rushed on the assailants who had been thrown into momentary confusion. Behind these stalwart Hawaiian chiefs pressed their followers, throwing spears and javelins at the rear ranks of the warriors of Maui, while with diabolical yells and a simultaneous movement, the entire body of the eight hundred rushed upon the dead, the dying and the living, giving no quarter to the wounded, slaughtering and trampling on their foes; as wild a tumult of carnage as was ever wrought on plain or in valley of these islands, more fruitful in bloody frays than they were lovely in crimson and carnation flowers.

Small chance then for the display of personal courage or skill; it was a *melée* rather than individual passages at arms; the *Alapa* shook off their assailants as infuriated tigers shake off packs of hounds; and they were rushing so furiously after the fugitives, that no one of them perceived the approach, stealthily as prowling panthers, of another band of spearmen coming upon them from the rear.

These new foemen had risen, as it were, out of the sands of the desert, to strike them from

behind before they could recover from their
first great effort against the unexpected assault in front. The *Alapa* had hurried forward too heedlessly in the flush of their success, when their wary antagonists fell upon
their flank and buried spears and javelins in
the back of many a warrior who could have
met and parried the weapons easily if fighting
face to face.

Not yet, however, were the giants of Hawaii
overcome or vanquished. Nearly the whole
force of Kahekili was needed to destroy these
war-seasoned veterans. The air was filled
with flying spears and javelins. War-clubs descended on the heads and shoulders of the combatants like hammers upon the anvil. When
darts and spears failed, and the short sword or
dagger was broken, the mighty champions
grappled in deadly struggle, often falling together in death on the sand slippery with
blood.

It was not a brief conflict; hour after hour
passed, and it was noon before the frenzied
combat ended. No warrior of the Alapa
wavered or fled. Two of them were somehow
pushed out into the plain in the rear of the
combatants, and seeing no reinforcements
coming up the valley and with no chance left to
ward off absolute annihilation of the Hawai-

ians, they left the field as a shout of triumph
and the cry "Beaten, beaten!" went up to
heaven. These two were the only ones of the
proud eight hundred to carry the news back
to the Hawaiian host.

During the progress of the terrible battle
the warriors in reserve and their chiefs could
scarcely restrain themselves from rushing into
the conflict. Had not the command of the
king been absolute and the penalty of disobedience death, it would have been impossible
for the chiefs to hold back their men. They
became more and more furious, and raged
about the camp like caged tigers. Their thirst
for blood and their desire to join the fray
made them frantic. Their cries and imprecations were fearful, as they stamped and bran-
dished their spears and clubs. Finally, when
they saw the last of the *Alapa* sinking on the
ground, the *tabu* having come to an end, they
rushed down among the victorious Mauians
and danced over the wounded and the slain,
utterly beside themselves.

Hookama, as one of the reserved contingent,
had no choice during the battle except to remain passive. With other young chiefs in
the reserve, he stood apart and viewed the
scene, quivering with excitement. When the
battle was over, he remained apart, for he felt

a new sensation, almost amounting to repulsion, as the fight seemed to him like a slaughter of brave men caught in a trap. An ambuscade was a kind of warfare hitherto unknown to him, and from that hour he hated Kahekili, the king of Maui, with his whole soul, looking upon his hordes as if they were assassins.

The Hawaiian army had lost but a fraction of its force in the destruction of the eight hundred. Its king received the news with surprise but recovered his composure as his thoughts turned to revenge. Another equally strong and brave band remained, the Piipii, gigantic chiefs, veterans, anxious to avenge their comrades. Besides, the bulk of the army had not been in the battle and all were animated with a frenzy of desire to meet the hated foe. The priests went among the warriors, urging them to fight with courage and declared the omens from the gods propitious.

In the camp of Kahekili there was great rejoicing over the destruction of the renowned *Alapa*, even though the victory had cost the lives of many braves, and not one of the eight hundred had fallen into their hands to be offered alive, the most acceptable sacrifice to the gods. The king's slaves cleared the battlefield of the bodies of his slain. His wounded were carried to the village of Wailuku, or laid beside the Waikapu stream where the cool water from the hills assuaged their sufferings.

During the evening, after the battle, the warriors of Oahu, led by their king Kahahana, arrived from Molokai and were assigned their quarters. The king received his subject, Hookama, very cordially. This king was a young man, amiable and brave, but weak as an administrator in the affairs of his kingdom, over which he had been placed by Kahekili, his brother-in-law. He had noticed Hookama during recent events at Oahu and had conceived a high idea of his ability and courage. As the adopted son of Numuku, who was staunch and loyal, the youth had often been at the royal house. Especially after his last exploit as a scout, the king took a strong liking to him and showed him great favor at court.

He now made a confidant of him, and treated him more as a companion than a subject, having learned the secret of his exalted rank; a secret known only to himself and Numuku, Hookama having no knowledge of it whatever.

The two friends were talking over the battle together when they observed a warrior climbing up to the crest where they stood. The king at once recognized the royal *moi* of Maui, Kahekili, to whom he presented Hookama, as one of his bravest warriors from Oahu. The *moi* received the youth with a courteous salutation.

This remarkable chief's nature was full of contradictions. He was calculating, cruel and unscrupulous, but when he wished to attract any one to himself, he could veil his craftiness under a smile of the utmost affability.

His personal appearance was startling. Notwithstanding his conciliatory manner towards Hookama, the young man thought he had never seen such a hideous warrior. One half of his face and body was tattooed in black spots, a color sacred to the priests and the highest chiefs. These spots gave him a most repulsive aspect in spite of the brilliant *malo* around his loins and his feather helmet with blood-red plumes. Around his neck was hung a hooked ornament, made from a whale's tooth and suspended by braids of human hair. Over his arm was flung a magnificent feather cloak, which he had removed from his shoulders during his ascent of the hill.

" Aha ! " said he to his noble brother-in-law. " Your gallant chiefs have my thanks for their prompt response to my summons. It is no small thing to come across the channels to aid me against the dastardly Hawaiians. They shall see such a slaughter to-morrow as Oahu-

ans have not witnessed since they were driven
from Molokai, when their king was sent to
join the long procession of ghosts. Pardon
me," he quickly continued, " I mean no dis-
respect for Oahuan bravery, but the sand hills
below us reminded me of the sands of Kawela,
even now full of half-buried Oahuan bones."

The cunning *moi*, choking down more sneering words that were almost spoken, then told
Kahahana the strategy of the coming battle
and accepted with ill-disguised disdain some
suggestions of the young king. Then he informed Kahahana that the warriors of Oahu
were not to enter the field at the first onset of
the Hawaiian army. He did not really mean
that they should fight at all if he could help
it. He wanted all the glory of the victory
for himself and his own men.

" I shall feel doubly secure of winning if I
can rely on such mighty allies in case of need,"
said he, " and you know, too, that as the heir
of my kingdom, [This was one of his treacherous promises] it would unnerve me for the
fight to think your royal life in danger.
But when I send you my messenger, then
spring forth like valiant sons of the god
of war and drink the blood of our common
foe. Till the message comes, hold your men
in check," and, without giving the young king

time to demur, the stalwart chief sprang down the slope with the agility of a wild goat.

The disappointed and humiliated king bit his lips with vexation, cast an angry glance at the receding form of his detested superior and, muttering: "Why did he summon me, if not to fight?" went back to his camp-tent, leaving Hookama to his own reflections.

CHAPTER V.

SAVAGE CHIVALRY.

THE first streaks of the morning lighted up
the eastern sky as the thousands of fierce Hawaiians set out on the march which the grand
council of chiefs had decided upon. Many of
their wives accompanied them, with calabashes
and food. Some of these women fought that
day near their husbands, shielding them by
parrying hostile spears, or even hurling javelins
at the foe. Many a brave woman is celebrated
in the annals of Hawaii for her prowess in the
field.

The wily Kahekili again disposed his
warriors in a partial ambuscade, the reinforcements from Oahu being held in reserve, as he
had said. But the Hawaiians were not easily
entrapped a second time. Cautiously and
slowly they marched across the sandy levels of
the isthmus. When they arrived near to the

army of Maui, a herald was sent forward, with a convoy of picked warriors, while the main body halted, awaiting a movement from the enemy.

Kahekili this time met the herald and, surrounded by a strong body-guard, showed his black side to the messenger and assured him that the ovens of Maui were already heated to roast the Hawaiian chiefs alive. To this the herald was about to reply when the leader of the escort, in a great rage, with the fury of a whirlwind, hurled a massive spear at the king, who dodged and left the weapon sticking in the sand.

Then throwing his own ponderous spear, which was caught by his opponent, he calmly turned and took the weapon behind him, saying, as he tried its point and weight : "A fair bargain, my *alii!* Now for the test." Immediately waving the spear high above his head, from the plain behind him that part of his army which was not in ambush rushed forward to the attack.

The shock between the foremost ranks of of the two armies was terrific. Now began a battle in the true Hawaiian way, hand to hand. The valley was wide enough for thousands to find room to engage in personal contests. Chiefs stepped forward and chal-

lenged other chiefs. Then chief sprang to
help chief. The war-club and bone dagger
came into play. The retainers of the noble
combatants crowded each other and fought
hand to hand like their masters. The air was
full of flying weapons. Cries and imprecations
were heard on every side. The tumult became
as the noise of the surf on a rocky shore. A
body of slingers, with stones weighing a pound,
plied their whizzing volleys like hailstones on
their enemies, while the mountains echoed
back shouts and war cries.

The Hawaiians gained a slight advantage.
They were driving the enemy back step by
step, a mighty force pressing upon the front
ranks and reinforcing their onset. Suddenly,
from the sand hills, what seemed to be another
army appeared as if rising out of the ground.

Astonished but undaunted, the Hawaiian
chiefs in command gave the signal to spread
out the front ranks that the warriors in the
rear might come on and meet the charge of
this additional force. Then, with hoarse
voices, the disciplined Hawaiian legion, the
Piipii, rushed to the front through the opening,
to receive the wild warriors of Maui, coming
down like an avalanche from their hiding
places.

Great deeds of valor were done that day, on

both sides. The combat waged hour after hour. It appeared as if neither side would yield until both were annihilated. Finally the tide turned a little in favor of the Hawaiians. Kahekili was himself well nigh spent with his terrible work of hewing down whole ranks of the enemy. He sent therefore a messenger, at this juncture, to the king of Oahu, and the eager warriors of his ally leaped into the field and retrieved the fortunes of the day.

The Hawaiians did not flee, but after hundreds of the bravest fell on both sides there was a lull in the conflict, many exhausted warriors throwing themselves on the ground, and others helping the wounded from the gory field.

The women went among the warriors, offering them food and water. The wives of the dead lifted up their voices in shrill, wailing cries, while the sufferers stoically bore the pain of their dreadful wounds. It was a shocking sight. Wounds on naked bodies looked ghastly and gaping.

Hookama had rushed in with the warriors of Oahu and had fought at the side of his king, defending him and at the same time engaging many a chief in desperate conflict.

Towards the end of the battle, the young brave singled out a herculean chief, who was unwounded but apparently much wearied with his tremendous efforts to save the day for the Hawaiians. Taking with him a small band of the Oahuans, Hookama determined to capture this warrior alive, as a prisoner of war.

Calling loudly to the hostile chief to defend himself, as island warriors were wont to challenge their equals, and followed by his band, he hurried into the fighting crowd and threw his spear with great force at the chief, who proved to be no less a personage than the chieftain in command of a large part of the Hawaiian army. He was the famous giant of Kona, who had pressed alone far into the ranks of the foe.

The grim old veteran smiled as he caught the spear and bade his youthful adversary not to court an untimely death. Then, as Hookama advanced a little in front of his own men, the gigantic hero hurled back the spear with terrific swiftness, its point grazing the shoulder of the impetuous youth, who dodged just in time and escaped with a mere scratch.

The two men simultaneously seized their long daggers and for a moment it seemed that the younger must be instantly slain by his huge opponent. But Hookama was fresher and his skill with the knife was greater than the chief surmised.

Making a feint as if to strike in front, Hookama, with wonderful agility, sprang to one side as the giant thrust his dagger forward, and, parrying the blow, struck at the chief from the left a blow which would have reached a vital part, had not the youth's foot slipped on the bloody sand, causing him to sink partly to his knees, leaving his antagonist unhurt.

Quick as thought, the veteran grasped the heavy butt of a broken lance from the ground and raised it to give a blow downward. The young warrior would have passed to the land of ghosts, had not his own warriors, unwilling to see such a termination of the duel, rushed in upon the mighty chief, front and rear ; a movement which gave Hookama time to fall on the ground, lessening the full force of the giant's stroke.

As it was, the blow stunned the youth and he lay motionless on the sand, while the Hawaiian battled with the Oahuans, calling on some of the few men of his own band to hurry to his assistance. These few Hawaiians made a desperate effort to rescue their chief, but were cut down to a man, notwithstanding the death-dealing blows of the giant himself, by which several of the Mauians were slain. It would have fared hard with the doughty warrior, had not another chief of Hawaii, seeing his imminent peril, cut his way, with several of his body-guard, and just in the nick of time added a new element to the conflict.

With renewed strength the giant seconded his brave rescuer's onset and, together with the remnant of Hawaiians that survived, the two hewed their way through the enemy and escaped. Is not this rescue of Kekuhaupio, the mighty Hawaiian, by the great Kamehameha, who afterwards subdued all the islands and became Lord of the whole group, celebrated in song by the bard Keaulumoku in the legends of the land?

Hookama, more dead than alive, was carried to the rear by two braves of Oahu. The blow he had received on the head proved a severe one, injuring him so much, that he fell into a stupor from which it seemed impossible to arouse him.

The king's own medicine-men, by his orders, applied all their art to relieve him. They used many remedies and the most approved incantations. They prayed to numerous gods, but without avail. The hut to which Hookama was carried was filled with the vile odor of burning offal to propitiate the inferior deities   Every device was employed to expel the bad spirit, which had entered the body of the warrior and had caused all the mischief.

The great *kahuna hoonoho* (a famous spiritual-istic exorciser), sought to reveal the "familiar" that had bewitched the patient.

It was well that Hookama had an iron con-stitution; otherwise, the extraordinary per-formances in his hut would have speedily ex-pelled the spirits that tormented him, along with his own, and our story, so far as he is concerned in it, would have to follow him to the realm of Kane, the "hidden land," where the good departed wander in a beautiful island, abounding in cocoa-nut groves and all sensuous delights. This indeed would not have been unwelcome to the *kahunas* in charge, inasmuch as burial services of chiefs always afforded them a richer harvest. With a newly-departed spirit of a chief, slain in battle, they might keep it in their service, by preserving the bones of its earthly tenement in a secret place. They had already matured their plans, with this end in view, making offerings to the gods in advance, that no obstacle might be put in their way.

Two days having passed, after a day of an unusual amount of incantation and perfumery in his hut, Hookama gave signs which the *kehunas* interpreted as positively preceding death. He suddenly relapsed into absolute unconsciousness and, with eyes closed, was growing rigid ; his fists were clenched and his limbs drawn up tightly.

Word was sent to Kahahana, the friendly king of Oahu, who came at once and stood beside the young *alii*, gazing sadly on the handsome face which had greeted him with genial smiles. The king lost some of his best warriors in the recent battle, but was more deeply moved by the expected death of Hookama, for whom a great affection had sprung up in his heart and from whom he hoped to have sympathy and aid in the days of danger which he foresaw with deep anxiety. Turning away, he gave orders that funeral rites be given to the brave warrior, as soon as death came, much to the satisfaction of the medicine-men and their attendants.

The great battle having been at last decided in favor of the king of Maui, the Hawaiians, bearing with them their wounded, retired to their canoes in Maalaea Bay, and the chiefs in council learned from the priests that their defeat was the will of the gods, to which it would be wise to bow, inasmuch as there was no help for it and not enough of an army left in fighting condition to renew the struggle.

A treaty was arranged between victor and vanquished, in which the king of Hawaii agreed to leave Kahekili in peaceable possession of his kingdom on the island of Maui. This solemn promise, ratified by the sacrifice of human beings, the king of Hawaii kept as faithfully as a believer in the Hawaiian deities usually kept his compacts; but, being a revengeful pagan, he forgot to keep it, as soon as he was strong enough to attempt another raid.

The battle of the Sand Hills was the death-blow of the proud, superior race which formed the real nobility of the land. " Their brawn and brain and vitality typified the enduring forces in an otherwise shattered and enfeebled race. Every one of them was needed in the struggle of the nation to survive. It was a fine example of heroism, but at an awful cost to the physical stamina and fibre of an already stricken race."

CHAPTER VI.

KELEA IN THE VALE OF IAO.

A MESSENGER having brought to Waihee the news of the first day's victory over the Hawaiians, the maiden Kelea managed to escape the vigilance of the old priest. Taking two of her *wahines* with her, she climbed the hills and forded the streams between Waihee and Wailuku, where at last she found her father, unhurt but bewailing the loss in battle of several of his bravest warriors.

He was angry with Kelea for coming, but having no one whom he could spare to send back with her, he told her to keep with the women till the next day's fight was over.

Kelea's mother had died some years previously, and the girl was, in a way, at the head of her father's household. At the women's camp, she was her own mistress and had her own maids. The women told her grewsome stories of the fight. She assisted them in caring for the wounded, and then withdrew with her attendants to a hut which she selected, on an eminence back of the main camp, where she was not likely to be disturbed. She obtained a *tabu* pole from her father and placed it before her door.

Kelea was named for a beautiful and capricious sister of an ancient king of Maui. Hawaiian legends tell of this royal maiden, as a wayward princess, petted and spoiled, but the most graceful and daring surf-swimmer in the kingdom. Her admirers, who watched and applauded her bold sport in the waves, were half inclined to believe that she was the friend of some water god, a supposition more credible because of her rejection of many suitors.

She was finally carried off as the bride of a chief of Oahu, and her adventures on that island form a very romantic story. This volatile woman was a remote ancestress of Kelea, whose father was also allied with the ancient *aliis* of Maui.

The Kelea of our story was not a delicate beauty like Pu' Aloha. She had a profusion of raven black hair which came low over her forehead and when unbound fell below her waist. Her eyes were full and lustrous; their dark pupils could grow soft when her heart was

touched ; her skin was light brown and surpassingly smooth ; her nose was regular in shape
and her lips full ; she bore herself like a stately
queen when she walked, and her robust bloom
made her a conspicuous figure among the
maidens of her tribe.

But she was haughty, imperious and capricious ; often unmanageable even by her father.
He seldom could divert her from a purpose on
which she had fixed her will. Not over-
refined in language, she could fascinate by her
words when she chose, and was as captivating
in manners towards her favorites as she was
passionate and pitiless to those who thwarted
her plans or wishes.

She was a fair type of the higher class young
women of her race. Her character was the
result of many pagan generations, with no re-
straining influences except the customs of her
people, and no elevating conditions except a
certain superiority which was the hereditary
quality of birth. The tone of life among the
people of Maui was somewhat lower than that
of the other islands. The men were more
ferocious and the women more perverse and
loose in manners.

Kelea's main reason for coming to the
camp was to obtain another meeting with
Hookama. She believed him capable of

doing wonders as a warrior and wished to witness his prowess. She was impatient of the
king's command that the men of Oahu be
held in reserve, but the bold rush of the allied
warriors towards the close of the battle roused
all the wild passions of her nature, and with
the women she entered the bloody field to
watch the conflict from a nearer point.

When at last the encounter between
Hookama and the gigantic warrior of Hawaii
ended with the collapse of the young *alii*, on
whom her eyes had been fastened with admiration, she could not restrain herself, but
rushed into the middle of the ensanguined
field; met the men who were carrying
Hookama away, and followed them, unnoticed
in the hurry and horror of the hour.

While the youth was in the hands of the
kehunas, Kelea hovered about the vicinity,
hiding in the bushes of the crags above the
hut. She watched every movement; she
even tried to bribe the guards to admit her
into the house. They only railed at her and
bade her begone.

At last, on the day that the king came and
found Hookama apparently near his end, she
followed him and falling at his feet, confessed
her rank; related to him, as she passionately
wept, a false tale of love and adventure, and

entreated him by all the gods to let her carry the inanimate form of her lover up to the sacred rock in the vale of Iao, where he might die in sight of the mausoleum of the deified chiefs.

She also told him of a small house, where some priests had lived near the sacred shrine, but which was now unoccupied, and she promised, as she clasped his knees in the agony of her entreaty, that if Hookama died, she would deliver his body to the *kehunas* for the rites of burial worthy of an *alii*.

The king was touched by her indifference to every consideration except that which was prompted by her love, and the same night sent Hookama in a litter to the place Kelea had described. He himself went with the bearers and met the girl, who with two of her *wahines* were found waiting at the house above the valley.

Every preparation had been made for the sufferer's comfort : the couch of mats was underlaid with dry moss ; calabashes with food, *kukui*-nut torches and hangings of *tapa*, with other needful articles, had been provided. The wealthiest chief could have added nothing.

Kelea had festooned the hut with flowers and there were mats on the floor, a great luxury. These evidences of loving care made a deep impression on the *moi*, and when the maiden, after the bearers were sent away, sat down by the inanimate form stretched on the couch, the sight of her sorrow brought the moisture to his eyes and he was in the mood to grant her anything she desired.

He asked her if he could do more for her, and she said "A *tabu* of the place, and may the gods bless you forever!" The request was instantly granted. The spear which the *moi* carried was planted before the door, and hung with a white *tapa* streamer, thus providing for the absolute seclusion and security of those in the house.

As the king went out into the night, the sound of the waterfalls came up from the valley and weird voices were wafted to his ears; the tops of the *koa* trees rustled in the breeze. In the midst of the ravine a pinnacle of rock sentinelled the vale and its crystal summit glistened in the moonbeams. When at last the streaks of the coming dawn dissipated the gloom of the night, the *moi* felt himself drawn, in deeper sympathy than ever, towards the two lovers as he supposed them to be. Again entering the grass hut, to his amazement and great joy he found Hookama sleeping; an unquiet sleep, but with renewed pulse and a regular beating of the heart.

The *wahines* had gently *lomi-lomied* his impassive body, arousing it to sensitiveness and a better circulation. A *kukui*-nut torch gave its feeble light, enabling the *moi* to observe the favorable change and also to see Kelea's graceful form, kneeling by the bed of mats, holding the youth's hand in her own. A smile of grateful pleasure lighted up her face as she whispered her thanks to him and to the goddess Lilinoe of Haleakala, her patron deity. Repeating his wish to hear often from the patient, Kahahana took his way down the path, with a lighter step and a more tranquil heart.

The valley of Iao, on the island of Maui, is among the most romantic gorges for which this isle is famous. On the western end of Maui, (the handle of the trowel, as seen on the map), it lies directly west of the Wailuku pass ; the valley, broad as its opening, gradually becomes narrow and the Iao river follows its tortuous course between *palis* (precipices) 4,000 feet in height. Stupendous peaks loom up to a loftier elevation, their tops in the clouds.

Mauna Eke is the name given to the circular range in the bosom of which lies the valley, whose sides, moistened with mists and trickling streams, are perennially green. Ferns and convolvuli adorn the precipices ; shining

The Pinnacle — Iao Valley

leaves, delicately stemmed, tremble and gleam with every breath of wind.

Through the opening to this romantic valley, a pathway with a southern trend leads upward, till the traveller emerges above the *palis*. This path, following the irregular sides of the cliffs, and climbing over crater-hills where the lava once flowed, finally comes out at the Olowalu pass, on the leeward side of Maui. Thence it descends to the coast, at a point seven or eight miles from Lahaina, an important village where the king of Maui kept his court and harbored his canoes.

This rough and toilsome road was the nearest route from Wailuku, where the battle was fought, to the southeast coast of the island, and the pass nearest Wailuku was the scene in after years of a terrific conflict, in which warriors climbed the path and clasped their foes, to hurl them, or be hurled with them, into the abyss below.

CHAPTER VII.

A MIDNIGHT ASSAULT.

It was at the close of a calm, bright afternoon, two days after Hookama was brought to the vale of Iao, that Kelea sat near the brink of the *pali*, in front of the grass house where Hookama was still lying in a condition of semi-unconsciousness. With her two *wahines*, she was weaving wild flowers into garlands, now and then tossing stones over the precipice and listening to the sound as they bounded from the sides of the ravine. The air was melodious with occasional notes of mountain birds and the music of falling streams.

Kelea was in a strange, uncertain mood, and her eyes wandered off to the lofty tower of rock, where, detached from the precipice on the opposite side of the valley, it stood like a warder, a thousand feet in height, its tapering top roseate in the light of the declining sun.

The half-disc of the moon traced its pale out-line on the blue sky, suggesting a night of serenity and beauty.

Kelea's expression, restless and anxious, was in strong contrast with that of the maid-ens, her attendants, who were carelessly happy, as most native girls usually were. Their mis-tress, suddenly fixing her eyes on the point of the rock where the sunset glow was rising to the vanishing point, broke the silence, as if speaking to herself, and said in a low tone : " I wish I had not gone up the hill this afternoon."

One of the *wahines* ventured to reply: " You told us to stay with the *alii*, or we would have gone. Glad I wasn't down on the plains. Did you see the funeral rites of the dead warriors, my princess ? Horrid things ! cutting themselves, knocking out their teeth after the war dance was over—and then it is dreadful, the way they treat the women after the dead are buried and they begin to drink *awa*."

" Hush ! " replied Kelea ; " you talk too loud. He might hear us. Come, go to your own hut and I will see if the *alii* needs anything." With that she led the way, wreath in hand, to the large grass house which stood back from the path.

Over the wall of the house clambered the convolvulus with its bright blossoms. On either side the door, was a *halapepe* bush, with long stems of lemon-colored flowers. As Kelea passed through the entrance she was surprised to find Hookama awake. It seemed as if his eyes were intently fixed on her as she approached. He appeared like one wakened out of too deep a slumber, not quite aroused, but catching a faint idea of her moving form. The contour of her figure, outlined in the dim light through the doorway, was all that was discernible; but the glimpse of a female shape caused him to strain his sight, while a smile spread itself over his face, which bore the marks of a severe struggle for existence.

With great effort he uttered, in a low tone, the words, "*Pu' aloha ! oli, oli !* " (the flower of love! joy, joy !), and sank back, as if overcome by his endeavor, or by the emotion which his voice expressed.

Instantly, Kelea, believing he had called her "the flower of love," sprang toward him, seated herself at his side, and took his hand tenderly in her own. His eyes sought hers in a confused, wistful way, as if he would fain reveal the fleeting impression which her coming had made upon him a moment before; then they closed, and he relapsed into **his** former half-conscious condition.

She called her *wahines* and they used all their skill in the *lomi-lomi* process till it was too dark to see clearly in the hut. Their work seemed to produce little effect. Hookama's breathing was more regular, but he did not awake. It was late when the two *wahines* flung themselves on the mats in their hut, where they soon fell fast asleep.

Kelea, torn with conflicting emotions, could not sleep. Hookama's words had given her new hope, but now perhaps he would die. Was she lifted into this great happiness only to have her lover ruthlessly snatched from her? She raved against the gods one instant and the next she supplicated their favor. Were the gods as ugly as their images, and wholly vengeful and implacable? She had never thought much about them, except that they were always having bloody sacrifices offered to them. One deity alone, the goddess Lilinoe of Haleakala, appealed to her because she had prayed to her once for a trifling thing which had been granted.

After watching long beside Hookama, she went out under the midnight moon to cool her blood, or, if that were denied her, to give vent to her feelings without restraint.

Sitting in the shadows, with the noise of tumbling waterfalls in her ears, and now and

then the whirr of a bat passing through the
air, she was sensible only of her loneliness
and a dread of something that might happen.
The supernatural gave her no terror, but it afforded her no solace. The mountain peaks
arose around her and the moon plunged
through the fleecy clouds over her head, but
she heeded them not. Her strong frame
shook with the violence of her emotions;
emotions chiefly of wrath because of baffled
hopes—a strange gust of passion, sweeping
across her fiery soul as the cherished object
seemed slipping from its grasp.

She might have rocked herself till daylight,
uttering her moans and cries, had not her ear
caught the sound of a footstep coming near,
down the path. With the sound came the
shadow of a figure, which rapidly approached
at a swinging gait from the higher ground.
Her first impulse was to flee, in order to conceal herself from a stranger.

Hesitating an instant, it was too late, for
stalwart arms enfolded her before she could
rise, and she was forced down upon the
ground.

The place she had taken for her midnight
vigil was on the side of the rough road leading
along the heights and down through the pass.
It was at some little distance from the hut.

which was now completely hidden in the gloom of the night. She knew that wild and reckless men traversed these lonely ways and made forays by night into the valleys, but she had trusted to the *tabu* for safety ; now, her only safety lay in her strength or her ability to outwit the man who had come upon her, as suddenly as a landslide.

She was used to rough treatment of a certain sort, and her muscular strength had often vanquished, in rude games, the young *aliis* of her tribe. It was not uncommon for women of the islands to compete with the young men in their rude sports, both in surf-riding, sliding down the hills on sledges, and even in trials of brute force. If her assailant were alone she did not fear him, and her instinctive presence of mind, joined with her courage, was equal to almost any emergency.

Finding, however, that the sudden assault was not as violent as it was abrupt, and that he was no churl who held her fast, she decided to try strategy instead of strength in order to escape.

Laughing saucily in the man's face, which she saw by the moonlight to be comely enough and youthful, she allowed herself to remain passive and waited for him to speak. She had wound her mantle of *tapa* cloth closely about her body in the chilly atmosphere, and the sudden transformation from intense anguish to the need of self-defence, put her at once in full possession of her faculties.

She sat perfectly still so that the bold intruder, seeing that she offered no resistance and that she could not rise quickly enough to escape him, loosed his hold and began to flatter her; " Kulia-nui (my beauty)," he said, and she started as if he had spoken her own name Kelea. Then he came a little closer to her; began to praise her charms and finally took hold of her mantle, as if he would unwind it from her form. " Why does my beauty watch so late, like the owl, if not in expectation of a lover? " he asked in a soft voice, as he tried to unclasp her hands which clutched her *tapa*. Finding her resolute, he was beginning to put forth more strength, when Kelea, with a look of supreme indignation, sprang from the earth before he could arrest her movements, and, with no careful choice of epithets, defied him to touch her again. She was in no mood for blandishments, but ripe for strenuous resistance. Not willing to be cowed by a *wahine*, the young fellow, having risen to his feet, closed in upon her with the intention of compelling her to sit down again. But her temper was now at white heat. She struggled violently against his attempt. It soon became a contest between two fairly matched athletes.

Soon, however, the man, being somewhat the stronger, was getting the better of the woman, when, with a wild cry, she freed her right arm and drew from the folds of her garment a short, white weapon and aimed a blow at her assailant. He adroitly seized her arm by the wrist, holding her hand aloft, and, with his right arm tightly clasped about her waist, succeeded in pushing her from the path and in the direction of the *pali.*

The frantic woman, seeing the danger, but maddened by the rough usage of her assailant, whirled around and with all her force urged the man towards the brink of the yawning chasm, determined to push him backwards into the gulf, even if with him she must fall to meet a fearful death.

The two reeled and panted, on the very verge of the precipice. With the awful fate threatening them both in his mind, the man, by a desperate effort, wrested the weapon from Kelea and sent it flying, while he grappled her with both arms around the waist and succeeded in flinging her on the ground towards the path, where she lay bruised and half-stunned by the violence of the fall.

Almost breathless from the struggle, her

assailant hardly gave a second look at his victim, but, muttering to himself that the game was not worth its cost, hastily started down the pathway, which a little further on passed between two huge rocks, as if the ledge at that point had been split in halves.

Glancing down as he started, he saw something white, glistening in the moonlight. Without thinking much about it in the excitement of the moment, he stooped and picked it up. Fastening it in his girdle, he hurried on and was soon out of sight.

CHAPTER VIII.

PAAO, THE TRAITOR.

THIS ruthless assaulter of Kelea was no less a personage than Paao, the enemy of Hookama. He had been hastily despatched by the chief Numuku, to carry a message from Oahu to Maui, urging the king of Oahu to return speedily to his own island, because of signs of rebellion in his kingdom. Numuku was loyal to the king Kahahana, and had been left by him as governor of Oahu in his absence.

With a swift war-canoe, manned by sturdy natives, Paao left Oahu secretly, at dead of night, and landed at Lahaina, the headquarters of Kahekili, early on the morning of the day previous to his appearance on the pathway over the Iao valley.

On his arrival at Lahaina he heard of the battle of the Sand Hills and that the king of Oahu was still there. That no time might be lost, he left his men and the canoe, and, instead of sailing to Maalaea Bay, decided to cross the Eke mountain over the pass. It was a laborious route, on the verge of dizzy precipices and through gloomy ravines; but he was sturdy, and when the moon rose he was already descending the eastern slope by a zig-zag trail, until at last he came upon Kelea, sitting by the roadside.

He supposed she was one of the native women, whom he often met in the course of his wanderings, and thought he would vary the hardships of the way by sporting awhile with her in the moonlight. If he had known how the affair would end, he might not have essayed the venture, for he was something of a coward and, even in his amours, preferred an easy conquest won by craft to any danger-ous trifling.

Now, as he passed through the rocky defile into the moonlit track, after leaving Kelea, he took a look at the small white weapon which he had mechanically picked up from the path. To his astonishment he recognized the dagger which he had given Hookama. It set him to thinking. "How did it come into that *wahine's* possession? Had she killed Hook-ama with it, as he had abundant proof from her reckless courage that she might have done? Why was a girl of superior rank out there alone?" he queried, as he recalled her looks and haughty manner. "And where was Hookama, if alive, his destination being the island of Hawaii and not Maui?"

Busy with such questions, he stowed the dagger away among the few articles which he had bound about his waist, carefully guarding the poisoned point from piercing his flesh; and at early dawn found himself looking out over the village and a thousand improvised huts where the army of Kahekili was encamped.

He soon reached the sand hills, where he was told the Oahuans lay, and, being at once brought to the king, delivered his message. Kahahana received the news with apparent calmness, but it caused him intense anxiety. He had already found out the ability and arrogance of some of the chiefs of his kingdom of Oahu. Signs of discontent with his rule had showed themselves even among the high chiefs who came with him on this expedition to Maui.

He therefore hastily called a council of his war-chiefs, the majority being loyal, and it was decided to send Paao back at once to Oahu, to announce that the king and his troops would speedily return. The messenger had orders also to say that the king's warriors had turned the tide, in the great battle, without losing many of the chiefs. This was a politic move, to allay the anxiety of the families of his attendant chiefs, and to announce the victory that they had helped so much to win.

The more important decision of the council was that at least four days must be spent at Wailuku, to allay all suspicion that a premature departure was necessary, on account of affairs at home. The coming of Paao and the intelligence he brought were to be kept a profound secret. He was to return immediately by the way he had come. But before he left, he managed to have a private interview with Kahekili, the *moi* of Maui, to whom he told the whole story. Thus Paao proved himself not only a scoundrel but a traitor.

As he was leaving the camp of the Oahuans he went to receive the last commands of his king and expressed the utmost loyalty to his person and his cause. Near the close of the interview he casually alluded to Hookama, as a dear friend, and asked if the king had heard of his whereabouts. Kahahana in reply told him of the young *alii's* gallant conduct in the battle, his brilliant dash against the Hawaiian giant, his severe wound and the present hopes of his recovery.

"Just now, he is in Iao Valley," said the king. "You will pass the house on your return."

"Could I see him?" asked Paao, with a sympathetic accent.

"You might look in upon him a moment; he lies about two hours up the valley," was the response, the royal speaker having forgotten the *tabu* spear, which would proclude even his own messenger from entering the premises.

Early the next morning, with two warriors as a body guard to the head of the pass, Paao started for the mountains. He was in high spirits and boasted to his companions of his warlike deeds and his amours, as they ascended the Wailuku pass. "Aha!" he said to himself as they approached the spot where he had encountered Kelea, "that girl had some muscle. I wonder if she was much hurt. What a superb form, and such flashing eyes!"

Then he thought, "What a fine story I can tell about Hookama to Pu' Aloha! She will wince when she hears that her devoted lover is infatuated with a Maui belle; the dagger will prove it," and he switched off the twigs at the side of the road with his staff as chuckling to himself he strode along.

CHAPTER IX.

HOOKAMA, OFF HIS GUARD.

KELEA, after the brutal assault on the night of her meeting with Paao, lay half stunned upon the bank where he had flung her down. Towards morning, one of the *wahines* in the hut awoke and, missing her mistress, aroused her companion; the two girls then went quietly out to find her. Coming where the poor girl was lying, they carried her in and applied the *lomi-lomi*. After their work was over, she dozed off into slumber and, in an hour or two, awoke to find them watching by her side; Hookama was still sleeping soundly on his couch of mats.

With some difficulty, her joints being stiff and her muscles sore, she went with the girls to the place near by, where they were wont to bathe, and plunging in came out much refreshed. It was a pool, into which a stream of cool water flowed with a rippling sound and over which drooped bright clusters of leaves and trailing vines. Shut in by lava rocks, it was a sylvan retreat fit for a goddess, and as Kelea, dripping from her bath, sat on the moss-grown bank, while the *wahines* dried her long hair with a fold of soft *tapa*, she might well pass for the goddess of the place, provided that Hawaiian goddesses had such ample proportions.

It was a pretty tableau in that romantic spot. The lights and shadows played through the tremulous foliage. The *oo* breathed a soft melody from the overhanging pandanus tree which, with its aerial rootlets and bright red fruit, gave tropical beauty to the scene. The *wahines* anointed their mistress with the sap of the *hao* mixed with liquid *poi*.

Paddling in the water with her feet, Kelea told her maidens of her encounter with the stranger, but cautioned them to say nothing to the *alii* about the affair. On returning to the house, to her surprise and delight she found Hookama awake and sensible of his surroundings.

She startled him when she appeared. He recognized her at once, and her unaccountable presence in this strange place excited him so much that he could hardly speak. With great

tact, Kelea quietly informed him at once of
the events since the battle, dwelling emphatic-
ally on the king's wish that she should nurse
him back to life.   He was too weak and dazed
to inquire further.

The girl pressed out the juice of some *ohelo*
berries, added *awa* to the draught and put it
to his lips.   Then seating herself by the couch
she bathed his hands, face and breast with
cool water from the pool.   Looking tenderly
at him as she recalled the words, "Flower of
love," which she supposed he had addressed to
her, she lifted his head to her shoulder as she
spread his *mamo* (scarlet cloak) over him, having found it among his effects that were
brought to the hut.

As she smoothed the bright feathers of the
garment, her luminous eyes, with a soft radiance (they were her one really beautiful fea-
ture) seemed so gentle and sympathetic that
they were grateful to Hookama's sight ; and
when she sang a love-song, while she stroked
his forehead and his arms, her low voice
soothed him and a contented smile passed
over his face, which Kelea interpreted in her
own favor.

She was older by two years than Hookama,
and an adept in all the artifices which Hawaiian maids practised with assiduity, having

abundant opportunity owing to the larger number of men than women on the islands.

But now, all conscious art was laid aside. Her affection was sincere, and when her raven locks fell over Hookama's face as he rested on her shoulder, the thrill which he felt passing through her frame startled and troubled him, although he was too weak in body and in mind to resist the pleasing touch of her arms and the glance of her tender eyes.

He lay, as it were, in dreamland, forgetful of the past and unmindful of the future. His passive spirit yielded itself to the witching presence and melodious voice of the flower-crowned maiden who knelt at his side, until at noon the *wahines* returned, laden with luscious fruit and fragrant blossoms from the hills.

The remainder of the day, after a repast to which the young *alii* brought a good degree of appetite, was passed by him in comfortable sleep, Kelea still watching beside him and gently waving her *kahili*, a brush of soft, long feathers from the wings of birds.

The day following, the dwellers in this little grass house awoke to the voices of the water-falls and the music of the wind in the tree-tops. It was one of the loveliest of the many lovely days in that land of semi-tropical warmth and beauty. The fragrance of the wild woods

was wafted with the early mists from the
lower chasms and the peaks sent down sun-
showers, the spray of which was shot through
with beams of light forming rainbows on
every hand.

Kelea determined that Hookama should
enjoy it all and be benefitted by it. He must
be coaxed into the sunshine, the elixir of life
for all Hawaiian ills. When she found that
he was willing to make the trial and could
walk slowly with her assistance, she led him
to a sheltered spot just above the hut, where,
spreading mats, she made him recline for a
sun-bath, such as no other land can furnish
more luxuriously.

Well may the savage refuse the inconven-
ience of clothes, when, in a climate of sub-
tropical salubrity, he can quicken recovery or
foster Nature's kindly aid in preventing dis-
ease ! He may live in a continual bath of light.

The Hawaiians of the last century violated
no sense of propriety among themselves, by
the absence of clothing from the larger portion of the body. It is the unusual that dis-
turbs. More or less covering with them was a
matter of no consequence. Their brown skin
was a covering in itself, just as a nude bronze
statue is differentiated from a white marble
one. A savage well tattooed was a dandy
well dressed.

Moreover, those naked islanders fitted into the wild scenery of their land. The flowers with which the women adorned themselves at all times, and their long flowing hair, matched the luxuriant vegetation. Lying on the red earth, their brown skin was in harmony with their natural couch. In the pools, their forms took the hue of the rich brown of pure, deep water. The garlands on neck, arms and waist were the native substitute for dress, and the gold and crimson helmets and cloaks of the chiefs rivalled the gorgeous flowering vines that hung from the trees.

There were few noxious insects or animals. Scorpions, centipedes, fleas and mosquitos are pests introduced by white men. Snakes have never been known on the islands. Clothing, not needed to conceal or protect the person, was therefore an incumbrance, except in higher localities among the mountains. Vanity might endure it, but neither comfort nor modesty demanded much of it.

No wonder that Hookama, lying at full length, with only a *malo* about his loins, stretched his brown limbs in the sunlight with a sigh of satisfaction and began at once to recover health and strength.

The spot, which Kelea had chosen as the sanitarium for her patient, was a commanding one, overlooking a broad expanse of territory, with the channel between Maui and Hawaii in the distance. Below, one could see the path-way, winding up the Wailuku pass, along which men and women were toiling, coming into view or vanishing as they entered or emerged from the many ravines. The shouts of these foot passengers echoed among the hills, and ever and anon spear points glistened in the sun, as bands of warriors passed along on their way from Wailuku to their homes on the southern coast.

Without disturbing Hookama, who lay in a delicious state of languor with his eyes closed, Kelea suddenly whispered to the *wahines*, bidding them watch by the *alii* and for no reason whatever leave him till she returned. Putting about her the garlands they had been weaving, she descended to the grass house and took her stand before the *tabu*-spear which the *moi* of Oahu had planted for her protection, in front of the dwelling.

Her quick eye had detected the approach along the path of the three warriors, Paao and the two men sent as his escort by the king. As they emerged from between the high rocks, a few hundred feet below the slight elevation above the path on which the hut was built, Kelea straightened her figure to its full height, and with arms akimbo awaited their approach.

Hawaiian Women Bathing

CHAPTER X.

A HAWAIIAN MAIDEN'S REVENGE.

PAAO, who had not told his companions of his encounter with the girl, slunk back behind the two warriors and was disposed to hurry past, keeping his eyes upon the ground. He was not prepared for this public meeting with his late antagonist, but intended to pass the spot, and then, bidding the escort rest awhile, go back and see if he could find Hookama, or the *wahine*. Now, the sight of this superb woman, evidently prepared to meet him on her own terms, disconcerted him and deprived him of his usual bravado of manner and speech. The two warriors involuntarily halted when they came opposite the place where Kelea stood and Paao perforce must delay with them, at least for a moment.

"Soho! My *maikola* (contemptible one), back so soon? You want another *honi* (kiss)

from my *pahoa* (dagger) do you? You *puaa*
(hog)!" Then changing her tone, she drew
herself up, pointed her finger at Paao and
cried out: "Had to bring a guard with you,
didn't you? to keep the *wahine* from flinging
you this time safely over the ravine to *Milu*
(hell)! Didn't dare come up alone? Or, have
you met some other woman on the plain, who
was your match? Sending you home with a
guard to keep you out of mischief, eh? or to
get well rid of a villain? Come take this skirt,
you woman fighter," and she whipped off the
outer fold of her petticoat and held it out to
him, with a sneer on her face.

These biting words had been uttered so
rapidly and with such tormendous force that
neither Paao nor his companions could get in
a single word in reply. Then Kelea rapidly
rehearsed the story, to a group of passers-by
who crowded around the three warriors.
When she came, in her recital, to the final
struggle, and, with violent gesticulation and
vivid mimicry, imitated the brutal attack upon
her by Paao, pointing at him as the *hero* of the
fight, the crowd fairly howled with scorn.

Then suddenly changing from sarcasm to
ridicule, she made fun of her late antagonist,
telling him to go home and look up his pedigree; "Go, feed puppy dogs for sacrifice

with the *wahines !* Change your spear for a
kahili (fly brush), and fight girls in a *pau*
(skirt.)"

This banter put the crowd, among whom
were some women and girls, into a perfect
roar of laughter; two *wahines*, who had laid
their burdens on the ground to enjoy the
sport, first tittered, then giggled and finally
rolled on the earth in a paroxysm of merri-
ment. The shouting natives then joined
hands and danced around the three warriors,
two of whom enjoyed the fun amazingly,
while Paao, the laughing-stock of the occasion,
hardly knew how to look or what to do. If
he ran away, the gibes that followed him would
be harder to bear than the jocose sportiveness
of the throng, huddled as they were together.

At last, their waggery nettled him and he
became angry; as they made themselves still
more obnoxious and pushed against him he
handled his weapons threateningly; and when,
as a final home thrust, Kelea called out from
the bank "*Luka, luka*, (beaten, beaten!) pick
up the cripple," Paao could contain himself no
longer, but broke through the crowd and
rushed up the slope towards Kelea, who, with
the utmost composure awaited his coming.

Stepping aside as he approached and pointing to the *tabu*-spear, she simply said: " The

Moi, your king." The weapon had been behind her all the time, purposely hidden by
her person. Paao, taken wholly aback by the
well-known, sacred token, recoiled a step, then
turned and calling his companions strode up
the pathway, foaming with rage, the crowd
cheering and laughing more loudly than before.

As the three warriors went out of sight at
a bend of the road, the natives gathered into
groups to discuss the incident and to mimic
the chief actors in it ; then they went on their
several ways, some down the valley, others up
the hill. As for Kelea, when she had watched
the crestfallen Paao out of sight, with a curl of
the lip betokening the utmost scorn, she took
her way up the rising ground back of the hut,
and rejoined Hookama and her *wahines.*
They had heard the shouting, but supposing
it the ordinary cries of travellers along the
path, were not even curious to know what had
occasioned the hubbub.

Paao's troubles, however, were by no means
at an end. The two warriors, who had been
selected as his escort, were from Waikiki, Oahu,
and knew him well. They hated him heartily,
as did most of the men who were his neighbors.
He tried to explain the story and said the
wahine who had made such a fuss about it was

only a crazy woman. True, he had met her on his way down the pass the other night, and she had accosted him, but being repulsed, had flown at him in a rage and he had been obliged to fling her off rather harshly, to rid himself of the incumbrance.

The two warriors said nothing in reply, knowing that Paao had influence with Numuku their own powerful chief of Nuuanu Valley; but a sly wink, one to the other, showed what their conclusions were, and suggested some fun at Paao's expense when they returned to Oahu.

As for Paao himself, he was completely mystified by the presence of the *tabu*-spear in that place. Could it be that the woman was one of the king's own favorites? If so, he might get into serious trouble if she told his chief what had happened. She was certainly of high birth; no common *wahine*, but a woman of blood and spirit. Well, he would think it over, and if the king should ask him about it he could invent a plausible answer. For all that, he was uneasy in his mind, and his journey was not a very happy one. He was relieved when the two warriors left him at the head of the Olowalu pass, but still his thoughts busied themselves with the events of the day, so galling to his pride.

Besides, he was not sure now about Hook-ama, and how did that ivory dagger come into the girl's possession? He might not have the laugh at the young *alii* after all, or even find it safe to show the dagger to Pu' Aloha, much less to accuse Hookama of what he might never have done.

"I wonder," said he, half aloud, "if those miserable men who escorted me, will stop and investigate the real truth, as they return: what stories they will tell at the camp, if they do! Well, if it comes to the worst, I can turn priest and get even with all my enemies!"

Then he thought of his treacherous inter-view with the king of Maui and wondered how his plotting would turn out. Trying to console himself with these evil counsels, and yet in a very crestfallen mood, Paao reached Lahaina, went aboard his war-canoe and sailed for Oahu with all despatch.

The day after Kelea had taken her revenge, she experienced a terrible reaction. Her *wahines*, whom she scolded for slight faults, began to sulk and complain to each other; she herself took a large draught of *awa*, which she had brought to the hut, ostensibly as med-icine for Hookama; even the young *alii* noticed the change, the cause of which he attributed to his lack of response to her ardent expressions of affection on the previous day. He pitied her after a fashion; he liked her in a way, and she had nursed him back to health, as he learned by questioning one of her maidens. But then he had saved her from a horrid death when in danger from the shark, and so they were quits, according to the Hawaiian idea of justice, which set one deed off against another, whether it were the killing of a man or the desertion of a woman.

He was able to walk slowly to the place where he took his sun-bath and siesta. There, the girls *lomi*-ed him till the warm blood coursed through his veins. They were skilled in playing on the nose-flute and the *ukeke*, a sort of jewsharp with two strings, and the plaintive music accorded well with his own feelings.

Kelea was with him much of the time, but there was something strange in her actions which he could not understand. The fact was, she had begun to realize, as Hookama gained strength, that this dream of love must soon come to an end for her, and the thought almost crazed her brain, her nerves having been strained to their utmost tension by the occurrences of the past week.

She thought of flinging herself off the *pali*

if Hookama would not take her with him, as
chiefs often took their wives and other women
even on their warlike expeditions. Then
came the dreadful temptation to poison herself and him, rather than to lose the object of
her heart. She stifled this suggestion, saying :
" Kà, kà! only a *kanaka* would use poison—or
a *kahuna*." Then she tried to offer the
" prayer to enlist the affections," but nothing
calmed or relieved her. She was revolving
several schemes to detain Hookama or to follow him to Oahu, when one of the *wahines*
came hurriedly to announce the arrival of
King Kahahana at the hut.

He asked to see Hookama at once, and Kelea
led him to the cosy retreat where he found the
young *alii* luxuriously reclining in the midst
of ferns and flowers that Kelea had tastefully
arranged.

" Aha! my fine friend! It is a joy to see
you again with the blood of your noble
ancestors showing in your face." He checked
himself, aware that Hookama was ignorant of
his birth rank.

" You have a snug nest up here, for a bird-
catcher ; but come now, if you are equal to it,
let us talk on some important matters ; and
my time is short."

Hookama took his friend's hand. unable to

rise and give the customary obeisance, and
the king then told him of a terrible sick-
ness in the camp at Wailuku, owing to the
unburied bodies of the enemy slain in the
recent battles. The situation was alarming.
Hundreds of the villagers were escaping to the
hills, which accounted for the numbers of them
coming through the pass.

He said Kahekili had given him permission
to retire at the earliest moment; a great relief,
as he was anxious to get back to Oahu. Then
pledging Hookama by a sacred oath, he explained the disaffection of some of his own
chiefs.

"Now," he added, "I must entrust to you
a secret mission, which will require both boldness and tact. It is an embassy to the defeated
king of Hawaii. I cannot trust the crafty
moi of Maui, who has designs of his own with
reference to Oahu; but the Hawaiian king,
knowing this, may come to my help if the
rebellious chiefs prove too powerful for me to
cope with them."

The plan was for Hookama to embark in
the king's war-canoe. Out at sea, he would be
transferred to another war-canoe with trusty
warriors. Then steering for Waipio, Hawaii,
where the Hawaiian king held his court, he
could land as a bird-catcher and get a chance
to confer with the king alone.

"There are so few that I can trust," he concluded, "but I am sure of you—you must go."

Hookama pleaded his feeble condition, his
youth and inexperience, but the king was persistent. "The voyage," he said, "will restore
you to perfect health." There was nothing
for the youth to do but to yield, and he
promised to do his best, if it cost his life.

"But," said Hookama, "I must tell Kelea
at once; the girl has been very good to me
and I am afraid," he added with a feeble
smile, "that she has taken a fancy to me, to her
own ill-luck, for she can never be anything to
me but a *hoalauna* (friendly companion)."

"I will look after her," said Kahahana,
"and I will send a litter for you, the day after
to-morrow, when we embark."

Then calling Kelea, who had retired during
the interview, he thanked her for her kindness
to Hookama and presented her with a string of
the precious *achantinella* (land shells), a variety
found only on trees, very exquisite in tint and
vivid in changing hue. The girl received his
praises with a blushing face, but refused his
gift. The king insisting, she finally accepted
the shells and hid them in her girdle, thinking
she might need them in the furtherance of her
plans.

Bidding her look well to Hookama and with

other pleasant words to his friend, after the usual parting salutation, the touching of noses, the king rejoined his escort and was soon out of sight down the ravine.

Hookama, exhausted by the interview, sank back into the long, soft grass and resigned himself to the luxury of the genial tropical sunshine.

CHAPTER XI.

A HAWAIIAN WOOING.

AFTER the king of Oahu had gone, Hookama's announcement to Kelea that scarcely more than a day remained before he must accompany his king to Oahu, made her heart sink within her. All that the young *alii* could say failed to cheer her. His words seemed cold and heartless to her fervid thirst for his love.

She hurried away on a slight pretext, and, in the secluded dell near the bathing pool, gave vent to her passionate feelings. She burst into angry imprecations at one moment and the next, calming a little, conjured up various schemes to attain her end. Finally a plan shaped itself in her mind, and bathing her face in the cool water of the pool she went back to the hut, and chatted gaily with Hookama till evening, of a thousand trifling matters.

The *wahines* played and sang to him, while Kelea fantastically arrayed the youth in festoons of vines and blossoms. He yielded to her caprice and was glad that her brow had lost the cloud which settled there at the beginning of the day.

No *kukui*-torch was lighted in the little grass hut that night. The *wahines* slept soundly in their own house and Hookama was happy to yield himself to sleep when the first darkness settled down upon the land. It is needless to say that Kelea, filled with the hope which her new plan inspired, slept only by fits and starts, while her mind was busy, in the intervals between waking and sleeping, with the details of the venture, into which she threw her whole nature with desperate disregard of whatever consequences might follow either its success or failure.

Another bright day dawned on the morrow, even more delicious in its balmy odors and its invigorating air. Early was Kelea in the hands of her maidens at the pool, which she playfully called her "city of refuge," a term applied to enclosures which no enemy could enter on pain of death.

The *wahines* caused her skin to shine after her bath like the polished *koa* wood, and placed about her neck the circlet of shells

which the prince had given her; around her
ample waist they arranged the marvellous
shining skirt (*pau*), constructed of spires of
sword-like grass, from which after the outside
was stripped a long, silvery fibre remained.
Hundreds of these flexible, glossy ribbons
made a gauzy covering from waist to knees,
clinging light as air, for the most part, to
the limbs, although some of the streamers
floated outward when touched by the faintest
breeze.

Kelea then wreathed her head and arms and
bust in flowers and delicate ferns and gave
directions to the *wahines*, who received them
with a most demure expression of countenance.
She told them to go back at once to Waihee
and say to her father that they had all been
to visit some acquaintances among the hills.
"You need not go into the hut to get the
tapas and calabashes," she added, "but hurry
down the pass as fast as you can go, and say
that I am coming after you, as soon as I have
made my offering at the shrine of Lilinoe,
where I must spend the night, according to a
vow made for my father's safety in the battle."
She saw them on the path, but she did not see
their amused looks, as they began to laugh
and chatter together, as soon as they were out
of sight.

Not long after their departure, Kelea returned to the hut and in her most playful, fascinating manner, assisted the invalid to come and see her " city of refuge," taking the *tabu*-spear with her, and planting it just outside the little dell. Never did fairy bower look more enchanting and never did queen appear in more bewitching mood. Kelea had hung wreaths of ferns and blossoms on the branches overarching the pool. Fresh moss was piled upon the bank and flowers were scattered everywhere. There were *tapa* cloths on which luscious fruits were laid, and a large calabash was filled with *poi*.

The fragrance of the Hawaiian begonia pervaded the air. Its delicately tinted pink flowers covered the spray-blown face of the waterfall, and a rippling streamlet made soft music as it fell from the rocks over a low ledge into the clear, bright water.

Hookama needed no urging to get down at once into the pool. It was hardly up to his shoulders, and as he stood in the midst of the circling wavelets after his cooling dip, he was more like the vigorous man of former days to the smiling girl upon the grassy shore, than he had appeared since the battle.

When he came out and lay on the mossy couch prepared for him, his muscular limbs

were tinged with a ruddy hue and a new color
came over his strong body, which his brief ill-
ness had not wasted. To Kelea, he was like a
god come down to earth to visit her, such as
she had seen in her happiest dreams.

With gentle yet firm touch, she dried his
dripping skin, using thin *tapa* cloths, and then,
applying her soft palms till the surface was
like polished marble, she anointed his body
with fragrant oils ; wreathing his neck and
breast with garlands, she set before him the
food, and with skilful fingers peeled the
breadfruit and bananas, causing him to eat
them from her hand.

When the repast was over, she seated herself at his side and suddenly flinging a roll of
tapa over them both, exclaimed, " Now thou
art my husband (*kane*)," and nestled towards
him, the silvery fringe of her skirt lightly falling on his body. The young man rose to his
feet in an instant, and upbraided her with
alluring him into the trap. It was a custom
of the country that a marriage ceremony was
complete when both parties, by mutual consent, were covered by the *tapa* cloth. In the
case of a chief or *alii*, it should be of a peculiar color. Had Hookama seen such a roll
near by, as if provided for the ceremony, his
suspicions would have been aroused and he

would have given Kelea no opportunity to claim him even in mock espousal.

Now he was thoroughly angry and denounced the trick. He defied her to publish to her kindred, (as was the custom when a marriage was secretly consummated,) the deception she had practised. Besides, no mutual consent was possible in this case, for, by all the gods, he declared he would not have her for his wife.

But the young man had overestimated the strength derived from the momentary glow imparted by the bath and the food he had taken. His exertion, under the excitement of his aroused indignation, was too much for his still feeble condition, and with a dizzy feeling he sank to the ground. His head reeled and he could not steady himself enough to rise, although he made an effort to get upon his feet.

At first, Kelea, hearing his angry exclamations, stood ready to respond with wrathful words; her hands were clenched, her eyes aflame and her whole frame trembling with passion. But the instant Hookama fell, she was kneeling by his side, bathing his head with water and putting the *awa* to his lips, in order if possible to revive him. She spoke no word; her face expressed nothing but concern

and pity. She had nerved herself for this
supreme effort to make the young *alii* all her
own, and she had failed. But what was
that compared with harm or suffering to
Hookama !

When the youth revived and sat up, looking
not at her but at the reflection in the pool of
her kneeling figure, the sense of her discomfiture and the hopelessness of her endeavor returned upon her like a torrent, and she felt as
if she had received the overwhelming shock
of an ocean wave.

She was crushed, humiliated, baffled in this
last effort to achieve a triumph which she
thought was almost in her grasp. She fell at
Hookama's feet, and, with her face in her
hands, buried her head in the deep moss,
crying and moaning as if her heart would
break. The flowers, with which she had
adorned her neck and brow, were crumpled
and awry ; the band, which held her silvery
skirt, parted and the shining folds of streamers,
wound round and round to form the fluffy
garment, lay unrolled, a disorderly mass half
covering her limbs. She was the picture of
abject despair.

Hookama could have met the situation, weak
as he was, had Kelea faced him with threats
or even with spiteful ferocity ; but this was a

new experience; he had never seen a woman in such a state before. He tried to lift her but found his strength insufficient. He was too feeble physically to realize that she was giving herself to him body and soul. Indeed, he felt something of the same fear and repugnance towards her that made him break away from her importunities at Waihee. Besides, he was bewildered, knowing that he was the cause of her despair, although without any such intention. He also knew that he had too easily yielded to her caressive attentions, and at Waihee had made to her some rash promises.

At length, he said to her, in as kindly a tone as he could command: "Kelea, listen! You have planted the tree, not I. If its fruit is bitter, am I to blame? The gods are unkind to you. The crab with its shell broken cannot cling to the rock; the waves carry it away: but a man can pick up the shell-fish and set it in a place where it can at least live. This is all I can do for you. I did not break the beautiful shell; I am sorry it is broken. I cannot make you my wife; I am only a boy; you are older; you are my 'elder sister' [A Hawaiian figure]. I have royal blood in my veins, they tell me, but I have no inheritance. My name, Hookama, means 'the adopted

one'; it carries nothing but the barren right
of an *alii* to serve another greater *alii*. I
don't know who were my parents; I only obey
my chief and my king; if I were free——"

With a sudden start, and fixing her tear-
streaming eyes upon him, Kelea cried, "Then
it is another—I feared it was; but she would
pity me. I'll be her slave, her *kauwa*, anything you wish, if you will only let me go with
you, be yours to love and care for."

There was a touching pathos in her tones.
This proud woman, who could meet a cowardly man and fight him for her honor; whose
superb strength could wrestle with the surge
of the ocean and conquer it; whose haughty
bearing had overawed many a chief that
sought her hand in marriage, was now suing
this unknown youth, whose lineage she did
not know, for the smallest favor which a man
could bestow, the wretched boon of being the
servant of one he loved and whom she had
never seen.

"Aole, aole!" he replied. "No, Kelea, some
evil spirit has suggested this to you. It is not
another, but I do not love you; I do not want
you. You are *tabu* to my heart. I do not
know why, but it is the will of the gods. The
sea-bird never dwells with the bird on the hills.
Even if I loved you, I could not carry you

with me to my distant home. The aromatic shrub has no sweetness when broken off from——"

"Then swear to me," cried the wretched girl, "even if you cannot love me; swear to me only this—will you, Hookama? If you will, I will trouble you no more. I will do all you say; you shall be my star in the sky and I will worship you as too fair, too bright for me, except as it shines on me from the clouds."

"Swear what?" he quickly asked, as if a chance to escape from the pit into which he had fallen were suddenly offered.

"That if I should appear to you in your distant home—alas! too far for me ever to reach it—you will not shun me, hate me, even if you cannot do more. I will not claim you; I will never burden you, but you will not hate me, kill me, or thrust me from your sight. Swear this to me, by Kane, Lono, and her whom I worship, the goddess Lilinoe, and I will try your patience no more. We will be brother and sister till you sail away,—lost, lost forever to your Kelea, whose spirit you will take with you, while her body wanders like the wind in the evening twilight."

"I swear it," said Hookama, soberly, "by Kane, Lono and Lilinoe. If I do not keep the vow (it is not a hard one) may their curses come upon me like the blast from a red crack of the volcano, where your goddess holds fiery sway."

As he said these words, he turned and slowly wended his way back to the hut and threw himself on the mats, exhausted in body and mind. The shock had unnerved him; he could not think of anything, except that he remembered how on the morrow he must be strong enough to reach the coast, for he had given his word to depart with the king, when the sun went down on that day.

CHAPTER XII.

A VISION OF KELEA'S ANCESTRESS.

As soon as Hookama vanished out of her sight, and Kelea's heavy eyes had watched his steps beyond the dense foliage of the dell, this strange creature of good and bad impulses seemed to change into a savage with all the inherited tendencies of the wildest of her barbarian ancestors.

She tore off the flowers that still clung to her hair and breast, and flung them into the pool. Her silver circlet was snatched, as if it were a poisoned garment, from her form; this she threw with violence after the garlands. *Tapa* cloths, calabashes, fruits, mosses, everything, even the wreaths she had hung on the trees, went into the water as if they had been witnesses to a deed of blood. Then, climbing upon the ledge, she rolled the largest stones she could move into the basin; breaking the

limbs of the overhanging trees, she bent them
down till the trembling leaves swept the surface of the pool, and, when all was done that
could be done by her main strength, she leaped
in after the tangled mass, as if to drown herself in the midst of the meshes of the net she
had madly woven.

But she did not mean to drown herself.   She
must live.   Her leap was only the last blind
movement of her savage fury.   Buoyed up by
the debris, her hot limbs sank but knee-deep
in the water; then she scooped the water with
her hands and bathed her fevered forehead.
Scrambling out, she lay upon the bank as if
her paroxysm, not of rage but of reckless
frenzy, in departing, had left her a wounded,
wretched creature, heedless of everything but
her own misery.

She might have remained in that condition
till the darkness came on, for all that she
cared.   It mattered little to her what happened now.   A numbness at last came upon
her and she felt as if she had no power to
move.   Then, to her tired brain, as if it were
a vision in sleep, there appeared the spirit-
ancestress whose name she bore.   Kelea, the
famous surf-rider of Maui, of whom the bards
of Oahu and Maui love to sing; Kelea, the
beautiful but capricious sister of Kawao, king

of Maui ; she who had called the surf-board her husband till the gods summoned her to Oahu and Lo-lale made her his bride, indulging her in every whim.

As if an ocean billow had flung this queenly form before her on the beach, Kelea recognized in the apparition a kindred spirit that had come to succor her in her hour of need. The goddess held out her arms and her feet were dripping with pearls of dew. Her face was radiant as she gaily told the story of her joy with the water sprites in the deep sea at Ewa bay, where now she sported beneath the breakers which she had breasted in her lifetime long ago, when she drove the white-maned steeds of the surf and lay upon the sandy shore with the wavelets lapping her feet.

Her mysterious disappearance from Maui, when Lo-lale's cousin, commissioned to find him a wife, carried her off to Oahu to the brighter home she found on that beautiful isle, is it not all written in the Myths and Legends of Hawaii?

Strangely enough, the exact route taken by the Kelea of centuries past, as the canoe of her abductor sailed by the stars bearing northward to escape Molokai, seemed clear to the Kelea of the present.   The wandering stars, the five planets known to the ancient Hawai-

ians, directed the course then to the west, and
the entire journey over the restless seas, end-
ing with the royal welcome by Lo-lale dressed
in his richest trappings, became as real to the
dreaming girl as if she were herself passing
with her captivating ancestress through it all,
to be decked with pearls on her arrival.

Then a cloud settled over the water-queen,
as she spoke of the gentle Lo-lale, who had
relinquished her to his royal cousin, when the
fitful bride longed for a home nearer the sea
than the royal *hale* on the mountains of Oahu.

The half-awake, half-sleeping Kelea thought
in the vision that she was the wanderer, but
as an outcast driven from her own island and
having no place to call her home.

Yet when the spirit of Kelea, the beautiful,
disappeared in the mist of a rainbow, diving
back into the blue depths of the sea, the look
she gave her sorrowful descendant was so
reassuring that it said, "Follow me, where I
found happiness in a lover," and the girl awoke
from her trance in new and vigorous hope-
fulness. She had received, she believed, a
message from the god that ruled the sea,
Kane-huli-koa, whose votary her ancestress
was, bidding her trust herself to him and all
would be well.

From that moment, her strength came in

full flood upon her again; her love for Hookama quickened her pulses and her whole being
was suffused with the glow of a new purpose,
which, as the will of the gods, she determined
to carry out, even to the minutest details as
the water-queen had revealed them. She
knew the story of Kelea by heart from her
early childhood, but now it became a reality
and a prophecy.

She arose from the bank, with a new light
in her eyes and a joyous feeling in her heart.
She looked down at the pool, then she turned
her back upon the scene of her discomfiture
and went away as if a victory were already
won. She said to herself: "He shall see
what a wife I might be to him," as she allowed
her hair to ripple over her comely shoulders.

One piece of *tapa*, which had escaped her
ruthless hands, she wound about her, as the
matrons of her tribe were accustomed to wear
their sober garments. With the *tabu*-spear in
her hand, she went back to the grass house
and planted it before the door. She saw
Hookama through the opening, as he lay
upon the couch, but she did not go in.

She busied herself heating stones in an
earthen oven. She cooked delicious cakes of
poi ; plucked the ripest fruit of the pandanus ;
chose the most juicy berries, and, when all was
ready, carried the tempting food into the hut.

When she stood before Hookama, her face
was serene, but not bold. Her eyes sought
the ground, not as if she were abashed, but
modestly. In subdued tones she invited him
to eat. As he ate sparingly, she waited in
silence. When he finished she quietly took
away the remnants of the repast, and returning sat in repose at his feet.

He saw that she wore no flowers, the first
time he had ever seen her without them. He
noticed that her bosom was covered with a
coarse brown *tapa*, a choice of vestments very
unlike her usual clothing of bright and varia-
gated cloths. But he could not avoid seeing
also a look of relief on her face and something
like exultation in her eyes.

When she had given Hookama the *lomi-lomi*,
usually performed by her *wahines*, she spread
the night-*tapa* cloth over him carefully, and,
with a pleasant *Aloha* and a smile, went out
under the stars. He heard her go to the
little hut of the women, and then all was
silent, except as the stillness was broken by
the occasional hooting of a distant owl and
the sound of melodious cascades.

There was no change the next day in Kelea's
manner or actions. She brought him water
and food ; asked if he wished to go out for a
sun-bath ; helped him collect the things that

belonged to him, rolled them into a bundle
and cleared up the interior of the hut, making
ready to leave in the afternoon. To Hookama's surprise and satisfaction, she did not
allude to the events of the previous day.
She said nothing to him about his "oath."
She made no affectionate advances, but acted
like a woman who looked after her master's
comfort, and accepted his whims as a matter
of course.

When the litter, a wattled netting swung on
two stout bamboo poles with cross-pieces, was
brought by order of the king, she filled it with
long grass, helped the carriers lift their heavy
burden to their shoulders, and, taking the
bundle of goods tied up in *tapa*, followed at a
little distance in the rear, as the little troop
marched down the valley.

The natives as they passed her gave the customary salutation, *Aloha*, but noticed nothing
that distinguished her from the peasant class
except her stately manner. Only a few turned
their heads and looked back to scan her more
closely. In her mind, however, there was
maturing an intense purpose. She meant to
reach Oahu by some means or other; what the
means might be she did not know, but it was
an absolute certainty to her that the home of
Hookama was the goal of her life henceforth.

This idea was fixed in her mind when she awoke from her vision of Kelea, the surf-rider and queen. It had calmed her. It gave her self-control. It dominated her temper. It gave Hookama a respite for the present from her importunity. It put her into harmony with Nature and its forces, for on the universal powers about her, supernatural or visible, she relied to accomplish her aim.

Her savage mind felt this vaguely but fully. In her thought, it was simply : " I will go where he goes, and sea, sky and land will aid me ; I can swim, walk, leap. Men are nothing to me ; there is but one man and he has sworn."

As she came down to the sand hills, the camp of Kahahana was breaking up. The ground was littered with torn bandages of *tapa*, remnants of food, bones, and broken calabashes. Warriors were collecting their few effects, and tying their javelins in bunches with cocoa-nut fibre. It was a busy and a mournful scene. The wounded warriors lay apart, ready to be transported to the canoes, some to die, and to be lashed in a large canoe, provided for the dead that their bones might be buried in their native soil.

A few gruesome bundles of bones of chiefs killed in the recent battle, cleared of flesh, were heaped in a pile, and the entire hillside was disfigured by foul materials, while the odors from the valley of death beneath came up like steam from a witch's cauldron.

The king of Oahu and his high chiefs had left the camp days before for a healthier location near the beach. After the battle the chiefs left the loathsome results to their low-lived followers, whom they used as fighters but despised as serfs.

Hastening forward, as soon as it was known that the king had given orders to bring the sick *alii* to his own quarters, the little band went through other collections of improvised huts, where the army of Kahekili, king of Maui, awaited orders to depart. Many had gone by the passes to Lahaina, but the bulk of the forces was to take canoes for the passage by sea, in attendance on the king.

Arriving at King Kahahana's house, with its low verandah overlooking the sea, Hookama was cordially received by his chief and the net of twisted fibre was swung in the coolest part of the *lanai* for his comfort. Kelea quietly deposited her bundle at his feet; took from it a few of her own articles of clothing and looked into the young *alii's* face for his parting words.

The king stood by and had already said some kind words to the girl, thanking her for

her care of his friend. He also placed in her
hand a small sandal wood box of precious
shells, more valuable than those he had for-
merly given her, and which could be exchanged
among the natives for any necessary articles.
Kelea inwardly revolted from the idea of
wages, but in her assumed rôle of nurse or servant and, remembering that she might need
them, as the king's first gift had been flung
into the pool, she took them with a stolid face,
thanked the giver and waited for Hookama to
bid her depart.

The young man, for the first time, had to
choke down a rising lump in his throat; he
had become accustomed to Kelea's friendly
offices and graceful presence. She had nursed
him back to life and he was loath to part with
her.

Drawing her nearer to him, while the king,
with a consideration hardly to be expected of
a barbarian, turned his back and looked off
towards the ocean, Hookama held her hands
for a moment and then, in the grotesque fashion of those times, touched noses with the girl,
a token of friendliness and familiarity which
carried with it hearty goodwill if not always
the sincerest affection.

As their faces touched, Kelea flushed, and,
carried away by a transport of love, whispered

in the young man's ear: "*Aloha nui !* Remember you have sworn !" Then turning quickly, with an obeisance to the king, she left the house, her bundle on her head like a common native, and walked towards the beach. Hookama's eyes followed her and a sigh broke from his lips, which caused the king to remark: "Yes, she is worthy of an *alii* for a lover." But he said nothing more and Hookama did not reply. The two friends then busied themselves over the details of the embassy to the king of Hawaii, which Hookama was about to undertake.

CHAPTER XIII.

A SAVAGE TYRANT FOILED.

THERE were signs of bustling life and preparation for departure all along the seashore, as Kelea, with a step of assumed gaiety, entered the groups of warriors and women, busy in loading the war-canoes and for once hurrying at their work. The reason for this show of activity was apparent, as a chief, tattooed over half of his face and body, came striding along, jesting brutally with some natives not quite as nimble as the rest and glaring at the women who involuntarily stopped their labors and crouched on the sand at his approach.

Seeing Kelea, who had laid her bundle down and was standing erect, not knowing that it was the king of Maui to whom the other women were so obsequious, Kahekili was taken by her figure and the freshness of her face. The savage beast in him, which usually

asserted itself, changed to an assumed court-
liness of manner which he could command at
will.

As he drew near to her, the crowd drew off,
that they might not cross his shadow, an
offence liable to the penalty of death, if he so
willed, and, also that they might not over-
hear his conversation, a still worse offence.

"*Wahine!* These brave fellows from Oahu
are not your tribesmen, I am sure? By Lono,
they are an ungrateful set. Not a single
Hawaiian chief after the battle left alive for
sacrifice, and several they killed instead of
giving them to me for my new *heiau* up there
on the hill. See it, my dear?" and he took
her chin in his great rough hand and twisted
her neck to look in the direction towards
which he pointed.

"They leave at dark; good riddance to
their shadows! May they never darken my
shores again: I've no faith in them; a race of
sharks."

Then lowering on her, with a grimace which
was meant for a smile, he said under his
breath: "Come to my *hale-alii* to-night. I've
a present for you. I'll send my *kahili*-bearer
to show you the way, when the canoe of the
king of Oahu, the last to go, leaves the shore."

Kelea, frightened and abashed, for no *alii*

had ever used such language to her before, did not dare raise her eyes to the devilish face and could only see the leg that was tattooed all over with black spots like the plague.

She had heard of the dreadful Kahekili and now her appehensions of her fate at his hands and in his power made her quiver with fear. All her courage left her. She felt a dragging sensation at her heart and hardly suppressed a shriek of terror.

The king did not want to frighten her ; that was not his aim. " *Milu* (hell) seize me!" he quickly exclaimed, as he saw her trepidation and attributed it to her sense of his exalted rank, " but it's only an ivory talisman I mean to give you, to protect you from evil spirits, if there are any, and bad men.

" Who are you, my *wahine ?* Not a low-born child, I'll swear."

Seeing that he must be answered, Kelea, without lifting her eyes, told him who her father was, and that he was the chief of Waihee.

" Then what are you doing here ? Come, come, I'll take you to the *hale* myself, and to-morrow send you to your father. He is one of my best warriors ; I must protect you for his sake," and the ferocious old sinner took her by the shoulder, as if to carry her along with him to his house.

With a sinking heart, and fearing the worst, which was to her the loss of a chance to join the war-canoes of Oahu and somehow get to Hookama's island, she walked with him a little way. Then, as if a sudden thought came to her, she looked up, and, summoning all her courage, said meekly to the old rascal, " My great and honored *Alii nui*, Kelea of Waihee is your humble slave. How can she touch the finger of her king! Your favor is better than any talisman ; it is my part only to obey."

Then Kahekili, pleased with her voice, as well as with her person, said, as gently as he could :—

"We go to-morrow to Lahaina and you shall go with me. Your father will esteem it an honor. I see you are as modest as you are fair. What say you, my daughter?"

Emboldened by his softer tone, Kelea replied : "I like it well ; to see your famous palace at Lahaina, my eyes have ached for many a day. Good *alii !* might I find my *wahines*, and have them with me here when the canoe of Kahahana departs? Then, without your guidance, we will find our way to the *hale*, or, perhaps you will meet me here and lead the way ? "

Thinking he had made an easy conquest, and that the girl, however nobly born, would not dare to evade his authority, which was supreme on the island, even if she were not won over by his large offer to make her one of his household at Lahaina, the sly old debauchee gave her leave to go, and, touching her face to his hand, Kelea quietly and with a proud step walked inland, moving slowly, this time with her bundle in her hand. When she reached a wooded path, well known to her, she quickened her pace to a rapid run, and came back to the shore about three hundred yards above the place where she had met and outwitted the craftiest and cruelest *alii nui* of all the islands.

Creeping along the edge of the beach where there was a growth of bushes, she gained a spot on higher ground, where a stream of considerable size flowed into the sea. The war-canoes of Oahu extended to this point, and there were many warriors and canoe-paddlers at work here as elsewhere on the shore.

She knew that the old king would not come so far from the main road to the beach, and that the men at this place could not have seen her with him. Assuming, therefore, the bold air of an ordinary native woman, she saucily approached the working crews and bandied jests with them; told them that the surf boards of Maui could outsail their crazy ca-

noes; asked them if their paddles were turtle-
fins; whether they did not want to take her as
a nurse, to go with them for good luck; or
would they prefer a *hula*-girl to dance on the
waves in the moonlight?."

The warriors gathered about her and chatted
with her, pleased with the diversion, and from
them she learned where the king of Oahu's
war-canoe was preparing for the voyage.
"Not far from here," said one of the merriest
of the young men, hoping to allure her away
from the rest. Then he counted on his fingers,
"*Akahi* (one), *alua* (two)," till he came to
umi (ten); "There," said he, "and I'll meet
you in the slinging of ten stones," meaning in
about half an hour.

Kelea wound towards the royal canoe by a
devious path through the bushes and came
out abreast of it to find a better class of warriors lounging about. They were on guard
and not at work, for the *moi's* boat was ready
among the first, and it was near sundown.

What was her surprise, as she watched the
lazy warriors, to see two of them get up, and,
going away, return, paddling a canoe, which
made her heart jump and her blood tingle.
She recognized in an instant the canoe of Hookama in which he had come to Waihee. The
men beached the boat, drew its prow on the

sand, brought a mast, sail, a bunch of javelins, some bundles tied up in *tapa*, and finally the very load she had carried on her head down the Wailuku pass that afternoon.

Stowing these things carefully away, they added calabashes, covered with skins, which Kelea knew contained food. A lot of fresh fishes, that wriggled and shone as the men handled them, were thrown into the canoe hap-hazard; and finally a roll of *tapa*, very securely fastened, was laid on the bundles towards the stern. Then the men spread a stout matting over the canoe, covering it wholly. This cover was secured by a cord of fibre, tied to the outrigger and drawn over and across the matting several times. This was done to keep the contents from the waves and the rain.

Having finished their work, the men sat on the top of the canoe and began to eat their *poi* with an evident relish. At this moment, Kelea, covering her head with her *tapa* mantle, ran very rapidly to the canoe, and, as if weary with running, leaned upon it to rest herself. The men offered her the calabash containing the *poi*.

She knew she was forbidden by *tabu* to eat with men. The *tabu* was very strict on that point. So she declined, but said if they would

leave some and go away till she had finished,
she would gladly share their food; and she
showed them some of the shells that were
given to her by Kahahana, to pay for it, saying that their *wahines* at Oahu would prize
them highly.

The men agreed to her proposal, took each
two handsome shells and went off to the royal
war-canoe. In fact, they told her that they
belonged with the king's war-canoe, and were
going to draw this small canoe after the king's
by a long rope. She asked if they were coming back again to the canoe, and they said,
"Yes, when the sun shows its back behind
Mauna Eke, and we have set the king's canoe
into the surf."

She ate her *poi* greedily, for she had scarcely
tasted a morsel since morning, and then, leaving the calabash on the canoe, she went
through the wet sand, for the tide was coming
in, and hid herself to watch and think. Suddenly she said to herself, " Be silent, O Sun!"
and her heart leaped into her throat as she
conceived a desperate "leap in the dark," to
escape the dreaded Kahekili and to attain her
dearest wish. " The canoe! the canoe!" and
she could hardly keep from shouting at the
thought, as she watched the sun, sinking in a
blaze of golden light beyond the hills.

Speedily the twilight came on, and still no
sound of the feet of the coming warriors who
were to embark in the war-canoes lying quietly,
and in them their crews with paddles ready in
their hands.   At last, with the first stars, the
beach was alive with warriors and she saw
dusky forms passing between her and the sea.
She thought a dark object like a litter passed
by and her pulses quickened at the thought of
Hookama so near; it gave her courage for her
daring venture, and when the last form glided
by, with rapid feet she tore through the
bushes, leaped across the sandy beach, quickly
untied the ends of the lashings at the stern of
the canoe, squeezed herself through the small
opening, after pushing in the bundle she carried, and replacing the withs of fibre as well as
she was able, crawled as near the bow of the
boat as she could crowd her body.

No sooner was she safely in her place, her
heart beating like surf upon the shore, than
she heard a voice, and the canoe, half im-
mersed in the water, moved as if some one
were leaning against it.   Then the voice came
again to her ears, as it said, " That *wahine* is no
fool; of course she wouldn't wait for a Maui
man as a companion, when all these *aliis* of
Oahu are about."   It was the youth who had
counted ten upon his fingers.

Kelea heard his retreating footsteps, and soon after, the sound of regular strokes in the water. She knew that this meant that the war-canoe of the king was breasting the surf.

The two men who had given her the *poi* (she knew them by their voices) came running at full speed: "Quick, with her into the surf," one of them cried out. "Did they mean *her?*" was the thought that passed like lightning through Kelea's brain, but it was only the canoe, which they shoved into the curling breakers, and sprang upon its covered top.

One of them bore down hard with his foot on the trembling body under the matting, but he noticed nothing unusual, as the craft danced on the waves and shot over the rollers into the smooth water where the war-canoe was waiting. She heard shoutings, and splashings of the water as of many canoes getting under way—sounds which seemed to recede from her as she felt her own little bark fairly afloat; and a great relief came to her spirit.

Kelea's perils, however, were not over. She felt the prow of the canoe strike a hard substance; it was the stern of the war-canoe. Hands clung to the smaller craft, and commands were given in a voice which she recognized as Kahahana's, as he sat in the stern of his war-canoe.

Of the two men in Kelea's canoe, the one in the prow leaped on board the larger boat; the other, who was steering in the stern, started across the cover to follow his comrade. He stumbled along as he went, and at last planted his foot squarely on the side of Kelea's head. Fortunately her head lay on a roll of *tapa*, but the man's weight was no small burden to the girl. She then heard him say, " Kà, hà, hà! I've left the *alii's* bundle in the boat; the *moi* says he must have it, if it costs my life. What's my life to him!" So back again to the stern he plunged; then dropping into the water he fumbled under the covering, (fortunately where Kelea had left the lashings loose,) and began to search for the roll of *tapa*.

Kelea felt the roll at her feet, and pushed it with all her force; it came near the man's hand, and, grasping it, he sprang again upon the cover, ran across it once more, and soon the voices of the men on the war-canoe sounded far away. There was a jerk at the bow and the poor, frightened girl in the frail boat behind knew that twenty stout paddlers were carrying her towards the west—and Oahu.

The sea was comparatively calm, but as the canoe was pulled rapidly through the waves, Kelea, rolling from side to side, could scarcely keep from being dashed against the contents of the boat, which had been left loose; her sides were bruised; she protected her head with her *tapa* which she slipped off, but the strain on nerves and muscles was fearful; then the strange reaction, which follows strenuous and prolonged effort in daring deeds, came upon her: "Would she live through the long voyage? How long would this dreadful strain continue? If the war-canoe stopped in any harbor this side of Oahu, would they send her back?" These and countless other possible perils, added to the fatigue of her uncomfortable position, made her brain reel.

But when she saw before her that monster, the king of Maui, with his body half black, and almost felt his foul breath in her face; and on the other hand, remembered Hookama's oath, she preferred the tossing canoe with all possible disaster, to the soil of her native island, with its cruel tyrant and his iron hand.

Hours passed and the light that came through the sides of the now loose and flapping covering, suddenly vanished; all was inky blackness. "Was it death?" she asked herself, "then welcome death, if the gods so willed." But she was still alive, and the gods were with her as she supplicated their aid. The god of the sea, on whose bosom she had so often ridden the angry waves, would protect her.

At any rate, she must do something for her own safety and the flapping of the now loose covering suggested the effort. She had a sharp shell which she always carried in a piece of *tapa* for cutting up food and separating the stout stems of plants and fruit.

Reaching out her hand with the shell in it—then her arm, she found the taut rope by which the canoe was dragged along. With the edge of the shell she sawed the wet rope. The moist fibre cooled her fingers but held fast. It was of many twisted strands. She made little impression upon it.

Then she determined, come what might, to tear the covering from the prow and work with better hope of success. Lying on her breast, she made an opening for her head, then for her shoulders. Soon her arms were free. She clasped a little block of wood, lashed upright in the prow; it was the "totem" of Hookama, but she did not take much notice of it; she laid her head against it for support and in order to steady herself for the work. Cutting, cutting, the edge of the shell became more and more dull, and to her horror, the moon, which had risen in a cloud, began to glimmer along a narrow pathway, bringing her canoe into plain sight, as the line of silvery light lay on the water between her and the war-canoe.

To her joy, clouds again shut in the disc, and the rope, as she felt it with her fingers, had one strand severed. With renewed energy she sawed across the remaining fibres. Fortunately for her, the strands gave way gradually, one by one. Had they all parted at once the men in the war-canoe might have noticed the result. Some of the fibres still held firmly, when, at last, her hand, cramped with the work, let the shell fall and it sank into the sea.

Sick at heart and exhausted, Kelea threw herself back into the canoe and lay down, expecting no help from the gods, since she could no longer help herself. She was tossed and rolled about, at the mercy of the pitiless waves, conscious of nothing but her misery —dreading her fate.

Soon, a new motion of the canoe added to her fears. It tipped and as it tipped it plunged. The sea came in upon her head ; it revived her, but only to increase her sense of danger. The moonbeams now fell full upon her face ; she gazed up at the sky, which showed stars twinkling but no clouds. She would soon be clearly seen. But the rapid forward movement had ceased. She crept to the fixed block of wood ; in the moonlight it grinned at her horribly, yet it looked like idols she had seen on the walls of the *heiau*. Perchance this god had come to her aid.

She raised her head and looked about her. The waves were high; their white crests danced under the moon. The nebulous " star with a blind eye " faintly glimmered above her.

But where were the war-canoes? There was not the sign of any moving thing on the face of the waters. High cliffs were on one side, afar off ; an immense waste of waters spread itself before and behind ; nothing could be seen save Nature's ever-rolling tides hurtling against the shore, and the twinkling stars which now thickly studded the heavens.

With a deep sigh of relief, she thanked all the gods whose names she could remember, and, laying her head lovingly on the little idol in the prow, she rubbed its ugly nose with her own, as a friend greets a friend.

Then she tore off the covering of the canoe, seized the paddle, and seated herself in the stern. She had never paddled a canoe, but she had guided her surf-board without a paddle through the roughest seas ; and now, with peace in her heart and hope in her soul, she sat like a sea-goddess commanding the waves, and the " totem " grinned at her from its perch in the prow.

CHAPTER XIV.

HOOKAMA, A PRISONER AT HAWAII.

THE king of Oahu, after setting sail from the island of Maui, sent his flotilla ahead, his own war-canoe, with Hookama's in tow, bringing up the rear, together with another, sent a short distance ahead as if for look-out. So it was that when Kelea's little craft dropped astern there was no one behind to see it; and when she gained courage to look out, the whole flotilla had passed on out of sight.

The solitary war-canoe preceding the king's was rowed by eight stout warriors, and when a good offing in the open sea was secured it was hailed and brought back. To it Hookama was transferred for his secret mission to Hawaii.

The canoe was stocked with provisions and weapons, and to the young *alii* the king presented a scarlet helmet and feather cloak with

the *palaoa*, an ivory ornament, the token of exalted rank. Hookama also carried rich gifts
from the king of Oahu to the king of Hawaii.

The canoe was not so magnificent as the
royal war-canoe, but it was twenty-five feet
long, carved at both ends, with a gaily-painted
sail and a red pennon, which only high chiefs
could use. No wonder that the young commander felt some pride in his new position, as,
after receiving the king's last commands and
adieus, his eight broad paddles swung the
craft away into the darkness, the warriors
singing a war song to which their strokes kept
time.

Hookama's course was due east for about
thirty miles; then southeast for sixty more,
with Waipio on the northern shore of Hawaii
as his destination.

Kalaniopuu, the king of Hawaii, had lived
all his life in the midst of carnage; he had
won his throne by being victorious in civil
strife. In the final battle, being told that his
only hope of victory lay in the killing of a
priest on the opposite side whose prayers and
powers prolonged the contest, he had the
priest singled out and slain by his warriors.
He showed great cruelty in his raids, and his
captives, men and women, were unmercifully
beaten on their heads by the war-clubs of his

men. Before him, neither friend nor foe could
stand without balancing the chances of life or
death. The caprice of the moment, or the expectation of some advantage to himself, turned
the scale in favor of or against the victim.

When then Hookama, who knew the *moi's*
reputation, saw a hundred warriors, armed
with spears, awaiting the thud of his canoe
upon the beach at Waipio, it required nerve
of the steadiest sort, to shoot the breakers and
to leap on shore without a weapon, leaving his
warriors in the boat, with orders not to allow
a spear or a dagger to appear in their hands.

Although the young *alii* had not yet fully
recovered his strength of body, he had matured
in the primitive virtues of daring and endurance during the past few weeks. Something
large had come into his nature, the manifestation of a spirit which occasionally appears in
those whose circumstances seem wholly un-
favorable to such a development. Not that
the savage was eliminated, but in place of
ferocity like that of wild beasts, there was a
germ of self-respect; instead of recklessness, a
conscious superiority to adverse surroundings.

It was therefore with an elastic step and a
courageous heart that Hookama landed solitary and unarmed at Waipio, for the voyage had
given him new vigor both of body and mind.

A tall, muscular chief met him as he set foot on the sand, and demanded his business. To this gigantic warrior, whom Hookama recognized as the chief that had felled him to the ground on the battle field, the young *alii* replied that he sought an audience with the king.

As he spoke, he removed his feather helmet with one hand, while with the other he threw back his cloak and displayed on his broad breast the ivory clasp, the token of his high rank. Then pointing to the scar of the wound on his head, he said: "Your weapon glanced when you struck me down at Wailuku, noble chief, or my visit here would be that of a ghost seeking revenge, and not, as it is to-day, a mission of peace."

At this the giant, as chivalrous as he was brave, held out both hands, which Hookama took in both of his own, a mode of salutation precluding treachery, and the two men touched noses in token of amicable relations between them, at least for the time.

Hookama's warriors were then allowed to disembark, and two of them, bearing the presents to the king, followed the two chiefs to the royal house, the others remaining on shore, apparently free, but really under guard. Hookama himself, as he well knew, was in reality a prisoner, and both he and his men, on this hostile shore, were in danger of imprisonment or even death, if the king of the island should prove unfriendly.

The old king was on the broad *lanai* of his house when the little company arrived. He was a lean, hard visaged savage, rather small in stature, with a cool, gray eye, and having the habit of expanding and contracting his eyebrows, which gave him the look of one whose ferocity might break forth at any time in terrible earnest. Woe to any one from whom the savage chief averted his eyes, and on whom the dread sentence, " Face down," was passed! There was no chance of reprieve when once the fatal words were spoken.

Hookama felt that the king was not a pleasant object to contemplate. He had just been defeated in battle. His two bands of choicest warriors had been absolutely obliterated, and his bitterest foeman, the treacherous Kahekili, was master of Maui. The wounded warriors, whom he had brought back to Hawaii, were lying yonder, in huts just over river, and their women were sitting in black *tapa* before the huts. In a few days the funeral obsequies of the slain were to be celebrated, an occasion calling for more human victims, whose heads would adorn the walls of the *heiau*. Under these circumstances it was by no means a safe or pleasant thing to have audience with the baffled and cruel tyrant.

At a signal from the king, who was surrounded by guards, the giant warrior, with Hookama in charge, went forward leading his prisoner, who prostrated himself as was the custom of the land. Being commanded to rise, he threw off his feather helmet and cloak, tightened the *malo* on his loins, and stood before the wizened little man, in all the pride and beauty of his young manhood.

If the king had averted his face, the doom of the young *alii* would have been sealed; but the king had other reasons for deferring sentence.

"Aha!" exclaimed the king, "why has the king of Oahu thrust you into my hands, just when I want victims for the god of war? A fine thing for him to do with his choicest fighter, after joining against me with that cursed king of Maui!"

Hookama met the scowling face and threatening words of the king, with steadfast gaze, as he said in a mild voice: "Noble *alii*, warlike deeds have no part in my embassy to Hawaii. May I present to your *moi*ship Kahahana's gifts, which he sends in token of his high respect for your valor, and to win your favor for his chief bird-catcher, who brings in his hands no snares for men, but only traps for birds?"

The king's lip curled with a sneer as he replied, "Ha, ha! A bird-catcher in a feather helmet and cloak! A fine rig for such service! Do you trap the *oo* and the *mamo* on Oahu with their own feathers? Kakuhaupio here, tells me you tried to catch a pretty big bird with a dagger at Wailuku the other day; I'm too old a bird to be caught with your sticky gum or your flowery speech," and the old man grinned at his own witticism, looking around to see if his followers caught the expression, at which of course they all grimly smiled.

Taking advantage of the favorable moment, Hookama quickly turned to his two men and took the presents, which he laid at the king's feet. The king picked up the carved spear and tested its sharp point, with a sly word to his giant warrior about poisoned tips. Then he examined the costly ivory clasp, as he turned it over in his skinny hands, and said, "My mother named me after this bauble at my birth and she came from Oahu; but the Hawaiian chiefs changed my name. It was a shrewd thing for your king to send me this gift."

Finally, he examined the precious feather

cloak and placing it on his bony shoulders, took up the necklace of priceless shells and counted on his fingers the number of them.

"That is for the comely neck of your majestic and beautiful queen," said Hookama, venturing a remark as he saw the king's face lighten up while gazing at the ornament.

"Which queen?" quickly asked the king. "Kalola," said Hookama on the instant; for he knew that she was his "love-queen," and that the king took her with him when he went on his raids.

There was a look on the king's face, as if he saw the shrewdness of the answer, but immediately the fierce scowl returned, for he needed victims for the sacrifice to the war-god, far more than witty speeches and rich gifts. The old man rested his elbows on his knees and held his head in his hands, as he fixed his stern, gray eyes on the handsome youth, muttering under his breath, "A rare prize for the altar, and eight warriors besides; what could be more acceptable to the great blood-drinker?" And, without changing a muscle of his face, the tyrant, whose first thought was to appease the deity who seemed angry with him, commanded, "Put them in ward. They must die. The gods so will. I have spoken."

Then, turning to Hookama, "You may ask

one favor before you are slain. It shall be granted, but it must not be a request to live."

Hookama, with folded arms and a proud bearing, looked into the cold eyes of the king, but held his peace. No muscle of his countenance quivered. Not a nerve of his compact frame twitched.

"Make the request!" angrily exclaimed the king. "I give it because you are as brave as you are rash. What could Kahahana mean, to send you here? There is treachery in it."

At this charge, Hookama, stung to the quick, replied: "There is no treachery, great king; I make no request."

"But I must grant you one; I have said it."

"Then, let it be death in a spear contest with your bravest warrior; I am of noble blood," and he glanced at two stalwart braves standing near the king.

"So be it," said the king; "lead him away, Kakuhaupio! You are responsible for his head with your own. Throw his men—eight of them, did you say?—into the prison; let the spear contest be this very day; Kamehameha shall hurl the death blow. He will not need to use all his strength. I have spoken," and the king went into his royal house, with tottering steps.

The savage chief, chosen by the king for

the antagonist (or executioner) of Hookama,
was the warrior, now thirty-six years of age,
whose fame was in all the islands. He was
named "The Lonely One" (Kamehameha)
and he it was, who rescued the giant from
Hookama and his band, in the recent battle on
Maui. Within a score of years, as has been
said, he was destined to become master of all
the islands, and already, as nephew of the
king of Hawaii, he held large possessions.

Unprepossessing in appearance, and with a
harsh, rugged face, " he was so strong in limb
that ordinary men were but children in his
grasp ; in council, the wisest yielded to his
judgment ; he was barbarous, unforgiving
and merciless to his enemies, but just, sagacious and considerate in dealing with his sub-
jects. He was more feared and admired than
loved, and in any age would have been a
leader."

"Well, stranger," said this burly chief to
Hookama, as he joined him and his giant
keeper on their way to the latter's dwelling,
" the king, my gracious uncle, says you are
chief bird-catcher to the *moi* of Oahu. Me-
thinks you listen to the singing of javelins
more joyously than to the music of the songsters, although both wear feathers. Is it not
so ? "

" You are right, my *alii*," replied the youth. " The *ihe* (javelin) is pleasanter to my ear than the *iwi* (bird), unless my doom is sealed beforehand, as seems now to be the case. But, if I must die I am glad it will be by the hand of the mightiest warrior of Hawaii."

" Truly sorry am I," rejoined The Lonely One, " to be chosen for this office; but at least I save you from the hands of the executioner and the game shall be fair, I promise you. We will fight as warriors and not as an assassin and his victim. The gods so will it and the king commands." Then he turned on his heel and went off to make arrangements for the contest.

CHAPTER XV.

A DUEL WITH SPEARS.

A SPACE was marked off for the spear-contest between Hookama and Kamehameha, and every advantage of ground and relative position towards the sun was given the prisoner. A rude platform afforded the king and his body guard a full view of the scene. Warriors and women formed a semi-circle about the arena; drum-beaters were stationed near the king, and spearmen stood at intervals to keep the enclosure free.

Kamehameha strode into the arena, and carelessly tossed six javelins, handed to him by an attendant, into the air, and by a dextrous movement caught them as they fell. Hookama came forward and when his keeper, the giant warrior, handed him six javelins, he tested their strength, breaking three of them, using only his right hand in doing it.

The two combatants abstained from the usual taunts, which rival chiefs flung at each other before battle. This conflict was looked upon by Kamehameha as well as by the spectators, more as a solemnity with a foregone conclusion, than as a trial of skill. It was almost as if they had assembled to witness an execution.

Some of the Hawaiian warriors, who looked on, regarded the affair as a matter of course, but the younger braves wore doubtful faces, as if their sympathy inclined toward the intended victim. If he had been one of the king of Maui's warriors, all would have rejoiced in his death, but as a warrior from Oahu, many deprecated his fate.

Some of the women, who had lost husbands and sons in the late battles, were stolid and accepted the sacrifice as a just vengeance ; but many others, especially the younger ones, admired the handsome young athlete and were sorry for him as he stepped into the arena with only a white *malo* about his loins and proudly confronted his massive foe.

Among these young women was a girl of nine or ten summers, whose dark eyes, even at this trying moment, attracted Hookama's attention as he walked towards his position. She was a bewitching little sprite, with raven

locks, a supple figure and clad in a rich *tapa*
mantle, flowers covering her head and neck.
She stood near the king in a haughty attitude,
but with her keen eyes full of sympathetic
interest. Hookama, ever susceptible to female
charms, even though displayed by a mere
child, was about to take a second look at the
proud beauty, when he caught sight of the tall
figure of his antagonist and, forgetting all else,
strode forward to meet him.

The young *alii* was allowed to throw his six
javelins first. Then he must stand as a target
for the six spears of his opponent. If he
caught or parried these, (a thing which the
spectators thought to be impossible,) even
then the king might order him to be slain.
Sometimes, an exceptional display of skill and
courage resulted in the reprieve of the victim.
In this case, however, it seemed as if his fate
were sealed which ever way the contest turned.

Hookama noticed, as he advanced towards
The Lonely One, that the eyes of the warrior
were searching the crowd, as if to discern the
presence of some one. It was in fact, to
catch a glimpse of the dark-eyed maiden
noticed by Hookama that the warrior turned
his gaze away from the young *alii*. But it
was only a moment before Hookama felt the
power of his terrible eyes fastened upon him-

self, and when at the signal the young man
threw his first javelin with little force, as if
husbanding his strength, the big chief smiled
as he caught it between his thumb and finger
and laid it on the ground.

Before Hookama had flung his fourth
weapon, Kamehameha perceived that his
antagonist was no mean opponent. The fifth
taxed the warrior's utmost skill in parrying,
and when the sixth hummed through the air,
it was only by the most agile dodging that he
escaped its point.

As it was, he failed to catch the javelin,
which struck the earth, entering the hard soil
the full length of the tip. The warrior bit his
lips with apparent vexation and only a wholesome fear of his wrath prevented the chiefs and
warriors that stood around from applauding
the stranger. A half-suppressed laugh from
the pretty child who stood near the king
reached the big chief's ear and brought an
angry flush to his face, which boded no good
to the young man, whose prowess the little
witch had so unadvisedly commended.

The good sense of the chief, however, gave
him control of himself, and, with a show of
magnanimity, as if dealing gently with the
young man, he hurled the first spear and
the second in such a way that if they were not

caught or parried, no injury would be inflicted by them. The third javelin he aimed more directly and the fourth with still greater precision and force. All these Hookama caught but there were two left and the spectators held their breath, fearing that the young *alii* might not be able to catch or parry them. The feeling throughout the assembly was intense.

The fifth javelin, coming with terrific swiftness, Hookama avoided by a quick movement to the left, but as it passed him it grazed his shoulder, inflicting a slight wound. The sixth and last weapon was poised and there was a profound hush, as the crowd watched the giant gather himself up, by a supreme effort to finish his adversary.

The heavy javelin was raised aloft by his strong hand. The muscles of his arm swelled with the tension of his grasp on the weapon. Then leaning backward to gain the utmost leverage, the mighty chief, with all the tremendous force of his huge frame, hurled the spear straight at the breast of the young man, who stood firmly on his feet awaiting the dread missile.

There was a scream, as the child near the king fell on the earth. The dust from the ground where Hookama had been standing rose in a little cloud, and the form of the youth, prone on the ground face forward, lay extended at full length.

It was but an instant; and before the spectators could recover their breath Hookama arose and without the movement of a muscle of his face, looked first at the child who had been assisted to her feet, then at his huge opponent, who immediately came forward and took him by both hands.

The youth had not caught or parried the weapon, but, with admirable presence of mind, he had dropped, when the javelin was in mid-air, and it had passed over his head, leaving him unharmed. It was a display of coolness and alertness, which, if not so wonderful as the catching or parrying of the spear, was a feat of which few were capable. The women and warriors crowded into the arena, and were giving vent to their admiration of the stranger's bravery, when the king's harsh voice was heard, commanding Kakuhaupio, who stood at his left, to despatch the youth offhand.

The shouts of the crowd about Hookama subsided, as the rasping voice of the king fell upon their ears; but the towering form of the chief, to whom the royal command had been given, remained motionless, in spite of the angry glances and excited gestures of the king.

"Your august *moi*ship," said the chief in a loud tone, "I am your loyal servant, but I am not your *mu* (assassin). Let your executioner perform his office!" and the speaker looked unflinchingly towards the king, who foamed at the mouth, swore vengeance by all the gods and called to two stalwart spearmen of his guard to slay the young man or take the consequences of their disobedience.

The men sprang forward, but were met by the bulky antagonist of Hookama, who waved them back with his spear. The king cried out in his fury, exasperated beyond measure: "Treason! Seize the traitors and——" But before he could finish the sentence, Kamehameha, saying, "No treason, my *moi*," stepped to his side and whispered words, inaudible except to the king's ear. The effect was instantaneous and surprising; the king's countenance changed from wrath to astonishment. He looked into the warrior's eyes as if to be reassured of the truth of what he had said, and received the reply, "As true as you are *moi* of Hawaii."

Before the king could formulate a further command, from the other side he heard the voice of his most trusted and shrewdest priest, who also spoke to him in an undertone. Then the king raised his head and in words tremulous with excitement ordered Hookama to be bound and led away to prison.

"See," said he, sternly, "that a double guard be placed around the strong cell; you will answer for the prisoner with your heads."

They bound Hookama's arms behind his back with a strong cord, and leading him away, placed him, without further indignity, in a small enclosure reserved for prisoners of state.

CHAPTER XVI.

MENEHUNE, THE DWARF-GIANT.

DAYS and weeks passed and no tidings came to Pu' Aloha at Oahu from the absent Hookama, for whom she longed. The old chief, Numuku, having received some vague rumors, which he interpreted in accordance with his own wishes, was wary and showered every favor known to him upon his poor victim, who saw in his gifts his desire to keep up her spirits till her lover's return.

She seldom spoke of Hookama in his presence and when she did talk of him, he managed to hide his real sentiments and started some other topic of conversation. It could hardly be called "conversation," inasmuch as the old man grunted his assent in most cases and let the girl say what she pleased.

He grew more and more fond of her, after his savage fashion, admiring her increasing roundness and amused by her attentions to himself. She made much of him, weaving fresh *leis* for his adornment and sending her women for the choicest fruits, which he gulped down, with the gusto of a gourmand. Sometimes in the evening, when he stretched himself on the royal mattings, she chatted gaily to him of the little incidents of her daily employments and sang for him the love-songs of the people. It was remarkable that he made no amorous advances, but perhaps he thought the right time had not come.

As the weeks lengthened into months and Hookama did not come, Pu' Aloha's heart grew weary of waiting. Each sunset she stood looking for the expected canoe, which she felt must come out of the bright glow of the west; and it was on one of these days, just at the quick turn of twilight into a cloudless night, that she stood as we have depicted her, watching, with eyes shadowed by her hand, that she might see farther towards the lessening horizon. Intent on her quest, and espying a speck in the far distance which might be the long-expected approach of Hookama, she did not hear the heavy step which came behind her, and her name was twice spoken before she turned her head.

It was Numuku, whose eagle eye had already

discovered the dot on the blue expanse of waves, with a point upwards which he knew was the peculiar tip of the three-cornered sail of Hookama. The chief had come hurriedly to the brow of the cliff, to spy out the thought of Pu' Aloha, to whom he whispered as he came near, " I think 'tis he ; now go and be happy. Your Hookama [he almost hissed the word], will be here before the white crests of the reef are lost in the darkness."

As the night came on with the least possible twilight, he gently took the young girl's hand, and together they slowly walked towards the houses of the women. Pu' Aloha trembled as he left her, bidding her sleep to-night and wake in the morning to embrace her lover. In a tremor of excitement she obeyed and went to her own house, where her servants were squatting outside the low door, and then, dismissing them, she loosened the folds of her *pau* and flung herself down, not to sleep but to dream—the waking dream of innocent love and hope, now almost a reality.

The chief quickened his strides as she disappeared, and sent for one of his most trusted inferior chiefs, to whom with stern voice he gave command to send a party with spears to transfix any stranger, coming through the opening in the reef, whether swimming or in a canoe; he added fiercely, "Bring his head to the *heiau* and leave his body to the sharks." On pain of his utmost displeasure, he commanded him to watch the whole night rather than fail of his errand. He warned him not to enter his presence, if the man he was to kill was not slain. He threatened him with the dread sentence " Down face," if he failed, and almost shouted with anger, as he answered "Hookama!" to the man's question who the victim was, that he was to kill.

In her house, lying quietly and looking up at the stars, through a crevice in the thatched roof, Pu' Aloha heard that name, faintly borne by the light wind to her ears, and the hot blood coursed through her veins and mounted to her cheeks, as the sound seemed to tell her, by invisible messenger, that her beloved was near at hand. With a prayer to the goddess, the protector of virgins, she at last fell asleep.

No one had seen a pair of glittering eyes, belonging to a queer head, peering out from a bunch of cactus only a few feet high and growing near the chief's house, where he had given his orders to the assassin; but Menehune's ears were long though his body was short; his heart was in the right place, if his mouth was somewhat awry; and he had scented mischief when he heard his master order the

men to the reef. When the name of Hookama
vibrated in the air, he knew what it meant to
Pu' Aloha, but he lay low till the chief had
turned into his house; then, slipping along
close to the ground, he crept out of the
enclosure under a patch of broad banana
plants, and once in the open ran like a deer
for the beach, where he ensconsed himself in
a snug hole in the sand, which he scooped out
far enough from the scene of action to be
unobserved by any of the natives watching
the inlet through the reef. The tide was coming in and the dwarf grinned as he felt the
muscles of his legs and knew what they could
do in swimming and running, and of his arms,
strangely attached to his sturdy body, but equal
to any arms of a more symmetrical trunk.

Nobody knew whether he was called a dwarf
because, when he stood up, he was taller than
other natives, or because, when he sat down,
he was much shorter; but perhaps the term
dwarf-giant, by which he was sometimes known,
would be more appropriate.

Menehune, though a clown with many of
the peculiarities of an animal, had a native
shrewdness which resembled the instinct of a
dog. There was something merry and wag-
gish about him, too. He was full of pranks
and antics. He could climb a cocoa-nut tree

for the fruit like a monkey; crack the nut with one hand; swing around crags where no one else dared to venture; the superstitions of the tribes had no meaning for him; his head could not go far enough in that direction to see the reason for the performances in the *heiau*, but he could look on and wonder what it was all about.

The ugly heads of protecting images along the outside wall of the priest's enclosure had a queer fascination for him. Perhaps he saw a certain resemblance, in the hideous shapes and faces, to himself. At any rate, he was not afraid of them, nor overawed by them as other natives were. Once he had a freak, during a sacrificial ceremony which was performed by night, and climbed up and seated himself between two of the ugliest of them, squatting down as if one of the spectral conclave. It tickled him immensely when several of the underlings passed by without recognizing him in the gloaming, and ever after, when he wanted amusement, he took his seat among the gods. He even conceived the idea of taking the place of one of the idols, which he lifted off the wall and hid in the bushes, while he sat motionless, with all the gravity and hideousness of a worthy substitute.

At such times he carried with him some red

and black paint, which he had stolen, and with which he smeared himself into quite a striking resemblance to the deity whose function he had temporarily usurped. He certainly was far more worthy of worship, and could have defended the *heiau* more valiantly than the painted wooden stumps humped on the broad parapet of loose stones.

Leaving Mene' to his own musings in the sand-hole, which gradually filled with water as the tide came in, we catch a last glimpse, for this eventful night, of Numuku, who, after his cruel mandate had gone forth, entered his own door and hung a piece of *tapa* before the opening. There the savage nursed his hatred and wrath, which were soon, as he believed, to be appeased by the death of his rival. Like a fierce tiger he rolled over and over on the figured mats, gnashing the teeth that were left to him, and praying, after the imprecatory style, to Lono, Pele, and all the wrathful deities, to make his plans succeed.

On the beach at Waikiki the sound of the breakers was louder than usual, for a stiff breeze was blowing from the sea, and dark clouds after the sun had set filled the western sky. The crest of Leahi (Diamond Head) stood forth in gloomy majesty, as the spray of the waves was flung over the rocks at its base.

Menehune crouched in his sand-hole and watched the white line of the shore, where dark figures ran to different points to catch a glimpse of any object appearing on the billows as they rolled tumultuously toward the beach. He kept a sharp eye also out to sea, as he chuckled to himself at the thought of outwitting the wily *alii*, whose murderous designs he had discovered.

The storm came rapidly from the south, as if the god of the winds had uncovered the cavernous gourd in which it was believed he held the blast, letting loose the fury of a tempest. At last the dwarf's eager search was rewarded by the sight of a canoe at a long distance outside the foamy reef. It was a mere speck, hardly discernible by the sharpest eye. It had no sail, and whether it contained a human being or not was a matter of conjecture. There was no possibility that if it had an occupant he could pass the breakers in it, much less find the one inlet through which in calm weather it was safe to pass. The dark watchers along the beach had lighted a fire to illure the imperilled mariner toward the entrance.

They knew he could not stay in the canoe in the midst of the squall, but as Hookama was a mighty swimmer perhaps he could reach the shore alive ; they sought to attract him, in such a case, to that part of the beach where they could despatch him in his half-drowned condition, or easily find his body if it were washed ashore. They hoped that the god of the sea would save them the trouble of engaging in a struggle with such a powerful fighter, even though exhausted in his contest with the waves.

But they congratulated themselves that he was only one, while they were ten stout warriors, every one armed with a spear.

Their eyes were so intent upon the limited space where such an experienced sailor as Hookama would attempt to land, that they regarded the southern circle of the shore with less scrutiny. Besides they had seen the canoe once or twice as it rose on the highest crests and always nearly opposite the point where they stood watching.

The storm increased every moment in violence. It was one of those fearful tornadoes which occasionally swept over the islands with great power, coming up rapidly and accompanied with more or less of tidal phenomena and a trembling of the earth.

It was at the very height of this tornado, with vivid flashes of lightning and the rolling of thunder, that Menehune, quaking with fear at the unusual manifestations about him.

lifted his head out of the hole in the sand and saw, far off in the sea, as a flash of extraordinary brilliancy lighted up the entire horizon, an immense wall of dark water, apparently rolling in towards the reef. It was not surmounted by the usual white foam; but when it reached the coral rocks, it rolled completely over them and in a surge of boiling spume, rushed with a loud roar over the shallow spaces towards the land.

There was no time for the dwarf to escape it, even if he had kept his wits about him, and, dumbfounded as he was, the immense mass struck him before he could even rise upon his feet, lifting him like a feather and, carrying him far beyond the straggling line of bushes back from the beach into a low-lying thicket a hundred yards inland, left him half-drowned, clinging to a small tree top, bent to the ground by the violence of the onset. Fortunately for him, his involuntary clutch upon the tree saved him from the less powerful thrust with which a second volume of water, following hard after the first, struck him and took away what breath he had left. It was like one of the tidal waves, not so tremendous and destructive as sometimes swept over the Hawaiian coasts, but sufficiently strong and high to break several of the cocoa-nut palms, hundreds of feet

away from the beach, which had withstood
the storms of half a century.

When Menehune came to himself, lying in
the sand and ooze and seaweed which the
refluence of the waves had left, he was too
startled and exhausted to extricate himself at
once. The jungle, in the midst of which he
was lying, with its tangled growth of young
trees, vines and bushes, was beaten flat, a
thickset, compressed mass, the supple stems of
the plants and trees having yielded to the force
of the wave. He lay in the center of the mass,
covered with slimy débris, stupified for a moment. Soon, the dogged pluck of his nature
returned to him, and by a strong effort he dis-
engaged himself, his long legs greatly assisting
his exertions. His first thought was of Hookama ; what had become of him ?

Fearful as he now was of the sea's angry
might, he yet mastered his terror in his anxiety
to know the worst concerning his friend. He
stood on the shore straining his eyes, as flashes
of lightning came, to discover any object
thrown on shore by the waves, but keeping a
good lookout towards the horizon lest the
great wave should return. He ran up and
down the beach which was hollowed out in
places and heaped up in huge piles of sand.
The soles of his feet slipped on thousands of
fishes flung on the shore, but not a trace of

any living creature could he discover and no object as large as a human body, except one immense sea monster, which lay wriggling and gasping, but which he did not even think of stopping to examine.

After he had made sure that there was nothing for him to do but to go back to his home in Nuuanu Valley, he found a gap through which he could reach a field and so gain the path by the plains to which he was accustomed.

The storm still raged, but its greatest force was abated. Occasional gleams of lightning helped him find his way. He stumbled on and was nearly to the line where the tidal wave had spent its flow, when in the glare of a vivid flash he saw a lumpish mass, lying in his way.

Seeing that it was a human body, without stopping to think whether it might be one of the spearmen or any other, his one idea being Hookama, he lifted the limp form without examining it and slinging it over his broad back hurried on in the darkness to gain a safe place where he might deposit the load. With his great strength he easily carried the body, that seemed to grow warm in contact with his own flesh, and, though he tripped now and then, he reached a grassy slope under a clump of trees and put the inanimate form on the ground.

CHAPTER XVII.

AN ASTONISHED DEITY.

THE dwarf was utterly aghast as he stood over the body, looking down at it and seeing, when the forked lightning threw upon it a fitful glare, that it was *a woman*.

His disappointment because it was not Hookama made him recoil for an instant from the object at his feet, which somehow he felt had cheated him of his prize.

Soon forgetting his first impulse to leave the body to the scavenger birds, he stooped down, partly out of curiosity and partly with the instinct of humanity, and feeling with his hands, perceived that the woman was alive. The signs of life were very feeble pulsations of the heart; the limbs were cold and the skin was clammy, but as he rubbed and kneaded the body, he at last heard a moan and felt a slight tremor of the muscles.

SURF-SCENE

He had brought the woman to this resting place in a most rugged manner, with head and chest hanging down, so that the sea water, which filled her lungs, had run out, and the very jolting of the rough porterage had been of use in her resuscitation. It was a miracle that she was alive at all; either the tidal wave had caught her on the beach, or, what was barely possible, if she had been the occupant of the canoe, the gigantic wall of water might have lifted her over the reef and brought her on its mighty crest to the shore.

Seeing that the woman lived, the dwarf renewed his exertions, the rain still falling in torrents, till, by and by, partial consciousness returned and the woman opened her eyes, closed them, and breathing regularly moved her legs as if in pain.

Menehune was in doubt what to do next, but remembering that there was a cave, at the base of the cliff Leahi, (Diamond Head) which jutted out into the sea, he determined to carry the woman there, and wait till the storm was over. This time he took her up more gently and carried her with one of his arms around her waist and the other about her lower limbs, with her head resting on his left shoulder. It was quite a distance, but the dwarf had found the trail which he well knew

and at last deposited his burden just within
the opening of the cave, and sat down on the
ground to rest.

He was no expert in the *lomi* process which
he had administered ; his pounding and pinch-
ing were rather severe ; he had left the torn
tapa cloth around the woman's waist where it
had been tightly bound with a cord ; and
now, as he sat at the mouth of the cave, he
wondered if he ought to continue the exercise
in order to restore the woman wholly.

He squatted beside her ; took hold of her
hand and as the lightning's brilliant glow
illuminated the place from time to time, he
felt of her fingers one by one and tried the
joints ; drawing through his big hands the
long locks of her dark hair, he gathered them
in two bunches and spread them carefully over
her neck and bosom.

He had rolled the body over and over like a
log, when he was working at the inanimate
form. He had squeezed the muscles as he
would have pinched a banana, or, perchance, a
dog—but now that consciousness had returned
to what had been only a substance to be handled, the woman became a reality to him ;
something to be treated as he had treated his
mistress Pu' Aloha ; to be touched, if at all,
with a sort of reverence.

Menehune had never before known the sensation of holding a woman's hand in his own.
So far as any palpable contact was concerned,
he was wholly without experience. The women of the chief's enclosure, who let him play
around like a sort of pet animal, regarded him
as a senseless creature, with a sort of canine
attachment to his friends.

But now, a new sensation came to him ; a
vivid, acute feeling, at first like a twinge of
pain ; then something akin to the satisfaction
he had felt while basking in the sunshine. It
was the dawning of a rude sentiment in his
nature, which changed him ever after from a
loutish, clownish animal with affectionate instincts, into a perceptive soul, alive to experiences in which the higher faculties find play
and development. The glimmer of the new
light was feeble, but the dawn would deepen,
even if it never came to perfect day, in his
simple soul.

The storm still raged without. The dwarf,
revolving vaguely his new sensations in his
feeble mind, took his usual attitude, with his
knees higher than his head, and waited pa-
tiently, watching the slightest movement of
the woman as the light came at intervals
through the entrance of the cave.

Turning at last uneasily and flinging her

arms above her head, an action which caused
the blood to circulate more freely, the woman
opened her eyes, looked about her with a
dreamy gaze, and tried to sit up. Instantly
Menehune was at her side, and placed her
body in a leaning posture against a stone
which jutted from the side of the cave ; then
he resumed his former posture, and fixed his
eyes upon her.

The young woman tried to pierce the gloom,
which was now and then illumined by a flash
of lightning. She could dimly discern the uncouth figure silently staring at her, with knees
and head like the idols she had seen on the
walls of her father's *heiau*.

The trembling of the earth and the strange
noises within the cavern, like the wailing notes
of imprisoned voices, blended with the rever-
berating thunder-peals without ; and altogether
the effect on the girl's half paralyzed brain was
overpowering. She shut her eyes, but even
the anxiety created by the situation could not
keep her from venturing a look, now and then,
at the grotesque being whose eyes gleamed
like a basilisk's. Seeing him remain as still as
if cut out of stone, she became more tranquil
in his presence, and at last was emboldened to
break the oppressive silence.

Covering her face with her hands almost in-

voluntarily, with a tremulous voice she said:
" Dear god! tell me, I beg; am I in heaven or
hell? What god are you?"

Having put these leading questions, as if
frightened at her own audacity in speaking to
the only real, living and present god she had
ever known, she sank back against the wall.

The sound of the woman's voice, which had
conveyed little meaning to his ears, brought
the dwarf-giant again into the realm of his
former consciousness and he tumbled himself
into a heap at her feet, as he was accustomed
to do in Pu' Aloha's presence. Then, with
the return of the new feeling which his recent
experience had awakened (a sort of reverent
regard for a higher being than himself,) he
prostrated himself before her, making a still
more extraordinary, amorphous spectacle of
himself.

His gaunt, misproportioned body, with his
monstrous legs and bulging joints sprawling
behind him, seemed even more than ever in
harmony with the girl's idea of a deity, such
as she was accustomed to imagine. Trembling
with a new anxiety, her agitation increased as
she almost shrieked: " Do not spring at me,
O, Kane;" she thought his attitude that of
one preparing to leap on a victim. " Only tell
me which god you are and I'll be your slave;

serve you; feed you; bring you squid, any-thing. Don't kill me, I beg, I pray——" and she clasped her hands in an attitude of intense supplication.

The cave shook with a louder peal of thunder and the dwarf, too simple to see the absurdity of it all, cried out, in a shrill voice as if to overcome the noise of the elements, " Me no Kane! me Menehune, Menehune." The girl mistook his name, which she heard only in part, owing to his thick utterance and the loud clap of thunder, and thinking he had said *mali-u* (the word for a deified, deceased chief), she fell on her knees and pleaded with the supposed incarnation of a warrior's ghost to spare her from the " oven," in which, she had been taught, the spirits of departed chiefs in Hades cooked those who descended whole; that is, without their flesh having been separated from their bones at burial.

Menehune was sadly nonplussed at the attitude she assumed and did not understand what she meant to say; but hearing the word, " oven," he thought she was hungry; so up he jumped and ran out into the storm as fast as his legs could carry him. Near by was a tall cocoa-nut palm, which nodded its plumes violently at him, as, with the agility of a monkey, he climbed and brought down a nut;

cracking the shell on a stone, he carried it to
the trembling captive in the cave and deposited
it in her lap.

During the "deified chief's" absence the
young woman had settled back to await de-
velopments, in great perplexity and anxiety,
not knowing whether or not her new master
had gone to heat the oven in which she was to
be cooked. When he brought the cocoa-nut
and gave it to her she was somewhat relieved,
and when he said, "Eat," her first exclamations were the natural queries of an Hawaiian
woman, "Do the gods let *wahines* eat before
them? Can women have cocoa-nuts in heaven?" (A fruit *tabu* to them on earth.)

No wonder that the poor thing was dazed,
almost crazy and sadly demoralized by what
she had been through. She was drenched
and had been half drowned; and now the
tempest, the gloomy, resounding cavern, the
thunder and lightning and more than all this
creature, half-monster, half-man, as seen in the
fitful flashes, unsettled the little reason she had
left. Disregarding her question, Menehune
held the cocoa-nut to her mouth; made a
gesture for her to drink, and when she had
drained the reviving draught, being assured
that after all she might still be living in her
usual fleshly tenement, she put another ques-

tion to the dwarf, this time in a more natural
tone of voice, and asked him, " Where am I ? "
His only answer was " Cave."

Again when she said " Oahu ? " she got no
reply, for Menehune never before had heard or
known the name of the island on which he was
born. She tried other words, but there was no
intelligent response and it reassured her to
think the " god " was perhaps only a half-
witted fool.

The storm cleared away as suddenly as it
came on. Two hours after midnight the sky
was clear of clouds and the stars shone with
unusual brightness. Light came in at the
cavern's mouth and Kelea had the first full
view of the dwarf, standing outside in the star-
light, whom she had before seen only in
shadow.

She saw at once that she had been frightened
without cause. The grotesque figure did not
appear to be formidable at all, although she
had never met such a creature in her life. She
took in the situation in a moment and when
Menehune came to her in a quiet way as if to
receive her commands, all her courage and self-
possession returned.

Stepping out under the stars she took an
attitude of dignity and repose ; she made signs
indicating that she had come far over the sea,

and when Menehune, showing more compre-
hension, pointed to a collection of huts, Kelea
said "*Mauka*!" (towards the mountains,) and
holding out her tattered skirt, added "*Pau*"
(petticoat): She wanted him to understand
that he must take her to the hills and that she
needed a larger sample of *tapa* around her
waist.

The dwarf was really abashed and timid in
her presence, after she resumed her natural
manner. When, in a little while, he found her
kind he began to understand better what she
tried to tell him. After a time, her gesticulations proved more effectual than her ejacula-
tions, and the dwarf picked her up in his arms
and started in the direction she indicated. The
ground was strewed with fallen branches, heaps
of stones, and earth which the torrent had
brought down the sides of Leahi, so that
Menehune stumbled along, sometimes nearly
falling; finally, he put the woman on the
ground and grunted out "*Auwe! auwe!*"
(Alas, alas), as if it were useless to try to go on
after that fashion.

Motioning him to get down on his knees,
Kelea mounted his shoulders, and placing herself astride of his neck, held by his head and he
crossed his arms over her limbs in front. The
good-natured fellow, with a guffaw, which

showed that he took in the situation, at once started off with steady step, and Kelea, all unwittingly, thus inaugurated the fashion which Hawaiian women eagerly adopted, when years afterwards horses were introduced into the islands.

There was not a four-footed animal on any of the islands, except dogs, swine, lizards and mice, until Vancouver, in 1793, landed a bull, a cow and afterwards some sheep.

The general public of Oahu had, however, very little chance of seizing upon Kelea's invention in a practical way, since the darkness left the novel combination in befitting obscurity. Had any chance observer happened to meet the composite pair during that droll promenade, he would have fled for his life, spreading broadcast the story of an apparition of the god of the sea, by whom the furious tempest had been aroused.

The device of Kelea answered every purpose ; she was too weary and bruised to walk ; Menehune was equal to the emergency and strode onward, over the wide plain ; by the entrance of Manoa valley, around the back of the extinct volcano now called Punch Bowl ; over the ridge leading towards a round hill, now known as Tantalus, and climbing along the western side of Pauoa valley, he at last arrived with his burden at a lonely spot, where stood a grass house with a *lanai* (verandah), close against a beetling cliff. All along the way they had come were uprooted trees, deserted or dismantled huts and signs of fearful devastation from swollen streams flowing down the hills towards the plains and the sea. But the strong fellow cared nothing for torrents or obstructions, carefully wading through the one and picking his way over the other.

The spot he had chosen for the end of the trip was in a nook of the mountainous ridge which looks down upon the magnificent pass of Nuuanu. From the top of Tantalus, one can see, across the valley, the terminus of five or six ridges which, like the fingers of a man's hand, stretch in a northern direction far away. These ridges have steep sides, and except near their summits are clad in perpetual green.

Through the nearest ridge, the pass of the *Pali*, which leads to the plains of Kailua, cleaves its rugged way. On the left of the pass is a precipice, a thousand feet in height. Above it rises a peculiarly sharp-edged, rocky peak, and the scenery on all sides is surpassingly grand. The high mountain on the right side of the pass is called Kouahuanui.

It was on a secluded cliff of this mountain.

overlooking the sublime prospect, that Kelea dismounted from her improvised steed. The earliest rays of the morning sun began to light up the scene and revealed to her the dim outlines of the lofty peaks. An abrupt termination of the path by which the dwarf-giant brought her showed that there was no further passage in that direction.

Turning towards the house where all was dark and silent, she saw a large grass dwelling, a garden of flowering plants and shrubs, a patch of ground for yams and a clump of sugar-cane, which in the islands flourishes even at an elevation of fifteen hundred feet.

The house stood against the side of the cliff, which formed a high wall; above the habitation, the beetling crag, with vines and *ohelo* bushes, made a sort of flowery protection, for it projected over the house and shed the water from above into the ravine. After the heavy rain of the night, quite a stream poured over the cliff, and the spray diffused itself throughout the atmosphere. When the sun shone upon this occasional water-fall, a rainbow arched the place; a romantic spot, ever green and bright.

Kelea caught a momentary glance of the beauty of the scene, but hurried through the spray to the verandah, where Menehune im-

plied by a gesture that she should wait till
he aroused the occupant of the interior.
Shivering in the cold, which at this altitude
was rather severe, the girl paced impatiently
up and down, wondering what would befall
her. Only a moment or two passed when
Menehune came out, leading by the hand an
aged woman, whom he guided towards Kelea.

The woman, thin, wrinkled and with a scar
on her otherwise pleasant face, was evidently
blind, for she felt of Kelea's countenance and
then passed her hand downwards. Finding no
tapa except the ragged *pau* and its tattered
pendants, she began to talk fast to Menehune,
in a jargon of which Kelea could understand
only a few words. The dwarf comprehended
if the girl did not, and went into the house,
returning with a roll of thick *tapa*, which the
old woman at once wrapped around the
chilled girl.

Evidently, Menehune had told his mother
(for such she was,) all he knew about the
wahine, and it was not long before she led
Kelea gently indoors and made her sit down.

When the dwarf saw that the stranger, after
eating a hearty meal, dropped into a sound
sleep on a couch of mats, he at once started
down the cliffside, and when Pu' Aloha awoke
the next morning she found her faithful Mene'
as usual before her door.

CHAPTER XVIII.

"FEATHER-MANTLE."

WE left Hookama a prisoner at Hawaii, after the angry king of Hawaii had ordered him to be kept under strict guard. The exhausted and dispirited youth sank down in a corner of the dark cell in a state bordering on prostration. The strain on his body and mind produced a numbness of the nerves and a torpid condition of the brain. The reaction made him indifferent to life or death. He suffered no apprehension, but fell into a sort of stupor, a dreamless, deadening sleep.

It was midnight when he was partially aroused by the flicker of a *kukui*-nut torch and the heavy tread of human feet. Half-conscious, he felt the cords on his cramped arms and remembered that he was a prisoner. The approaching figure he thought was the king's *mu* (assassin) and, as it was of no use to resist,

he lay passive, awaiting his fate. What difference to him whether the end came sooner
or later?

He was aware of rough fingers untwisting
the ropes from his arms, and with a sigh of
relief he stretched out his hands. Somebody
was talking, whether to him or not he did not
know or care. Soon, another figure came in
and kneeled beside him. The two strange beings rolled him over on his side. He made no
resistance; why should he? Then they took
his limbs in their hands and twisted the
joints; they pounded his flesh and muscles.
He wondered if it were the torture. They laid
his passive body upon mats and rubbed the
skin, pouring on a liquid, till the prickling
sensation resembled that of the tattoo process
with thorns.

By and by, a feeling more pleasurable than
painful ensued, and Hookama wondered if it
were that preceding death, which he did not
dread in the least. Finally, conscious of being
not only alive but fairly comfortable, he
stretched his legs, sat up and found a gourd at
his mouth from which he took a long draught
of the stimulating *awa*, mixed with water, and
a gruel of *poi*.

His eyes by this time were accustomed to
the dim light in the cell, and he recognized the

face of the big warrior who had refused to
kill him at the king's command. The recognition was so joyful to Hookama that he smiled
and managed to utter the difficult name of his
friend, "Kakuhaupio." At this, the other
man left the cell.

Without giving in detail the conversation
which followed, the substance of it was as
follows :—

It was the little witch of a child, who stood
near the king during the contest with spears,
that prolonged Hookama's life. The burly
chief, Kamehameha, was infatuated with the
girl, whom he meant to have for his wife by and
by, although she was now betrothed to the
king's son. She was an arch-coquette and had
been greatly taken with Hookama. When
she heard of the intended duel, she went to
the fascinated chief, over thirty years her
senior, and cajoled him to promise not to kill
his antagonist. Otherwise Hookama would
certainly have been slain by one of the six
javelins.

The change that came over the king when
he ordered Hookama to be bound instead of
being killed off hand, was occasioned by the
mysterious words, whispered in his ear by
"The Lonely One" and Hewahewa, the
priest.

The one had said, "The young *alii* is an envoy from Oahu with an important, secret message. If you kill him, you will regret it." The other, the priest, whispered: "The youth is the son of a god; I have learned his pedigree, and you kill him at your peril."

"Now," continued the chivalrous chief, "you will be brought before the king tomorrow. He is capricious, and just now he chafes at his disappointment in not securing any prisoners alive to sacrifice to the war-god. Yet you may possibly save your life if you are shrewd. You told me you came as an envoy from the king of Oahu, on a secret mission. You did not tell me what it was. If the king is favorable to your message, he will not want to destroy the messenger. However, the old man is an odd being. There is at least a chance for your life."

Hookama thanked him for his kindness and then said abruptly, "Who is that little maiden that has such power over the men? She surely has bright eyes and a charming form. But how does she get such influence?"

"Aha," replied the big chief, "you ought to know. I saw you look at her, when you started in for the fight. She is Kaahumanu, Feather-Mantle, the daughter of Queen Namahana, who is the sister of the king of

Maui; curse him! He drove them away
from the island. Our king has taken them
under his wing and he is very fond of the
child. But now, get some more sleep; you'll
need all your strength. The guards here are
my own men. They will take you for a bath
in the river in the morning. Aloha!" and
the large-hearted chief hurried out of the
prison.

At early dawn, the guard led Hookama to
the river where he plunged in and disported
himself as if no care ever weighed on his
mind. He displayed his wonderful skill as a
swimmer, and the guards were looking on with
admiration, when suddenly from a clump of
bushes Feather-Mantle appeared and, leaping
into the water, swam like a water-bird towards
the young *alii.*

When she approached him she shook her
raven hair over her face so that the youth
could see only the glances of her keen, black
eyes. In the friendliest manner, Hookama
praised her skill as a swimmer, whereupon she
tossed back her locks and allowed her face to
be seen. He thought her smile more attractive than her bewitching form : but he had
no time to improve the acquaintance. She
quickly said, "*Alii-nui!* Don't be afraid. The
king shall not kill you. I came out to tell

you, and the guards must not hear me; Aloha!" Before the young man could reply, she turned and swam for the shore.

Hookama thought it best not to follow her, and so waited in the stream, till she emerged and her *wahines* threw over her shoulders a gay mantle of *tapa*, decorating her head and neck with wreaths of fragrant flowers. Then he swam to the shore; but with one arch look behind her, the charming creature hurried away and was soon lost to sight.

When Hookama stood before the king, his arms having been bound again behind his back, the two giant-chiefs, his keeper and his antagonist, stood on either side, ostensibly to guard him, but really to reinforce his courage.

The king, after the young *alii* had prostrated himself, commanded him in a stern voice to approach, and motioned the chiefs to stand back. Then in a lower tone he said to Hookama, " My priest tells me that you are the son of a god. Is that true? Answer me on your life."

"Alas! your *moi*ship, I know not my parents. I am of noble birth, but whether my ancestors sprang out of the earth or descended from the stars, I cannot say."

The answer satisfied the king better than if Hookama had affirmed a divine pedigree and named the god from whom he had come ; for it was the mystery of his origin that assured the king of the truth of what Hewahewa the priest declared.

Again the king spoke : " You have a secret message for my ear alone, I am told. Speak, and let your words be few. I like not a secret message from an enemy."

" Fling me from a cliff," calmly answered the youth, " if either my king or myself can be counted your enemy, even if we fought with Kahekili against you. It was by constraint. Your *moi*ship has an eye that searches my heart. Kahahana sends no hostile message. He has a word for your ear alone. He trusts you, as he distrusts the crafty king of Maui." The king's face assumed an expectant and interested expression. " Kahekili would rob my king of his kingdom. My king wants your mighty hand to crush the robber. The day that sees Hawaii and Oahu united will shine on one tyrant the less. Maui will be yours, and Oahu free."

There was excitement in the old man's eyes as he replied almost in a whisper : " Kahahana's warriors will never fight against the king of Maui under the war-gods of Hawaii. Would to Kane that we might join forces against our common foe. But the gods do not so will.

Your king will again join the dastardly robber
against me, and a bard from Oahu will chant
my death-song. But I shall not have long to
await the ghost of Oahu's king in the realm
of Kane. The king of Oahu is the tool of
Kahekili; I will not betray him, but the
tool will suffer at the hand of him that uses it.
I have spoken."

The old chief dropped his head and was
silent for a moment; then raising his eyes, he
said: "But *you* are the son of a god. I see it
in your face. There is only one like you in
the land. Yonder he stands, and the child is
holding him by the hand. He will rule after
me, and you will serve him."

Astonished at these words Hookama simply
replied, "But I am to die by your hands.
One more request only and I am content.
Send a trusty messenger to my king, that his
mind may know the mind of Hawaii's king."

The king looked hard at the youth, to see
what would be the effect of the announcement
that he was about to make, and then said:
"You will go back to your king. The gods refuse to receive you as a sacrifice. My priest
has sought the oracle. You are free.—Here,
guards, unbind the prisoner!—Only the warriors who came with you shall be laid on the altar. You can go whence you came."

"What!" exclaimed Hookama, forgetting his assumed composure, "My men sacrificed, and I go back? Never! never!"

"The gods so will it, and I must have victims to appease their anger. Go, young man, and thank the god you serve that you escape."

"Bind me again," cried Hookama in a loud voice, holding out his arms to the guards who stood with the cords in their hands. "Thrust me into your vile prison. I die with my friends, or we all return to our island. You call me the son of a god! As such, I say to you, king though you are, that the gods will have no such sacrifice. Kahekili himself could not perpetrate such a crime; if——"

"Seize him," cried the king. "Strangle him at once! Son of a god! We will see if Kahekili can be outdone; who cares——"

The priest who was standing a little distance away, came suddenly forward and laid his hand on the king's shoulder. "My king, have a care! You are forgetting yourself. The gods demand no such propitiation." Then turning to the two giant chiefs he said in a low voice, "An evil spirit possesses our mighty king. We have provided other victims."

The chiefs thus addressed consulted a moment and then said to the excited king, whose hands trembled as if shaking with palsy: " It is right that the young man expiate his fault. The priest forbids the sacrifice either of him or his followers. But the gods take vengeance on their despisers. Send him to the fire goddess. If he escapes her wrath he is dear to the gods and we are guiltless. If he is consumed in the flames of Pele, his doom is just."

The king, still unappeased, was weak in the hands of his two mightiest chiefs, and, finding these leaders of his army resolute and insistent, gave orders to pack the strangers off at once. He wanted them out of his sight. To Pele they might go, but they were never to see his face again. He cursed them as he retreated to his house.

Thus Hookama gained what he most desired, a visit to the domains of the Fire Goddess. He had intimated this desire to the giant warrior, and, as it was made known to him long afterwards, Feather-Mantle had won Kamehameha over to the scheme, in hopes of saving him.

Lest the decision should be revoked, the young *alii* was hurried to the beach; the eight warriors were released and sat with paddles in the canoe. A crowd of natives stood on the shore; the two friendly chiefs had given Hookama directions for the voyage

and a token for Keawe, the chief of Hilo.
The youthful chief stood in the surf ready
to embark, when suddenly Feather-Mantle,
followed by several of her *wahines*, rushed
from the crowd ; their hands full of *leis*
(wreaths), and dashing through the shallow,
rippling surf they covered him with flowers,
making him, much to his surprise, an animated
overgrown bouquet with all the colors of the
rainbow.

Gallantly the youth bent down to the laughing maiden and laid on her raven tresses one
of the choicest of the garlands she had given
him ; then he bent his knee, half in jest and half
in earnest, as if predicting for her the royal
honors which would crown her brows in years
to come. But he did not know that she was
to be the famous queen regent, who after
Kamehameha's death would break the *Tabu*,
and with Hewahewa's help abolish idolatry
from all the islands.

Waving his *alohas* to the chiefs, as he leaped
into his canoe, he noticed, the last object
meeting his eyes, a smile on Kamehameha's
face, as the "Lonely One" looked down at
his future bride and rejoiced that there was
one man the less, handsomer than himself, to
attract the attention of the flirtatious little
maid.

CHAPTER XIX.

PELE, THE FIRE-GODDESS OF KILAUEA.

THE northern coast of the island of Hawaii, from its western cape, Upolu, in Kohala, to the bay of Hilo, a distance of sixty or seventy miles, is a dream of beauty as seen from the sea. This windward side of the island presents to the voyager a succession of lofty ridges, stretching from the interior in irregular, curving lines, and cut off at the coast. Each end projects its smooth, precipitous front to the waves from the north, which fling their spray far up the cliffs.

Between these colossal, headland ridges, gloomy valleys are scooped out, submerged in shadow, impenetrable, and canopied by fronds of tropical trees and plants. No canoes lie at the mouths of these retreating vales, for the jungle of convoluted, tangled vines and shrubs, kept moist by constant showers, is too formidable even for a savage, bred to the work of forcing his way through pathless thickets.

High above in the distant background, the volcanic mountains, which dominate and often devastate the lower lands, wear their mantles of snow, except in unusual seasons of summer heat.

It was along this marvellous coast, with its picturesque and irregular outline, that Hook-ama, after his release, sailed gaily in his war-canoe towards the bay of Hilo, the most tropical and delicious of all the garden spots of this Liliputian group.

At last, the little party arrived at Hilo and were conveyed by the chief Keawe, to a little island a few rods from the main land, where preparations had been made for their entertainment. Cocoa-nut Island! a favorite resting place of royal chiefs. The tallest cocoa-nut palms wave over it. Branches of trees are there reflected in the stillest of pools. The breeze that stirs their fronds causes no ripples on the side of the island towards the shore. The sands that surround this lovely spot are the whitest, and the mossy turf under the shadows of the palms is the softest. The graceful pandanus trees, with a dozen or more supporting stems growing from the trunk to the ground, incline towards the mirroring

COCOA-NUT ISLAND

waters. Soft, gray mosses droop in rich festoons from branches and trunks, some even
dipping in the pools.

Here Hookama rested after a bath, while his
warriors were escorted to the village as guests
of the chief. The night was cool; the sounds
of distant revellers and the noise of their drums
scarcely reached his ears. The rippling waves
upon the sands were musical to him as he lay
on the mossy sward and dreamed; dreamed of
Oahu, of Pu' Aloha, of Kelea, and Feather-
Mantle; waking dreams, but all the more fascinating because they were real.

He dropped asleep, just as he called to mind
his purpose to seek on the morrow the strange
haunts of the goddess Pele, whom the dwellers
on Oahu worshipped only as a distant deity,
whose terrors scarcely troubled them in slight
earthquake shocks at infrequent seasons. Now
he is to meet her and her fiery ebullitions, at
the mouth of the volcano which was her home.

As he slept, there appeared to him a vision
of a woman divinely fair, of immense proportions and surpassing form. As she lay on
beds of black lava, her breasts were twin
mountains covered with snow and her limbs
were like fiery streams of molten gold. Her
face was like the sun in its brightness and its
expression was fascinating to his eyes.

He seemed to be kneeling in the presence of the goddess and professing ardent and enduring loyalty. Then, in his dream, the image of Pu' Aloha appeared, weeping and dejected. She reproached him for his devotion to a new deity, and at once the goddess, whom he had seen in splendid majesty, became a fury, belching smoke from her distended nostrils and shaking a forked lightning-flame with her hand.

Her hair, scintillating with sparks and brittle as glass, fell over him in hot showers and burned into his flesh and eyes. A yawning chasm opened at his feet and he was falling headlong into it, still gazing in terror at the apparition, when—he awoke with the sun's early rays full in his face and a lizard, the dreaded *moo*, was crawling over his limbs.

Beautiful as the Cocoa-nut Isle might be to others, it no longer had any charm for him. He arose, looked around and found his warriors, who had been brought back during the night, drunk with *awa*, and were sleeping off the effects of their debauch. Jumping into a canoe drawn up at the edge of the beach, he paddled to the main land and, inquiring the way, soon found himself in front of Chief Keawe's house with its broad *lanai* (verandah).

The chief was taking his morning meal, fruit and *poi*, and received him cordially. Dipping his fingers with the chief into a large calabash of the national food, which natives adore and which foreigners avoid, Hookama won the chief's heart by his frankness, and the two men planned the journey to the volcano, from which the chief tried in vain to dissuade the youth. Keawe discussed the dangers of the undertaking and the capricious nature of the dread goddess, but finding the young *alii* resolute, offered him provisions and a bird-catcher as a guide.

Hookama expressed a wish to go at once, before the sun was hot, and Keawe thereupon summoned a native who was not only a mountain climber but an expert bird-catcher as well. His name was Lou, meaning a fish-hook, and given to him because his bow-legs corresponded to the double bend of the fish-hook in common use.

What was Hookama's surprise to see in this chosen guide, a little man about thirty-five years old with an anatomical structure like a monkey; having a thin, scrawny body bristling with hair; a face tattooed with lizards; luminous eyes that sparkled with drollery; a puckery mouth; a top-heavy head, and legs as crooked as the limbs of a *hau*-tree.

"Here, Lou! Make your *Aloha* to the *alii*, and show him what wonderful things you can

do," cried the chief as this extraordinary specimen made his obeisance to Hookama. Keawe
then took a bow and arrow, such as chiefs used,
not in war but for shooting mice, (the only
hunting they had on the islands). Giving the
bow and arrow to the man, and, standing up
some thirty paces away, he made a circle with
the thumb and forefinger of his right hand,
extending his arm to its full length from his
side.

Lou drew the arrow to its head on the bow
and let it fly at the chief's hand. The arrow
passed through the circle without harming
thumb or finger, though the chief did not
move a muscle or show the least concern. Then
Keawe turned to Hookama and said: "The
little scamp can cut the stem of a cocoa-nut on
the tallest palm, but this is the only weapon
he knows how to use. He will, however, do
better by you than a dozen spearmen among
the mountains.

"Give my *Aloha* to the goddess," said the
friendly chief, "and be sure you sacrifice two
pigs; else you'll be food for her hot oven.
We will look for you after seven suns, or rake
in the ashes of the next lava-flow for your
bones." These were his reassuring words as
he started the ill-assorted pair on their perilous
tramp.

CHAPTER XX.

LOU, THE GUIDE TO THE VOLCANO.

LOU, the guide, was one of the many strange human products of this land, where women fondled puppies and left their own offspring to look out for themselves; where swine were allowed more license in the grass huts than boys and girls, and where a demigod, a defunct chief, was supposed to assume, at will, the form of an immense black hog; where aristocratic birth demanded obesity in the women of the court, and where mutilation of the features, in honor of a dead king, was common among the chiefs.

Lazy, reckless, half-tamed, no wonder that many of the young men were deformed, half-witted and diseased. Fortunately, leprosy was not introduced into the islands until the Chinamen appeared in the next century. Lou couldn't remember that he ever had any parents, but attributed his unique physique, when questioned concerning his history by Hookama, to his birth under a tree that was withered at the top, and his hairy body to the fact that a favorite puppy had been his foster-brother.

But the two bird-catchers, travelling ostensibly for that purpose, got on famously together. Hookama became much attached to the bow-legged little fellow and chatted gaily with him as the pair walked briskly along the side of pools where the natives were bathing and a few of them gathering fruit and flowers from the luxuriant vines. After an hour's walk, they struck into a jungle, by a path which allowed them to go only in single file.

The air was humid and hot, even in the early morning, but in no other atmosphere could be produced the wonderful growths of vegetation that revealed nature in her most prodigal moods. Ferns, tall as trees; fern-trees, with fronds pluming from their tops or hanging from their sides; immense *kukui* trees with mossy trunks, covered with clambering vines; wild fruit trees; spiked plants with long stemmed blossoms; vast wastes of tangled roots underneath and miles on miles of brilliant foliage overhead; all this variety, with luscious wild fruits, which Lou, who went ahead with sidelong strides, ached to pluck, but which even his agility did not enable him to gather from the impassable labyrinth.

The men walked in a sort of variegated twilight, although it was broad day; a revelry of color; heaven's blue hidden and earth's rarest hues everywhere prevailing. There was not a snake nor a reptile to make it dangerous to cross the mouldy bottom-brakes, but an entanglement quite as fatal, of roots and vines, clung to the limbs or clasped the body of any one who left the beaten track.

Hookama had seen no such jungle on Oahu. Only on this more southern island did the clear light of the sun give place to the myriad hues of overarching vines and flowers.

After two hours, the change to daylight and a ridge where huts were found and tall palms stood sentinel, was like emerging from a zone of roseate and amber tints into clear white light. Then passing over immense masses of cooled lava, where stunted bushes and tough grasses grew, the pedestrians picked *ohelo* berries and finally came at night to a grove of palmettos where they stretched out in the hollow of a lava-bed, in delicious rest after their toilsome march.

It was a little more than thirty miles from

Hilo to the volcano of Kilauea, and on the morning of the second day, the atmosphere became cold. Lou did not appear to enjoy the change. He hunted for cracks and seams which emitted vapor and steam. They were a better tonic to him than rarified air. He sat on the edge of a crevasse and hung his feet over the side of it in the comfortable mist. The sight of snow on Mauna Loa's curved summit gave him the chills, and as for going near the crater to get warm, he could hardly entertain the idea. With his cracked voice he repudiated the whole trip and wondered how Keawe had allowed them to attempt it.

Here indeed was a dilemma for Hookama. "Could he go on alone?" He saw the thin column of white vapor terminating in a cloud, which the risen sun gilded as it floated over the sea of fire, and Lou said, "That is the smoke of Pele's oven and her horrid house is down below it."

But if he went on alone, could he leave Lou behind? What sort of a guide was the little old man after all? Was he loaned to him by the chief, to be an incumbrance like this? And besides, where were the black pigs, which Pele exacted from those who entered her fiery realm?

To all these questions, as Hookama poured

them into Lou's ear with expressive gestures and vehement words, the miserable, crooked fish-hook of a man answered nothing ; he only kept on warming his toes in the cracks of the lava, looking longingly in the direction of his sunny home near the shimmering sea.

The detonations, occasionally heard from the direction of the crater, served but to harden his determination not to budge. He said Hookama might kill him if he chose, and toss him instead of a black pig to Pele; she would like him better than a hog, he did not doubt: but as for facing her flaming wrath, and looking into her face and eyes, he couldn't do it, and by Kane, he declared he would not.

It looked as if Lou were afraid. Hookama began to be frightened also, but for other reasons. He was fearful lest he should not win the fiery smile of the dread goddess, nor hear her deafening voice. Then, with the disappointment, there would come the ridicule of Keawe and the bandinage of Kahahana, Paao, and even of Pu' Aloha, at his return.

He stood and looked sorrowfully at the little creature, half hidden in the lava crack; that woe-begone face haunted him; the bony fingers, fumbling and twitching at the stick he held in his hands, indicated imbecility. Was the man becoming demented through fear?

That drivelling speech, as Lou mumbled in-
coherently to himself, was it delirium or giddi-
ness ? Hookama drew nearer, and saw big tears
running down the hollow cheeks of the stupid
clown, as he drooped, with his head over the
crevice, from which the sulphurous steam came
up in a thin, hazy, yellowish mist.

Then he laid his hand on Lou's shoulder and
shook him to arouse his wandering mind; but
observing him narrowly, he thought he discovered a gleam in those tearful eyes which meant
something very different from disorder of the
faculties ; there was a lurking keenness in the
orbs quite unlike the appearance of a dulled
brain. At that instant, a slight trembling of
the ground, like the first, feeble throes of an
earthquake, caused Hookama to spring back
from the opening with a vague apprehension
that the crevice might close up, calling at the
same time to Lou to take his legs out of the
crack. What a horror, if the fellow should be
caught by his lower limbs, and, clenched by
the tough lava, be held fast to linger till he
died !

But the *Kanaka* did not move a muscle and
Hookama saw at once that his apprehension
was groundless. It was a passing fear which
was soon dissipated, and a feeling of anger
took its place in the young *alii's* mind. He

started towards the misshapen creature, with an impulse to tear him from his stupid position, set him on his feet, give him a thrashing and make him lead on.

But the little chap was too quick for him ; before he had advanced two paces, Lou grasped the bow and arrow lying at his side and fitting the arrow to the string, aimed it straight at the *alii*'s eyes, while his expression changed in a twinkling from that of dullness to the most intense shrewdness. Hookama's hasty movement was arrested by this unexpected change in the situation, and holding up his hand to protect his face, he called out to know what was meant by this sudden performance.

Thereupon Lou gave a whistling sound from his lips and began to laugh and dance about in the most extravagant fashion. If he had acted like a muddle-headed coward before, his ridiculous antics now savored of the most irrational mirth. Hookama stared in wonder at his preposterous performance ; if it had not been for the fellow's half humorous look about the eyes, he would have thought him even more idiotic than when he sat gibbering, with his legs dangling in the crack.

When Lou found that the impression he had made upon the *alii*, whatever it might be, had worn off, he stopped his absurd exhibition and

assumed his usual attitude ; the change was so
instantaneous and the man fell into his customary voice and manner so naturally that
Hookama cried out, "What demon has got into you, to make you act so much like a fool?
You sit over the mouth of *Milu* (hell) like a
coward, and then you dance a crazy dance like
a maniac. What do you mean?"

"Mean? Noble *alii-nui* ! I always give
the foreign *aliis* a chance."

"A chance?" responded Hookama inquiringly, for he had not the remotest idea of the
man's meaning.

"*Ae, ae*; a last chance to go back. Many a
brave chief has come up here with me and when
I've sat in that 'yellow crack in the ground,'
has gladly seized the chance to go back and
let Pele alone. I tell you they are afraid of the
fiery goddess, and when they see that cloud of
white smoke from her ovens and feel the earth
trembling the least quake they get so scared that
they want to leave, without even saying *Aloha*
to Pele. And I always help them off," added
Lou, with a malicious twinkle in his eye and
a wicked grin on his face, which made the
wrinkles show from chin to forehead.

"Then they make me swear by all the gods,
not to say anything about it, and I always
swear my biggest oath and I keep my promise,

too. If I didn't, my game is over, and I can't do it again."

"But why do you want to do it again? Did you think you could scare *me*?"

"I do it again as often as I can, to get rid of climbing over the big heaps of lava in the crater, and getting the hogs for Pele, which is not a little *pilikia* (bother) I can assure you. I am always glad to get off and go back; they give me a larger reward, too, to shut my mouth; *They* never tell; they don't call me coward either. Most of them go back when I act like that. I tell you the biggest, bragging warriors are terribly afraid of Pele, but I don't care *that*," snapping his fingers, "for all her 'shooting fire,' if I only watch the signs at the crater and keep cool. Many a terrible fighter," added this queer little man, "can't bear the sight of a mouse. If he sees one run across his path in the village, he will go home and stay in all day, no matter what he wants to do outside;" and Lou, who never handled a spear in his life in a battle, chuckled over the foolish timidity, in ghostly matters, of warriors whose courage in war could not be questioned.

Having delivered himself of these sarcastic remarks, the clever little skeptic laughed and laughed till the tears ran down all his wrinkles.

"I wasn't quite sure about you, but I thought

I would try and see. You're the right sort,
my *alii-nui*, but there is a lot that ain't."

"Come then," said Hookama, growing impatient at the long delay, "let us go on; we
haven't much of the day left to us." So on
they went towards the home of the fiery deity
and her attendant goblins of flame.

It may be mentioned, before we pass on with
them, that the "crack" is called "Fish-Hook
Crevice" to this day, whenever tourists, having found it, ask their guides to tell its name.

CHAPTER XXI.

AN OFFERING TO PELE.

As they strode along, Hookama inquired of Lou how he managed to cry when he was fooling at the crevice. "Oh, that was easy enough," replied the *kanaka*, "you try it yourself over a sulphur crack and see if the tears don't come."

It was soon evident that they were approaching the lake of fire (Hale-mau-mau) with its nine miles of circumference, by the immense masses of cooled lava which through the centuries had flowed over the lip of the crater, and by the sulphur beds which lie towards the west.

About a mile from this sulphur plain, and before the travellers came upon it, they arrived at a depression in the mountain, covering hundreds of acres and filled with rank grass and a few scrubby plants. "Here," said

Lou, " are the wild hogs from which we will get a couple for Pele. It is the custom and we may as well conform to it, because, if we chance to meet Pele's priestess, who lives in Hilo and comes up now and then to sacrifice, she will tell Keawe that we did not give the goddess any offering. Then woe to me! Oh, she is a terrible woman. If she points out a native, the priests have him secretly strangled, and even the Chief Keawe is afraid of her wrath. But now take care; this low ground is full of pit-holes and seams "—and without further remark away ran Lou, as rapidly as if the entire area were safe as a road and smooth as a floor. It was only a few moments after the guide's disappearance, when Hookama heard his voice calling for help. His cries were intermingled with squeals. He followed the musical sounds and discovered Lou at the bottom of a big hole struggling with a porker. It was no easy thing to subdue a wild hog in a hole in the ground.

Hookama was inclined to take the part of an amused spectator, while the contest assumed a comical aspect, first the guide over the pig and then the pig on top. Occasionally the beast slipped one side and the scramble became lively. At last Lou managed to sit on the pig and having an interval of repose looked up at Hookama with a pathetic expression while his bowlegs were wound around the animal, holding him fast.

The guide's expression of utter helplessness threw the young *alii* into an uncontrollable fit of laughter, which angered Lou and gave him strength enough to grasp the pig by the tail and the long snout, and throw him up towards Hookama. The athletic youth somehow caught the animal, and now it was his turn to sit on him while Lou scrambled out of the hole. The scion of many generations of chiefs, with the help of the guide, managed to tie the four legs of the pig together with a cord of cocoa-nut fibre, and then Lou went off for a second offering to Pele, which was procured more easily.

To carry a pig, the natives usually strung it, back downwards, on a pole which they placed on their shoulders, two men to a pig. But this time, there were two men and two pigs. Each therefore was obliged to carry his own burden on his back. Under these conditions, it was impossible for Hookama, holding the struggling, squealing porker on his shoulders, to contemplate with appropriate solemnity the supernatural possibilities of the occasion. At last they emerged upon the brink of the immense circle whose cliff-like

walls enclosed the area of the crater. Down
into this chaotic depression they had to
scramble bearing their noisy and active victims.
And when the two men, with varying emotions connected with their melodious porterage, had descended the precipitous side of the
crater and toiled over vast mounds and billows
of cooled lava, grouped in monstrous and fantastic forms like petrified antidiluvian Saurians,
Hookama's chief thought was to rid himself
of his annoying burden as speedily as possible.
This he did the instant he arrived at the
" house of everlasting fire."

Each cast his struggling victim into the
seething cauldron of molten lava, and though
it was required of Pele's worshippers to invoke
her favor by a formula of submission, Hookama forgot all about it, and Lou thought
such a waste of good pork needed no waste of
words. Thus, the final squeals of the victims
were the only ritualistic utterances that accompanied the sacrifice.

When the offerings were duly acknowledged
by a sputtering hiss as they plunged into the
fiery waves, a marvellous change came over
the spirit of the young *alii*. If it is an easy
step from the sublime to the ridiculous, a
sudden transition in the opposite direction in-
volves indescribable emotions.

A Lava Cascade

It was at the verge of the less awful lake of fire (for there were two of them) that the twain dropped their burdens into the flames. Then Lou led Hookama across more rough surface of the great crater and, saying that he was going on watch, clambered to the top of a cone of lava about twelve feet high, perching there and munching a banana which he had brought with him. He threw the banana skins into the hole of the cone, which had served as a chimney for escaping gases, and looked down into the seething whirlpool of fire forty feet away as unconcernedly as if he were gazing at a calm landscape from the top of a tree.

Not so Hookama! Although somewhat reassured by the careless attitude of his companion, the emotions that took possession of every faculty of his soul were absolutely overwhelming. Lou had left him in a tolerably secure place, on a bank of hardened lava, overlooking the pit a thousand feet in diameter, where the fiery sea raged, leaping upwards and bearing on its molten billows huge blocks of red-hot lava—which were again sucked downward in eddies of the agitated mass.

Hookama had often stood on the verge of cliffs when the sea was lashed into fury by the violence of storms, and had seen the waves in the shock and recoil of terrific encounter with

the sharp pointed rocks. That sight he had
enjoyed, as any bold youth, accustomed to
wild scenes of nature, would enjoy a contest
in which familiar forces are engaged with boisterous fury. But here were new elements of
wholly unknown, bewildering and fierce agen-
cies on which his eye had never looked and
which his imagination had never conceived.
Storms, hurricanes and even earthquakes were
less appalling, in comparison with the fierce
rage and delirium of a fiery gulf, belching
steam and hurling hot masses into space.

One may brace himself to confront the sea
or a tempest; but the paroxysm of flaming
waves and fuming fire-spouts leaves him no
resources with which to wage battle. A fierce
jet of flame, reaching out to clutch an object,
be it a man, a tree or a tower of rock, is a
monster from the central depths of the earth,
which it is useless to oppose. The spirit of
man reels when it encounters the heat of effer-
vescing exhalations from boiling caverns underneath his feet.

Fling a tree-trunk into the angriest waves
and it appears again, but let a block of wood
however huge touch the surface of a whirlpool
of fire and it disappears at once and forever.

No whistling of the wind in the most furious
storm can equal the deafening noise of com-

pressed and heated air, suddenly issuing from a rent in the earth. No vortex, even of the spouting cave of Kaala, can devour the waves; as the centripetal action of a whirlpool of fire carries a wallowing mass of lava into the depths below.

Everything, below, above, was infernal; the shrieks, the flame, the moving mass, the mantling lurid clouds, the caving banks and glittering showers of scattered lava falling back into the horrible chasm, all raged and raved like fiendish embodiments of beings hot from the unutterable realms of agony and despair.

Hookama was overpowered by the awful scene; convulsive throes shook his powerful frame, and terror, for the first time in his life, seized him, and made his heart pulsate with throbbings so violent that he almost sank upon the lava hillock where he stood. Then the mysterious and tremendous sights and sounds fascinated and intoxicated him; cool-headed as he was under ordinary conditions, now he longed to get nearer the quivering monster, which seemed alive and conscious of his presence.

It beckoned him to its embrace. It was animate with a personality. Out of the foldings of gray, glistening lava surfaces, eyes of fire looked at him, as if claiming him and urging him to come. A great seam from which sulphurous steam escaped with deafening noise, warned him of the danger, but he heeded it not, although he was conscious of the peril.

He crossed the crack and stood over the abyss, as if ready to leap into its embrace. Suddenly the sound of a surge striking below was heard ; the ledge on which he stood trembled and shook; still the infatuated gazer hesitated, and would have stayed transfixed, had not something jerked back his palpitating form. A moment later and the projection on which he had been standing split off and was engulfed in the fiery lake.

A human voice recalled him to himself, as he lay panting on the ledge, at the very edge of the fissure he had so wildly crossed ; it was the high-pitched, squeaky voice of Lou, who sprang from his perch, as he saw Hookama drawing near the pit, and had caught him in the nick of time. It is hardly conceivable that the little fellow could pull back the stalwart man, but the peril gave him almost superhuman power and his friend was saved.

With eyeballs seared, hair and eyebrows singed, the soles of his feet like parchment and the *tapa* he had worn, scorched, Hookama lay supine and powerless ; the *Kanaka* stood astride his body, as if afraid he might attempt the perilous experiment again. "You're too good an egg for that oven, my *alii*," said the bow-legged rescuer. We gave Pele two pigs; isn't that enough? must she have an *alii* for a companion, too? I thought you had more sense than a hen; and I didn't want to deliver your ghost to Keawe, without your bones. Kà, hà, hà! But it's getting hot here; climb up on a blowhole, and look down into the pit if you want to, but we can't stay here. See, see!" he exclaimed, with terror in his voice, "the mound shakes! Jump—*jump!*" and the two men had just time to leave the hillock, when that too fell with a fearful crash, and they saw it rolling, till it tumbled with a splash and a boom into the molten sea below. The surface of the fiery lake was sinking.

The whole crust of the larger crater heaved and swayed; the inactive blowholes far and near emitted steam and gases. Even the one on which Lou had been seated gave out hot vapor, and on the right, a big stream of red hot lava burst forth and ran in a torrent down the side of the mound.

It was a fearful moment. Hookama had no time to think whether Pele had a hand in these disturbances or not; the two men ran for their lives. They dodged the steam jets from the seams; they held their *tapa* to their faces to enable them to breathe as they crossed the smoking sulphur beds, and had it not been for Lou's general knowledge of the surface and of the action of the larger crater, they must have missed their way and been caught in the erratic movements of the oscillating crust.

CHAPTER XXII.

A CHALLENGE TO PELE.

IT was two miles and a half to the place where they had descended from the cliff, which was like a wall extending nine miles in circumference around the volcanic basin.

When previously they crossed the surface of this immense crater carrying their pigs for Pele's maw, the distance seemed shorter to Hookama, so intense was his expectation of the spectacle awaiting him.

But now, the course stretched out interminably. They could not shorten the distance by climbing out at some other place, the wall elsewhere being almost perpendicular. To add to their distress, they saw on the cliff above them a strange figure, wildly gesticulating and shouting in a shrill voice unintelligible words. Lou was much more alarmed than Hookama.

" It is the priestess, and she is angry with
us." The *Kanaka* was more afraid of her than
of the fiery crater.

Sharply defined against the sky, the woman,
with dishevelled hair and rasping voice,
screamed her maledictions on the impious
intruders, who had dared to invade the
sanctuary of the goddess, without the aid of
her consecrated priestess. Invoking curses on
them as they ran breathlessly over the heaving
and swelling crust of the crater, she kept
abreast of them in their course, with the evident intention of meeting and confronting
them when they should come up out of the
black valley of death, in case her prayers for
their destruction did not take effect.

Lou's undevout and scoffing spirit could not
resist the terror with which the old *Kehuna* inspired him. He cared nothing for her sorcery
and incantations, but if she denounced him
to Keawe or the priests, his life would not be
worth the value of a shell upon the shore.
She soon recognized him, as he came nearer,
and all the passionate demonstrations at her
command broke forth in a flow of denunciation
like the fiery rush of a lava stream. The little
heathen trembled like an aspen leaf. He be-
sought Hookama to go on before, though both
were running as fast as their legs could carry

them over the unstable crust, and he declared
he would jump into the first crack they came
to, unless the *alii* would placate for him this
demon of a witch.

To pacify the *Kanaka*, Hookama climbed
up the zig-zag bank, as soon as the wall of the
large crater was reached, leaving Lou to come
on when he could muster enough courage to
meet his dreaded enemy. Much to his surprise, the aged hag met him as he emerged,
held out her skinny hand to help him up the last
steep ascent and bowed before him reverently,
calling him *alii-nui* (great chief), with various
posturings and expressions indicating good will.

"Why did you, oh, sorceress! curse me and
call down Pele's wrath upon me?" asked Hookama, as soon as he could interject a word.

"Ah! *alii-nui!* Son of the gods, of whom
it has been whispered in my dreams; behold
me the guardian and priestess of Pele. Those
she destroys, I curse; those she saves, I bless.
My curses were on you, lest you perish and I
had not cursed you. I curse whom Pele destroys and I bless whom Pele saves. How could
I know that she would save you and that miserable, bandy-legged despiser of the fiery goddess?"

"Then you must now bless us both, oh
Kahu! for Pele has saved both; and my

comrade Lou," (who was listening under the cliff and poked his head up at hearing this conclusion,) "he too has made his sacrifice to the dread ruler of Kilauea."

"Spoken like a chief and the son of a chief," replied the priestess ; and Lou echoed the sentiment under his breath, as if much relieved. "Come," continued the old crone, " and be safe under my roof. To-night will witness Pele's most sacred rites. See," pointing to the Lake of Fire, " how she lifts her columns of flame to the skies."

It was indeed a fearful manifestation of power; both lakes were sending fountains of red-hot lava into the air, which vibrated with intonations and reverberations.

The Priestess led Hookama (Lou following at a few paces in the rear and keeping behind the chief,) along the bank till two small huts were reached, on the western and upper cliff of the crater, from which point a view was had of the burning cauldrons, miles away and hundreds of feet below.

The darkness came on apace. But for the flames of Kilauea, the gloom would have been oppressive. In the glare of the fiery pit, the heavens were bright with lurid beams and the oval crest of Mauna Loa was seen beneath the stars. The clash and roar of the crater sounded like thunders of artillery as Hookama and the Priestess sat upon the cliff, near a fire which the *Kahuna*, human enough to shiver in the cold, had kindled. As for Lou, he crept into the hut provided for guests, and soon dropped off to sleep.

On a ragged mat, with a thick mantle of coarse *tapa* over her bony shoulders, her gray hair, thin and blowing in the wind, the prophetess sat gazing steadily at the coruscating fires. Higher and higher the molten jets were flung into the air from the awful laboratory of flame. So grand was the sight that Hookama felt the strongest impulse to worship that he had ever experienced.

"This must be the work of a god," he murmured to himself; loud enough, however, for the *Kahuna* to hear the words. Turning on him her strange, glittering eyes, she answered his thought, "*Ae-ae!* *K'Alii*, the terrible volcanic deities rule here; let him who denies it, light a *kukui*-torch and see;" (that is, compare the light of a candle with that of the volcano.) "Now, the most benignant of Pele's sisters, adorned with garlands, hangs her fiery flowers in the sky. But let her unappeasable sister, the heaven-rending one, show her might and we sit here at our peril."

"Then, you really believe in Pele and her

tribe?" said Hookama suddenly, as if giving utterance to the deepest questioning of his own mind.

"Believe in Pele?" the offended witch quickly and angrily replied. "Believe? I *know*—See, see, there she rises out of the abyss; my eyes burn with the sight—shame and grief to him who doubts!"

Hookama looked towards the smaller crater and from the incandescent abyss a fiery spray arose; out of the spray, a white cloud, thinning, spreading, glowing and sending abroad a radiant reflection like the arms of an aerial divinity dropping hot showers into the molten mass below. Then from the apex of the column, far up towards the stars, a burst, blood-red, revealed a fiery cluster like a crown resting on the head of the goddess of fire. A sudden movement of the arms—a boom—a crash—and the fountain of gold and blood and mist sank into the glowing furnace beneath.

The youth staggered to his feet, lifted his arms high over his head and cried in loudest tones, "*He-Akua-ia! He-Akua-ia!* (It is a god! It is a god!)"

The sorceress leaving him to his own further meditations, with a parting *Aloha*, crept under the thatched roof of her low hut and was seen no more that night. Hookama stood in wrapt wonder and gazed at the sea of burning lava and the fountains of fire at his feet.

"What then is a god?" he instinctively asked himself, as a child would ask "Who is God?" He recalled the salutation to him of the old king of Hawaii, when he said, "You are the son of a god." He thought of the salutation of the priestess of Pele, when he met her after escaping from the crater. "'Son of a god!' Is a god like me? I can fight, throw a heavy spear, swim, kill a shark, climb a *pali*— but I cannot set fire to the earth; I cannot mount the cloud and throw fire sparks around like handfuls of sand: 'Son of a god?' Then, of what god? Perhaps of a greater god than Pele,—or Lono, or Kane."

The youth, hardly conscious of his actions, thrilled and excited by the grandeur and sublimity of the scene before him, intoxicated by the vague possibility of kinship with higher being, as low savages are sometimes conscious of kinship with inferior animals, in a moment of exaltation, pride, presumption (call it what you will), assumed an attitude of command, folded his arms, raised his muscular form to its utmost height, and in loudest tones shouted across the chasm from the cliff on which he stood: "The son of a greater god than Pele commands her fires to cease!"

This, the visionary young man repeated thrice; each repetition in a louder tone; and when the reverberations of his voice sank into the clang and roar of the volcano, he stood still and waited for the result. The fountains of yellow and bloody fire continued to sparkle and leap into the air. The lava stream still flowed down the slope of the vast cone, and the blow-holes shrilly whistled as before. There was a slight earthquake, a trembling, a succession of eruptions and new seams in the surface of the larger crater, but no signs of important changes in Pele's fiery manifestations.

The youth had not really believed in his assumed prerogative as "a son of a god:" He had been carried away in a fatuous mood of bewildered feeling; and now that nothing followed his outburst of foolish assumption, and as he began to shiver with cold, the *koa*-wood brands hardly showing a spark of fire, his dream vanished, his strange sensation passed and a great loneliness came upon him, as if, amid these awful sights and sounds, his absolute powerlessness was uppermost in his mind, and his puny self was less than nothing.

The contrast of this state of feeling, with the vanity and arrogance of his half involuntary presumption, made him afraid that Pele herself, or some invisible power, might draw him into the fiery gulf and drown him in its waves. He felt small, and timid, and almost guilty, as he hurried into the hut where Lou was snoring loudly, and where he found, even in this vulgar, human sound, a kind of sheltering and reassuring companionship.

Lou had not heard his repeated commands to Pele to stop her fireworks, and would have considered it a good jest if he had heard them. But the priestess in her hut heard them, and muttered, "Pele will take care of the presumptuous youngster, whether he is the son of a god or not." Then she closed her eyes, too weary even to roll over on her mat to see what would be the result.

The morning sun arose, a radiant disc from the ocean, and the calm stillness of the air contrasted strangely with the din and turmoil of the previous night. Hookama, after fitful slumbers and uncanny dreams, crawled out of the low entrance of the hut where he had passed the night, and when he stood up to survey the scene which had so thrilled and intoxicated him a few hours before, what was his amazement to behold scarcely a thin thread of yellow vapor rising from the smaller lake with hardly a vestige of the flaming surface and not a fountain or a jet of flame.

The immense crater enclosing the two

lakes of fire had sunk in the middle like the
collapse of a suddenly cooled crust, leaving a
black ledge, hundreds of feet below the dark
wall of circumference. The orifices had en-
larged ; fiery masses were still falling from the
sides, but the great central mound seemed to be
gradually subsiding. The red-hot lava hung
over the emptied lake-basins like crags dropping slow cataracts into the bottomless cavities
beneath.

But far towards the southeast a line of
yellowish vapor, mingled with dark puffs of
upward rolling smoke, carried Hookama's eye
towards the Bay of Hilo, and told the story of
a lava-stream, bursting from the side of the
mountain from subterranean conduits, and,
like a flaming, sluggish river of fire, licking up
all vegetation and even the loose earth, in its
passage to the sea. Hookama gazed in wondering awe. He was dumb before the astound-
ing sight.

The changed appearance of the crater was
so complete and the dismal aspect of the
scene so depressing that the youth was more
bewildered than when he had looked the night
before into the fiery vortex of electric flame.

Not long, however, had he time to wonder
whether the scenes of yesterday were not a
creation of the fancy, and whether or not his

present vision was a reality, for hearing steps and turning around he found the prophetess, prone on the earth at his feet in the attitude of the *Kulou;* a custom which compelled all persons, on penalty of death, to prostrate themselves before a sacred chief, (*alii kapu*), to whom almost divine honors were paid.

Pretty soon, out crawled Lou from his cramped lodging, and seeing the priestess on the ground, he too, involuntarily threw himself down, his face in his hands and his hands in the black lava-dust of the earth. No native dared rise from this posture till the sacred *alii* had passed along, or had commanded him to get up. Then he must crawl backwards on all fours and only when the *alii's* back was turned, could he stand erect.

Hookama looked at the two grovelling figures with a quizzical expression on his face, and told them to get up, but as he did not use the proper formula, neither stirred a muscle. The youth seized Lou by the shoulders, set him on his feet, told him to get the bundles from the hut and come along. He then turned to the prophetess, whose sprawling figure was fantastic enough, with great folds of flesh hanging from her neck, and her brown, wrinkled skin showing through the rents in her ragged *tapa* mantle. He tried his best to get a parting word from her, but she was so seriously impressed by the power he had shown in putting out the fires of the crater, that she neither spoke nor moved till he was out of sight.

Hookama, without looking back to see if Lou was following him, walked rapidly along the edge of the crater, wondering at the transition from a scene of conflagration to one of black and smoking desolation. Taking a last look down into the immense abyss, he turned to the right and crossed the sulphur beds, where from seams and cracks the fumes were rising with a peculiar odor.

Holding his hand over one of these fissures, the steam gave him such a pleasant sensation that he took off his *tapa* mantle and his *malo*, and crouching over the aperture, while he shielded his face from the sulphurous jet, enjoyed the luxury, of which the gods, having no corporeal frames, might well envy him the delight. His joints became supple, his flesh soft. The warm vapor took away all stiffness and aches. He felt like a new being, endued with fresh vitality, and when he had revelled in the delectable refreshment to his heart's content he lay down on the soft, greasy, impregnated earth and was half inclined to go back and challenge Pele again to her face.

The Lake of Fire, Collapsed

The coming of Lou, however, put all supernatural affairs out of his mind, as the droll little man informed him that before he left the priestess, seeing that she was still prostrated on the earth and apparently oblivious of all the surroundings, he had slyly shot some mice and laid them on the threshold of her hut, "which will keep her out of it," said he, "a day or two at least, till the birds come and carry them off. If the old hag," he added, "gets back to Hilo before we do, she will tell every body what you did to Pele, and then we shall see fine sport on our return."

CHAPTER XXIII.

KING KAHAHANA'S RETURN TO OAHU.

EARLY on the morning of the tornado which landed Kelea on the island of Oahu, Numuku, who had slept uneasily during the latter part of the night, aroused himself, stretched his big legs, and, with a grunt of disgust, stood up and shook himself. A savage has the advantage of being dressed as soon as he gets upon his feet; he runs his fingers through his hair, adjusts his *malo*, possibly throws a *tapa* mantle over his shoulders if it is cold, and is ready to meet the new day. If a pool or stream is near at hand, he may plunge into it before he eats his *poi*, or in the case of a chief, his attendants may groom him, rubbing down his limbs and polishing him off with oils, or the fat of hogs, the odor of which announces his approach at a score of yards.

In the case of Numuku, his anxiety allowed him no time for this elaborate toilet ; he took a draught of *awa* from a calabash, and with sullen look, like a dog with a wicked eye, strode out of the door to survey the scene. It was a cheerless spectacle in spite of the clear sky and the glorious sunrise. On every hand devastation, trees broken down, huts unroofed, fruits scattered on the ground, while in the distance, the sea, not yet quieted after the storm, was white with foamy crests and tumultuous waves. The havoc around him did not serve to allay Numuku's irritable temper ; he was in a mood to wreak his vengeance for his losses on anything that came in his way.

Pu' Aloha awoke, that morning, filled with apprehension as to the fate of Hookama, and when the bright dawn appeared she aroused Menehune who had dropped off into sleep. His jerky, disjointed sentences, in reply to her hurried questions, did little to compose her feelings. She gathered from his words, however, that there were no tidings from Hookama and that possibly he might have been involved in the casualties of the storm.

When then she saw the bulky form of the chief striding towards the lookout on the bluff, obeying her first impulse she ran towards the place where he halted, her hair dishevelled

and her *tapa* twisted hastily about her ; but
his agitated manner arrested her steps, and in
a flutter of misgiving she stood trembling at
some distance behind him. When he turned
towards her she drew near, although her
heart was beating as if it would burst. Numuku said nothing, but, every now and then,
the grunt that escaped his lips, a sound between
a growl and a snort, showed the state of his
mind very clearly and increased the discomfort
of the young girl.

She thought of turning back and getting
away from the surly chief, when, glancing
down the path leading towards the sea, her
eye caught the sight of two men carrying a
third on their shoulders, while a fourth followed at a short distance with some objects
in his hands. The chief had already seen the
approaching group and as they came nearer,
he went towards the opening of the enclosure,
sharply bidding Pu' Aloha to stay where she
was.

Her excitement now became intense. Was
it Hookama, borne by the two men? Was he
dead or only hurt? She could hardly control
her over-wrought impulse to disobey the chief
and rush after him. As Numuku went outside the enclosure to meet the little party,
which halted at a place in the path that con-

cealed them from Pu' Aloha, she sank on the
ground, all her fortitude giving way, and
rocked herself to and fro, with cries and irrepressible wailings.

At last she saw the men pass the opening,
carrying their burden, and immediately Numuku entered the enclosure, followed by the
man who still held the things in his hands.
The pathetic sight of the disconsolate child
seemed to touch the rough savage, and speaking as kindly as he could, he told her that the
dead man was the inferior chief who had led a
party of men at the beach with orders to save,
if they could, any persons cast on the shore
during the terrific storm. There were ten
men in the company, and seven of the ten had
been drowned by the enormous waves, or so
badly bruised that their lives were despaired
of. All of them, except the chief in command,
lived down on the plains.

" But Hookama—? " cried the girl most piteously, and the chief, hardly able to repress a
scowl, answered, " Nothing at all of him, dead
or alive, *except his canoe*—and—and an idol and
a broken lance ; this rascal, one of the survivors, has them here," and beckoning to the di-
lapidated native, the fellow came forward, bearing two pieces of a javelin and the " totem,"
which had been firmly lashed at the prow of

the canoe. The canoe itself had lost its outrigger, but being made of tough *koa*-wood, it was washed ashore like a log and was found at some distance inland from the beach.

Pu' Aloha hardly heard these details, her whole thought being of Hookama; but when the man told all he knew, hope died out of her heart and a numbness crept over her as again she dropped to the ground. Numuku lifted her in his mighty grasp and telling the man to wait till he came back, carried the fainting girl to her house, where he laid her on the couch of mats and summoned her *wahines.*

The old savage, as he came out of the grass hut, muttering to himself, "She'll get over it," was somewhat less explosive than was his wont, owing to the fact that Hookama had been disposed of without giving him further trouble, or subjecting him to the necessity of vindicating himself for causing his death. "The gods are on my side," said the chief almost audibly to himself. "I'll sacrifice the first captive taken alive to Kane, and since the shark-god has got the rascally Hookama, he must get along with that, without an offering from me."

The grim smile that overspread his ugly face as he muttered these words showed that he was well satisfied to be rid so easily of the man he hated. In fact, so well pleased was he with the result, that he told the man who was waiting for his commands, that, as it was the will of the gods, he would inflict no penalty upon the survivors of the party although they had not delivered even the dead body of Hookama into his hands. "Beware, however," were his stern words to the fellow, "beware how you keep your lips; if you, or the other men, ever utter a word about this night's business, except to say you were on the beach as a look-out for wreckage, I'll get the flesh off your bones, before a dog can bark twice." The fierce look of the chief, as he gave the native this friendly warning, was assurance enough that the command would be obeyed. "Put those things at my door and go away," was the chief's final word, as he went over to a banana patch, almost levelled to the ground, to pick up a dozen of the luscious fruit for his breakfast.

He had many other matters of greater weight than the disposal of Hookama on his mind, or even than the condition of Pu' Aloha, crushed as she was by her forebodings of her lover's fate. The chiefs, who were disaffected, had shown a determined opposition to their young king Kahahana, and even when informed that he was on his way home, had openly avowed their purpose to force him to resign the *moi*ship.

Loyal as he was to his king, it was all that
Numuku could do, by promises and threats to
induce the rebellious *aliis* to await the *moi's*
return before proceeding to violent measures.
The real reason why these insubordinate chiefs
did not act at once, was their doubt concerning the mood of the large body of warriors
that the young *moi* was bringing with him
from Maui. They could not tell whether that
army would side with the king or with them,
in case of an appeal to arms.

Late in the afternoon, Numuku received
news that Kahahana and his war-canoes had
fortunately put in at Kalaupapa, on the northern coast of Molokai, and so had escaped the
tidal wave which rolled in from the south. A
few of the canoes had been damaged and
needed refitting, but the *moi* expected to arrive at Waikiki the following day.

It was the afternoon of the second day after
the storm that the watchers on Leahi,
(Diamond Head) gave the signal that the fleet
of Oahu was in sight, and immediately crowds
thronged the beach at Waikiki, or climbed the
heights to get a view of the war-canoes and
their brave warriors. Among the crowds were
women anxiously awaiting news of their husbands and sons, many of whom had been
slain in the battle of Wailuku, and no one

knew at Oahu who would return alive, or be brought back dead in the canoes covered with black *tapa*.

But the prevailing feeling was one of joy, and great preparations were made to give the fleet a triumphal welcome. All *tabus*, except those that could not be removed, including those respecting the women, were declared off for the day. Great heaps of drift wood were ready to burn. Large quantities of fish, fruit and *poi* were spread out on the plain for a feast. The ovens of hot stones contained hogs and dogs to make the feast more appetizing, and all the women were decked with brilliant flowers. The musicians with guitars, nose-flutes and drums of various sorts, were stationed at intervals, and *hula* girls, decorated with wreaths, dog-tooth buskins and ornamented skirts, were dancing in large companies, in anticipation of the arrival.

It was a gallant sight, when over the sea, now tranquil and glassy in the clear shining of the sun, came the hundreds of war-canoes,—the royal double canoe leading the van ; in it, a double row of two score stout warriors paddling with all their strength, and followed by the rest of the fleet, with sails set to catch the light breeze and streamers of all colors floating from the masts.

Sorry-looking savages perhaps, at close range, but as they moved to the rhythm of their war-songs, every paddle keeping time, it was an array of which any chief might be proud and in which the natives on shore took great delight. The young *moi*, Kahahana, stood in the stern of his red double canoe, decked in his yellow mantle and helmet, with all the insignia of his rank, while grouped around him sat the high chiefs, erect and lifting up their spears.

But the king, as he surveyed the crowd on the beach and saw the chiefs gathered into groups, the largest group apart from the rest, could hardly be said to be proud and happy, for he knew not whether his reception would be cordial or hostile. He was brave in battle but weak in authority. Would his return bring civil war, or a settlement of difficulties? His breast was torn with conflicting emotions; but seeing, in the midst of one large body of chiefs, his faithful and beloved wife, all other feelings gave way to the joy of once more clasping his Kekuapoiula to his heart.

He looked therefore every inch a king as his war-canoe swept through the inlet on a high roller, and gracefully breasted the surf towards the spot where at least some faithful adherents waited to give him welcome. The people, carried away by enthusiasm and excitement, set up a mighty shout, while the musicians sounded their drums and all their other inharmonious instruments, so that for the moment the *moi's* breast swelled with exultation, and apprehension fled away.

Soon all the war-canoes were beached, men and women swarming into the breakers to draw them ashore, and the scene was lively enough to satisfy the most ardent lover of noise and hubbub; warriors embraced each other, the women waiting for their turn to show their loyalty to their one or more husbands as the case might be. If some of the low caste warriors fell to boxing and slugging one another, it was only their way of manifesting exceptional delight.

Half a dozen canoes covered with black *tapa* were surrounded by a mourning company, wailing and tearing their scanty clothing. But these scenes on the beach were only preliminary to more extravagant performances. Who can describe the feast, which to these pagans was the consummation of their earthly joys? The women danced and frolicked and the men ate and drank *awa* till many were ready for the saturnalia which ended the feast. Girls, decorated with flowers, strolled from one group of warriors to another, laughing with the men.

One party coming to a squad of returning braves, became loudly convivial.

"Say, Maili," cried one of the *wahines,* "did you find any pretty girls on Maui?"

"Find any?" replied the good-looking youth, "Aole, aole! They found us. One of them came down to the royal canoe which I was guarding the day we left. A splendid girl. She wanted some *poi* and ordered us away with the air of a queen. But she paid us well."

The fellow fumbled in his girdle and brought out a beautiful shell, which he handed to the girl, saying: "There, Kamili, how do you like it. She said our sweethearts at home would be glad to get them."

"Oh," replied the girl, "that's nothing! a woman gave me one like it yesterday in Manoa valley, for showing her a path," and she took both shells in her hand to compare them. The youth sprang to his feet and insisted that his shell was the handsomest, at the same time putting his arm around the neck of the *wahine* to get a nearer view and to steady himself. The girl threw off his arm with an affectation of anger.

"Then that woman is somewhere on this island," shouted the tipsy warrior. "I'll find her. Where did you see her?"

"No matter where," replied the *wahine.*

" She is a chief's daughter, I'll swear, and you'd better not meddle with girls of an *alii*, Maili."

" I will, all the same," said Maili as he tumbled on the ground and the *wahine* put both the shells away in the folds of her girdle.

When the sun was setting, hundreds of warriors lay on the ground in a stupid sleep, while others staggered along, followed by the women, to take a dip in the sea. Then followed a briny saturnalia neither picturesque nor passable ; a little later lighted heaps of driftwood shed a glare on the revellers on the beach and in the surf. All that is odious in savage life was let loose, and as the moon begrudged her silvery countenance and did not illuminate the scene, it may be as well for us to throw as little light as possible upon it.

The only one among the frantic crowds, whose interest in the occasion was innocent and creditable to himself, was Menehune, the dwarf-giant. He had seen the bonfires and, led by curiosity and a vague hope that Hookama might somehow appear, came down to the shore.

The fires burned low, driftwood being scarce, so that Menehune was not noticed as he squatted in his usual grotesque posture at the water's edge. The predominant eccentricities of the occasion were lost upon him, but he was fascinated by the beating of the drums and the songs of the bathers in the waves. He watched one couple, a man and a woman, who had drawn apart from the groups and were disporting in the billows by themselves.

The fancy took him to join the revels of this particular pair as they were leaping, tumbling and laughing in the breakers. The dwarf hopped out as a frog jumps, till the shallow waves were passed. Along the line of the breaking surf, parallel with the shore, he reached the two bathers, before whom he suddenly appeared in preposterous ugliness, stretching out his arms, gaunt and monstrous in the gloom, while he uttered the most fearful noises, jumping up and down in the midst of the foam.

The improvisation was a success. Tumbling, running, screaming, the man and the woman scrambled for the shore, falling headlong, rising to be caught by a high wave and again overset; with Menehune rolling like a wheel behind them, his long arms and legs making admirable spokes. Now he comes upon them as they sprawl in the water; he puts the woman on her feet, much to her surprise; then sets her a-going again; he trips up the man and leaves him behind; then jumping like a leap frog he takes the woman's shoulders for a leverage and vaults over her head. A crowd, attracted by her screams, follows the capering dwarf. He leaves the woman to find her mate if she can and dives into the midst of the ranks of his new followers. Down they go as he tosses them over his shoulder or swings one after another far out towards the surf.

The dazed medley of men and women scatter in every direction. The dwarf runs for one, then for another. There are continuous shrieks from the women and shouts from the men. Were it not for the darkness and the noise of the breakers, the whole multitude would have assembled and the dwarf's fate have been problematical to this day. As it was, leaping and waving hands, jumping backward as the monster approached, the crowd left the field to him and reported all along the shore that the god of the sea had joined their revels and disappeared, carrying off a damsel for his bride.

This was the second enrollment of the dwarf-giant among the gods; and with a little more wit in his brain, coupled with his native drollery, Menehune would have stood a good chance of an apotheosis.

As for the damsel, the dwarf made a dive for her through a roller and came up grinning, much to her astonishment and fear. However, having no inclination to trouble her any more, he fled in one direction and she in another, as fast as the waves and the slippery sand would allow.

The bonfires on the beach were dying out and the dwarf, highly pleased with the general effect of his evening's entertainment, crept along a ridge of sand and escaped in very human and humble fashion; an eclipse of deity, with which, strange to say, the deity himself was more satisfied than if his fellow pagans had caught and worshipped him.

CHAPTER XXIV.

THE SONG-BIRD UNDER A CALABASH.

WHEN Kahahana, the young king of Oahu, retired from the feast of welcome, he summoned Numuku and other loyal chiefs to the royal house, to consider the situation. It was a grave question whether to attack the insubordinate chiefs with the army, on which the king believed he could rely, or to temporize and wait for a change in the sentiments of the rebels.

Finally it was decided to call an assembly of the disloyal *aliis* and try to win them over. The assembly was held the next day and Numuku presided. The king prudently remained away. Numuku's efforts at reconciliation were seconded by some of the older chiefs among the insurgents, but quite a large number of the younger *aliis* went home, to wait for an opportunity to renew their hostility.

Kahahana received the result of the conclave rather as a reprieve than a victory. He knew that the end was not yet, and as a precaution sent a trusty messenger to the king of Maui, asking for a reinforcement of warriors. It was a foolish thing to do, as it revealed his weakness to the king of Maui, and gave his own subjects a chance to accuse him of partiality towards their dreaded enemy Kahekili, the treacherous Maui *moi*.

The old chief Numuku, having these weighty matters of state off his mind for a time, had leisure to turn his thoughts again towards Pu' Aloha, and, though his affair with her was only an episode, he was not a person to be balked even in matters of small importance.

Kahahana had informed him that Hookama was alive and that he had sent him to Hawaii on a secret errand to the king of that island. The mystery of the canoe which had been cast ashore was partially explained by the king, who said it had been unaccountably detached from his own war-canoe on the voyage home, and had probably drifted in the current until caught by the tempest off Oahu. The fact that the sail was hoisted and that the watchers reported some one in the canoe just before the storm, left the matter somewhat in doubt, but so far as Hookama was concerned, it did not affect the case.

Numuku decided not to let Pu' Aloha know that Hookama was alive, but to act towards her as if her lover were drowned; and since Hookama would be coming back in a few weeks at the most, he meant to press the girl to marry him at once. Then on Hookama's arrival, he would see what could be done.

Pu' Aloha was inconsolable over her loss. Day and night, clothed in black *tapa*, she sat in her house, rocking to and fro, with wailings and sobs. Sometimes she sang a plaintive chant to give vent to her emotions.

> "*Eia ka uhuki hulu manu,*
> *Kau pua o Haili,*
> *Na keiki kiai pua,*
> *Ka lahui pua o lalo.*"

> "He is the picker of bird feathers,
> (Of birds) lighting on the flowers of Haili;
> The young ones watching the flowers.
> The multitude of flowers below."

But the refrain of every song was the requiem of love and grief, which *Ua* sang when the lover of Kaala, the Flower of Lanai, plunged into the whirlpool of the Spouting Cave to clasp the misty form of his bride. She changed a few words only, and the pathos of the song quieted her spirit as she coupled her own name with that of her lover.

" Oh ! dead is Hookama, the young chief of Oahu ;
The chief of few years and many battles !
His limbs were strong and his heart was gentle ;
His face was like the sun and he was without fear.
                    *   *   *   *
Hookama is dead and the black tapa is over my heart.
Now let the gods take the life of Pu' Aloha ! "

The presence of Menehune at her door was
a comfort to the stricken girl, and he was to
her a protector, like the giant Maukaleoleo
who watched over Umi, the peasant prince of
Hawaii, whose story she had often heard from
Hookama's lips. The dwarf heard the pathetic voice of his mistress as she sang her
mournful chants. Now and then he mysteriously disappeared, but always came back at
nightfall and no night was he absent from his
post.

Numuku let the poor girl take her own way
for a few days, thinking she would soon rally.
He gave special orders to her *wahines* to care
for her comfort and sent fruits to her which
she left untasted. As a particular mark of
attention, which showed considerable tact on
the part of the old chief, he sent to her house
the " totem " and the broken javelin, which
had belonged to Hookama.

Several days having passed and no change
in her being apparent, the chief went to see
her and was struck by her altered looks ; her

eyes lacked their wonted brilliancy and her countenance was pale. As she sat in a drooping attitude she was the picture of despair.

The sight of the girl in this condition angered Numuku. He felt that it was her own fault that her beauty and vivacity were gone. Why should she mope for the bird-catcher? It was opposition to his authority; a kind of antagonism to his wishes. Hating Hookama as the author of this state of things, he visited on the child the wrath which he could not inflict on her lover.

She had no idea why he frowned upon her as he stood looming up in her presence. Was it not right to mourn for a dead friend? Did not the chiefs disfigure themselves (she had heard of such things) at the death of relatives?

When then Numuku blurted out his indignation in the bitter words, " Isn't it time to stop this dreaming and moaning, Pu' Aloha? You can't gather berries from the clouds! What the gods will, must be submitted to!" Pu' Aloha was struck dumb; she could not answer; it was all so unexpected. Was this the Numuku that promised to be a father to her?

But she soon looked up with pleading eyes and the chief, touched perhaps by her silent misery, conscious also that he was deceiving her in regard to Hookama's death, softened his tone a little and touching her shoulder, said, "You need not be unhappy here with me. Is it an eclipse of the sun when a single star goes out?"

"Alas!" replied the girl in a low voice, "can the bird sing when covered by a cala-bash?" Numuku remembered that these were the very words which Hina of Hawaii spoke to Kaupeepee of Haupu, when he stole her away to make her his bride, and kept her a prisoner, till she forgot her bondage and accepted his love which gently wooed her thoughts from the past. Pu' Aloha herself had sung to him this *mele*.

The remembrance of that love story of long ago awakened the chief to a new strategy, and he began to say tender things to Pu' Aloha; that is, as tender as his uncouth utterance could frame. He asked her what he could do for her. Could he bring Hookama to life? Could he dry up the sea and find his body for her to fondle? Could he get her another Hookama that she would like as well as she liked this bird-catcher? "No!" he concluded, "these things belong to the gods. I am not a god, but I can marry you myself, as I prom-ised, and keep you from harm. Besides, you may select another husband if you will, and we will dwell together in peace."

These words had the opposite effect from that which the deceitful old chief intended to produce. Pu' Aloha burst into a passionate fit of crying and clasping her knees rocked herself in uncontrollable distress. To marry Numuku, with Hookama dead, was utter misery; she was fast losing control of herself; but what she might have said was prevented by Numuku himself as he abruptly left the house, muttering that the girl was a fool and might go to *Milu* for all that he cared!

Menehune, hidden in a clump of bushes, heard the word "fool," (he had a knack of getting ideas from separate words,) and he knew there was trouble. Creeping back to Pu' Aloha's door, he looked in for the first time since the girl had secluded herself, and seeing her prostrate, lifted her tenderly on the mats and, calling her *wahines*, went out beyond the enclosure, with a vague sense of the need of doing something for his mistress.

No sooner had he passed the opening towards the ravine, than he saw the figure of a man, hurriedly moving up the highway. The man turned as if to see if he was followed, and Menehune knew that it was Paao. The dwarf had taken an intense dislike to this man. Why, he could not tell. It was an in-

stinct, such as makes a dog cherish antipathy
to a person for no obvious cause.

Believing that some mischief was brewing
he kept himself out of sight, while he kept
Paao in view.   After a long time he saw
Paao strike off the main path, into a foot-way
leading in the direction of the house on the
cliff where he had left Kelea.   It was a path
seldom travelled, and with increased misgiving
Menehune followed on till within a few rods
of a lonely spot where another path from
Manoa valley crossed that on which Paao was
going.

Much to the dwarf's amazement, he saw a
second traveller, who had come up by the
path from Manoa, and who was entering into
a violent altercation with Paao.   It seems that
both men were about to ascend the same
path, when Paao, in a rude way, asked the
stranger, a strong and active young man,
where he was going.   The stranger replied, in
equally rough language, that it was none of
his business.   Whereupon Paao struck at the
man with a heavy stick which he carried.

Quick as a flash, the stranger wrenched the
stick away, and whirling it in the air, bade
Paao stand off or take the consequences.
Drawing a dagger, Paao made a lunge at the
stranger, who, too quick for him, sprang aside

and brought the stick with great force down on Paao's arm.

The arm dropped and the dagger fell to the ground. At this instant, Mehehune rushed straight at the combatants and thrust his mighty limbs between them. It was an easy thing for him to hurl the stranger, stick and all, into a low bush at the wayside. Having done this the dwarf turned to Paao and took hold of his arm, which was badly bruised but not broken.

The other fellow, who had made aquaintance with the scrub plant in the unceremonious fashion described, picked himself up and laughed heartily as the big dwarf bent over the crestfallen Paao. It was the warrior Maili of the king's war-canoe, who had given the shell to the girl on the beach. He had coaxed the girl to tell him where she met the mysterious woman, and out of curiosity, having a little leisure on his hands, he had come in search of her. He knew Menehune and regarded the whole affair as a joke.

Paao, on the contrary, aside from the serious injury he had received, was angry because Menehune had followed him, and, overlooking the fact that the dwarf had prevented his antagonist from following up his advantage, began to berate his deliverer in words which would have been highly profane if uttered in any civilized language. Seeing that the quarrel was over and that Paao resented any further assistance from him, Menehune coolly walked a dozen paces up the path and squatted in the middle of it, as much as to say " No trespassing allowed."

There was a moment's silence ; Paao glared at the two co-operators in the offence to his dignity and person ; then with a look of scornful anger, turned and walked rapidly down the path by which he had come, nursing his battered arm. Maili kept the stick and made a movement to pass the dwarf and ascend still further beyond him, along the path. Menehune allowed him to come abreast on one side and then by an adroit shifting of his leg, laid the fellow sprawling on the ground, at the same time snatching the stick from his hand.

This was too much for the warrior's goodnature and, resenting this second interference, he jumped at the dwarf, who coolly enclosed him in his big arms, placed him in his lap and began to fondle him as a *wahine* caresses a puppy. It was of no use to resist, and, as there were no spectators, Maili made the best of the situation and began to imitate the bark of a young dog. This tickled the fancy of the dwarf so much that he set the man on his feet and with a grim smile, pointed down the way that led to the Manoa valley and grunted out the word "*Makai*" (to the sea); the man, taking the hint, vanished instantly without even a parting oath.

Menehune then stood up and waited till the sound of retreating footsteps ceased. His eye fell upon something white, in the grass at the side of the path where Paao received the stroke from the stick. It was the shark's tooth dagger, and as the dwarf picked it up, he gave one of his customary chuckles and put it safely away in the folds of his *malo*.

The path from this crossing of the ways was an intricate one. Almost impenetrable by others, it was familiar to Menehune, who before long emerged on the plateau in front of the house on the cliff. There he found Kelea, beating out moist fibre for a *tapa* cloth. He was evidently a regular and welcome visitor and his advent was not a surprise. Taking his mother aside he told her that the girl must keep near the house, because her presence on the island was probably known to at least two men, who he supposed had come in search of her that very day.

Then handing to the astonished Kelea the dagger, the dwarf, as if in great haste, disappeared around the angle of the ledge.

The dagger was like a mysterious gift from the gods. How it came into Menehune's possession, or why he gave it to her she could not tell, but she placed it in her girdle, and felt as if somehow it was a recovered link between her fortunes and those of Hookama.

CHAPTER XXV.

A CRISIS.

TOWARDS nightfall, Menehune was squatting as usual at the door of Pu' Aloha's house, as unmoved in appearance and as grotesque in attitude as if his only occupation was to orna- ment the premises of his royal mistress.

Within a day or two, Paao had an interview with the chief. He represented to Numuku the need of keeping an eye on the dwarf, who, after that time, was strictly forbidden to leave the enclosure without permission. He also arranged with the chief that he should pay court to Pu' Aloha and win her for them both if he could. The chief gave him permission to make advances to her with that purpose in view.

Numuku rallied Paao on his arm, which was bound up, and the young man said that it was the result of a fall, when he was climbing a cliff. It was not a serious injury, but for a time it crippled the arm and rendered it useless for handling a spear or a club.

From this time, Paao's attentions to the sorrowful maiden amounted to little less than persecution. He intruded upon her whenever Menehune was absent from his post. He tried all his powers of persuasion and made the girl as wretched by his amorous advances as by the threats which he finally employed to bend her to his will. Finding her obdurate, he persuaded Numuku to see her, if possible to induce her to comply with their united demands.

The old savage arrayed himself in the most approved Hawaiian fashion for the interview. His feather cloak represented the labors of one hundred men for a year. Its airy magnificence was dazzling to behold. The *malo* about his loins was gaudy and fringed with red. On his breast was the *palaoa*, the mark of his rank, suspended from his neck by twisted strands of human hair. In his hand was a necklace of curiously wrought mother-of-pearl. When he entered her house he planted the *tabu* spear before the door. In such splendor was he arrayed that he felt assured of success. How could any Hawaiian woman hold out, in presence of these irresistible attractions, to say nothing of the odor of the cocoa-nut oil with which he was anointed !

Pu' Aloha was seated on the ground, covered with black *tapa*, her eyes lustreless and her face pallid ; there was little beauty, either in her countenance or form, to charm the savage heart. The drooping eyelids and the sombre clothing gave the chief a start; he was in doubt whether he cared to press his suit. He had overstimated the value of the prize.

But of one thing he felt assured ; a girl with no more to offer certainly must yield to one like himself who could give her everything a woman's heart desires. Besides, he had begun the affair and he meant to win, whether he cared much for the girl or not.

He seated himself on the pile of mats and looked about him in evident embarrassment. Pu' Aloha had risen, as was the custom, when her lord entered and she now stood near him with her hands crossed over her bosom. She said nothing except to give the usual salutation, " *Aloha !* " (Love to you), which meant more or less according to circumstances.

Numuku held out the necklace, and she took it, thanking him and laying it down on the couch. " I have come," at last said the chief, " to claim my rights as your *Alii*. I made a promise to you which I intend to keep." Pu'

Aloha's cheek flushed but she returned no responsive look or word ; neither could the chief give utterance to any of the soft speeches he had prepared for the occasion. He was completely stranded so far as any inspiration for love-making was concerned. It was a very awkward situation for him.

After some moments of oppressive silence, he began a sentence, " The—the choicest flower—the flower of my choice—Pu' Aloha is the—all the flowers in—in the garland—" and there he stopped, actually run aground and unable to go on.

Again he started, as he had sometimes tried to get his canoe off a rock, where it went round and round the more he paddled. " Why those [a grunt]—those tears, Pu' Aloha ? The sun-showers—shower-tears [another grunt] of the —tears of the winds—are—are—*Kà—Kà*," (he was getting angry) ; " By Kane ! will you have me, child, or not ? " He was getting down to the familiar vernacular once more ; " It may be only a *hoao* (trial to test the feelings) at first. Come, come, answer me, or I'll see who is master," and the ugly face of the chief assumed its most diabolical expression. Numuku was himself once more.

It only needed this return of the royal wooer to a threatening attitude for Pu' Aloha to gain all her courage and firmness. The "totem" of Hookama stood upright against the thatch and caught the girl's eye as she regained her strength and composure. Dropping on her knees before the image, in a strong, unwavering voice she uttered the following prayer:—

"Here is your body of a bird, O Lono!
May I be saved by you, O Lono, my god!
Saved by the supporting prayer!
Saved by the holy water!
Saved by the sacrifice to you, O god.
Here is the sacrifice, an offering of prayer."

Numuku fidgetted about on the mats as the prayer begun; he was too superstitious to interrupt an appeal to the greatest of the gods. When the supplication was ended and the suppliant arose to her feet and stood, with a look of serene composure on her face, as if defying him to harm a votary of the all-powerful deity, the chief also arose to his feet and said hastily: "I'll see the priest about this; you will marry me to-morrow, and Lono will accept the sacrifice." Then, with heavy tread he left the hut.

That night no moon looked down on the enclosure of the chief, and the clouds were piling up above the hills. It was near midnight when

Menehune felt a slight touch on his shoulder,
as he slept at the door of the house of Pu'
Aloha. Clad wholly in black, with a bundle
covered with black *tapa* in her hand, the girl
drew the dwarf inside the door, placed the
"totem" in his hands, uttered the words
"*Hele*" (go); "*Mauka*" (the mountain), and
showed him where her hands had cut away the
fastenings at the back of the hut.

The faithful dwarf needed no further explana-
tion. He crawled through the aperture, and
led the way, on all fours, the girl creeping after
him, to a gap in the hedge. She crouched
under the broad leaves, heedless of the sharp
points which punctured her soft shoulders,
while Menehune reconnoitered. On his return, she took his big hand and was led
down into the ravine, where the plashing brook
smothered the sound of their footsteps. Picking their way along the shallow stream and by
the smooth jutting rocks, the two fugitives
came out at the foot of a steep hillside; a dog,
in a hut near the bank of the stream, barked
loudly; they thought they heard a noise˙ of
hurrying feet behind them and held their breath
to listen. The mists came down from the hilltops and enveloped them. Pu' Aloha heard
what seemed to her a burst of laughter; it was
the hoot of an owl. They passed through a

collection of huts; the darkness of a cloudy
night settled on the valley; all along the way
the girl's fancy conjured up spectres of monstrous shapes from the trees and skirts of the
wood, along which they toiled. Never before
had she groped among the ghostly forms of
night. Had it not been for the strong grasp
of Menehune's hand, her courage and strength
must soon have failed.

When a path was reached, the dwarf lifted
the girl in his arms, carried her easily, and
moving steadily through the mists, climbed
with his burden the way he knew so well, till
the house on the cliff was reached. It was his
shrine. To defend it was his passion. To
make it the refuge and sanctuary of those he
cared for, was his one object in life. The
dwarf had a big heart, if there was but little
room for it in his body, and his soul was as
true as his face was homely.

A quiet signal and the ever-watchful mother
came to the door. Menehune said to her,
" Here, another foster child," and disappeared
in the darkness.

At bright daydawn Pu' Aloha's *wahines*,
coming to awaken and bathe their mistress,
found the dwarf-giant alert and watching as
usual at her door.

CHAPTER XXVI.

THE HOUSE ON THE CLIFF.

KELEA was aroused, the morning after Pu' Aloha's arrival at the house on the cliff, by the touch of the gentle old woman whom she had learned to love and to call "mother." She was told that during the night Menehune had brought a strange girl to the house. "She is a delicate flower," said the "mother," "and Menehune tells me that she is much *pilikia loa* (distressed). Will you come and look at her?"

Then the sympathetic old soul led the way, with Kelea following, to the mats hidden by a *tapa* screen, where Pu' Aloha was lying asleep. Her fair, round arm supported her head, and her flowing locks rippled over her glossy brown shoulders, while the long lashes, veiling her eyes, gave an inexpressible charm, heightened by the tears which hung beneath them, like dew-drops on the petals of a yellow *hala-pepe* flower. The tinge of lemon color in the brown of her complexion gave the skin the tint of a foreigner, and added a peculiar brilliancy to its transparent beauty.

Now and then, the sleeper gave a nervous start and her tapering fingers twitched with convulsive movement. The black *tapa* mantle she had worn was flung, half on the couch and half on the ground, an emblem of the woes through which she had passed.

Kelea was deeply stirred as she gazed on the sweet maiden. The surf-rider of Maui, with all her audacity and caprice, was a creature of affectionate as well as passionate impulses. The stranger appealed to her best instincts and she longed to befriend her, to hold her to her breast and comfort her.

It was a striking tableau : the delicate girl asleep, fair as a flower, inviting soothing and caressing care; the dark maiden, bending over her, strong, intense, with her raven locks floating loosely over her shoulders and swelling bosom. Her eager face and well-balanced pose showed that her susceptibilities were under control, while the unconscious movement of her lips and the moisture in her eyes revealed a deep sympathy for the distress which she could not at once alleviate.

In the background, the wrinkled, sightless "mother" stood motionless, evidently feeling the pathos of the scene. It was she who broke the silence by a whispered word to Kelea, and the two women left the side of the sleeper, as one would leave a flower with folded petals, not wishing to disturb it till the sunshine caused it to unfold.

Pu' Aloha slept nearly all that day. Occasionally, she partially aroused herself to receive a cooling draught, brought to her by the blind "mother." The *tapa* curtain kept the sunlight from her eyes and the two women walked softly that their footfalls might not awaken her. It was a day of mingled emotions for Kelea. She had no idea who the newcomer was, but a strange fascination led her to go quietly from time to time and look at the beautiful girl.

As Pu' Aloha grew stronger and received the kind ministrations of Kelea, the two girls drew together in close friendship. This was the first friend Kelea ever had, with whom she was frank and affectionate. She became devoted to the lovely maiden and was as tender toward her as a lover. It was a new revelation to her of a responsive, artless, clinging disposition, exactly the opposite of her own.

Adroit questions on her part drew from Pu'

Aloha the simple story of her life and even her relations with Hookama. Under other circumstances, the highstrung girl would have broken out into vehement words. But, as in the case of Hookama's refusal of her pleading love in the Iao Valley, her pride enabled her to repress all evidences of excitement and her love for Pu' Aloha kept her within bounds.

Only when alone, in a secluded spot further up the hill, to which she went in order to give vent to the tumult of her soul, did she find relief in tears and exclamations. Had her rival been a less lovable being, or had she failed to win Kelea's love, the jealousy of the savage would have overmastered all other feeling. Even the death of her rival at her hands might have been sought, if thereby she could remove the obstacle to her desires.

But Kelea's infatuation for Hookama did not obliterate her fondness for the girl, who nestled to her for protection and who guilelessly confided to her the feelings of her heart. Pu' Aloha believed that Hookama was drowned by the tidal wave. Sometimes that thought was overwhelming, and the poor child wept for hours, giving way to uncontrollable sorrow. Then Kelea would hold her in her arms, without saying a word.

In her own mind Kelea revolved the whole

matter, trying to think of some way by which both she and her dear friend might be satisfied. She thought of the possibility, allowed by custom, of a double marital connection! But this would be of little comfort to her, if Hookama gave all his love to her rival. Could she bear to see him in the arms of another and lavishing on her the fervid affection which she demanded for herself?

There was one hope: that Hookama might not reciprocate Pu' Aloha's strong passion. " But how can he help loving such a sweet flower," she said to herself over and over again. He had said, in the vale of Iao, that there was *no other* ; had he deceived her, to prevent a frantic scene on her part? Her mind was perplexed. She was sometimes plunged in despair. Must she lose everything for which she had imperilled her life and doomed herself to exile?

Hookama had told her frankly that the gods willed otherwise; that he did not love her; but at that time, she felt that she could, in some way, win his heart. Now, the appearance of another, charming enough to win the love of the noblest chief, changed the aspect of the case, leaving Kelea almost crushed in spirit.

Kelea believed that Hookama was still alive.

She knew, what Pu' Aloha did not know, that he had not been drowned, for she herself had been in his canoe. Where he was, she could not tell. Had he returned with the king? If so, why did he not come in search of Pu' Aloha? This was a thread on which to hang her hopes. Perhaps he did not care after all for the lovely child.

Then the question came, should she impart to Pu' Aloha her own belief that Hookama was living and would come back sooner or later? Was it not the part of friendship to offer this small degree of consolation. The picture of the dear girl's distress was vividly before her, as she decided to comfort her, if she could, in every possible way.

She found Pu' Aloha in tears; the girl had been in one of her paroxysms of grief. As Kelea approached, the maiden flung her arms about her and said: "At least, loving one! the wilted flower has the strong tree to cling to; what would Pu' Aloha do, with Hookama gone, if she could not rest on her *kuu poli aloha* [a Hawaiian term which means more than a mere relative] even though no one can take a lover's place?"

"My own darling," replied Kelea, with emotion, as she folded the weeping girl to her bosom, "perhaps your Hookama will come again to you." (She used these words with the greatest effort.) "How do you know that he has joined the brave warriors in the hidden land of Kane? Does the bee, that has once sipped honey from the choicest flower, stray away among common weeds and not come back? Your wild bee will surely long for his Pu' Aloha and thirst for the nectar on his blossom's lips."

"But the canoe was Hookama's, and Numuku said the idol was lashed in the prow of it," quickly exclaimed the excited girl. "If his canoe was washed up by the storm, he must have been drowned,—Menehune said so,—and his body lost," and the child sobbed on the breast of her friend, whose heart might have told its own secret by its rapid throbbing, if Pu' Aloha had suspected any reason for its unusual palpitation.

Kelea endeavored by her caresses to calm the maiden whom she held in her arms, and when Pu' Aloha became somewhat tranquil she told her the story of her flight from Maui, and, with some omissions and occasional divergencies from the truth, explained to her the reason why she thought Hookama might still be alive and come back to her safe and sound.

Telling her first about her own home at Waihee on Maui, she narrated the story of the battle of Wailuku and the attempt of the terrible *moi* Kahekili to carry her to his *hale-alii.* This attempt, she declared, led her to resolve to flee from the island over which he held absolute and tyrannical authority. Fortunately, she discovered that the king of Oahu intended to sail homeward and that an empty canoe would be towed behind his war-canoe. Then she gave a vivid description of her efforts to cut the cord and her final success.

She related other details of her voyage, its perils and adventures, at which Pu' Aloha shuddered while she admired the pluck of her new-found friend. Kelea concluded the exciting tale with an account of her experience with Menehune in the cave and her unique ride on his broad shoulders to the House on the Cliff. The latter portion of the story amused Pu' Aloha so much that she laughed aloud, the first time since her arrival at the " mother's " house.

It will be noticed that Kelea said nothing about her meetings with Hookama and Paao, but made the story so plausible that her unsuspecting listener did not even surmise that Kelea's use of the canoe had anything to do with Hookama. She asked one question. " How did it happen that the king was bringing the canoe back with him to Oahu?

Hookama meant to go in it to Hawaii, why should he send it back from Maui ? "

Kelea's ready answer was that probably the war between the kings of Maui and Hawaii made the continuance of Hookama's voyage to Hawaii too hazardous. In that case he may have returned to Oahu with the king. "If so, you will see him before long," she added with a brave attempt to smile.

Pu' Aloha was somewhat brightened up by the comforting words of her friend and began to grow stronger and more cheerful. As her vigor returned her beauty increased, and the bloom of her cheeks vied with her joyful eyes in giving her a magical charm which Kelea could not resist. She was more and more enchanted with the loveliness and gentleness of the flower which she tended with increasing fondness. It was the older girl's delight to make wreaths of the choicest blossoms that grew about the house on the cliff, and adorn with them the comely neck of her companion.

Pu' Aloha's beauty was so different from that of other native maidens, that it seemed to Kelea to belong to another and superior race. If tradition can be believed, then the one white woman, who centuries ago was cast upon these islands had transmitted a refinement, which now and then appeared in indi-

viduals, like the stars called "sporades" not included in any of the constellations. At any
rate, Kelea could not cast off the spell which Pu'
Aloha threw around her more and more. This
woman, savage born, fitful in her impulses, became almost a worshipper of the gentle being,
whose claim to adoration lay in her artlessness and her delicate beauty of person and
character.

But there were times when the surf-rider,
accustomed to the wild waves and the mountains, became restless and felt that she must
grapple with something in order to tame the
unruly spirit within her. She would plunge
into the thickest jungle, seek the highest crag
when the thunder was the loudest and fill the
ravines with her voice. Now and then the
sound of the sea, reaching her ear far up the
mountain, would set all her pulses beating for
a mad race with the billows.

One day, seeing in the distance hundreds of
bathers on the beach, enjoying a public festi-
val or contest in surf-riding, all her prudence
was swept away, and telling Pu' Aloha that
she was going off to find Hookama for her,
away she fled down the mountain. With the
single thought of her merry comrades, the
dashing rollers from the sea, and a longing for
scope and liberty to let herself loose, she be-

came once more a wild barbarian, impetuous
and heedless.

The crowds, excited by the exploits of
swimmers on surf-boards and in canoes, were
shouting and running up and down the beach,
so that Kelea reached the white crested waves
wholly unnoticed. Seeing a surf-board which
had slipped from some bather's hand, she
seized it and pushed it before her towards one
of the higher breakers which the rest of the
swimmers avoided.

Lustily breasting the heavy waves, handling
her board with consummate skill and watching
for the loftiest comber, she rode the surf so
audaciously and skilfully, that, drawing the
attention of all, she was watched and cheered
as the champion of the hour. When she
came near the shore, by an adroit movement,
instead of landing she dove into a wave which
came after others of less size, and, swimming
under water, emerged among a group of
natives, who, tumbling together in the rush
of the surf took no heed of her arrival among
them.

Again the spirit of reckless daring came
upon her, and borrowing a board from one of
the women, she joined a party of expert swimmers, who were contesting for a prize. With
her usual boldness, she sought the most dangerous surf, and, in the face of disadvantages,

distanced all her rivals, gracefully guiding her course so as to approach the shore in the deepest water possible.

This time she also mysteriously disappeared, and the crowd, searching for the fair contestant without success, declared that she must be some sea-goddess, a suggestion quickly caught up and repeated by the defeated swimmers, glad of any pretext to cover their failure. Somehow in the confusion Kelea managed to escape from her perilous position and to gain a covert in the fields and finally a safe return to the house on the cliff. She did not wholly avoid, as she supposed, the recognition she feared; one of the swimmers, Maili, knew her and made an unsuccessful attempt to follow her.

All she told Pu' Aloha was that she had taken a bath and that she had discovered no traces of Hookama.

She, as well as her companion, was becoming more and more impatient for tidings of the young *alii*, and intended, at the earliest opportunity, to find out if she could what had become of him. She dared not risk a meeting with Paao, whose relations towards Pu' Aloha had been disclosed to her by her friend. She was therefore cautious in her wanderings, as well as careful to avoid the path leading down to Nuuanu valley.

CHAPTER XXVII.

THE CONSPIRATORS' CAVE.

ON the morning after Numuku's rough wooing of Pu' Aloha and her hasty flight to the house on the cliff, the *wahines* came and found Menehune as usual on the threshold of his mistress' house. Not many moments afterwards, Numuku met these girls rushing towards his habitation, the dwarf following them, with the news that Pu' Aloha could not be found.

The chief became as excited as the rest, but all that he could discover was that the girl had gone away in the night. Menehune took refuge from the chief's inquiries in his accustomed brevity of speech and in a look of more than unusual imbecility. Once or twice the dwarf uttered an ejaculation: "*Auwe, auwe!* Alas, alas! Little song-bird gone!"

Numuku immediately sent out a scouting

party of natives. Menehune went with them and managed to lead them astray. After hours of searching they returned with no tidings of the girl. The dwarf appeared to be more distressed than any one at the failure of their efforts and persuaded Numuku by various signs and gesticulations to let him go by himself to find his mistress.

Then he slipped off and went rapidly by a round about way to the house on the cliff, and, having satisfied himself that Pu' Aloha was there and that no one had been there to search for her, he returned the second time and assumed the disconsolate air of a dog baffled by a false scent.

Paao was absent the night of Pu' Aloha's flight. He did not come into the enclosure till noon ; when he heard the news he was in a quandary. He felt the need of great caution. He had been at a secret meeting of conspirators on the mountain and he was suspicious of Menehune's movements. He could neither give the chief a good reason for his absence, nor acquaint him with his distrust of the dwarf.

He met Numuku with an expression on his face of the deepest concern and offered to make immediate search himself. The chief counselled waiting, as he had sent out a second scouting band. Towards evening, no tidings being received, Paao became frightened, lest his own movements be discovered, and insisted that the perplexed chief should allow him to make a more thorough search. Numuku finally yielded and Paao left for the mountain to notify his accomplices of danger.

The time for Hookama's return from Hawaii was calculated by Numuku as not far distant. It made Numuku anxious, and he redoubled his efforts to discover the missing girl. His scouts penetrated the thickets and found the house on the cliff. They reported that there a poor, blind old woman lived alone and complained that her son, the dwarf, never came near her and sent her nothing to live on day by day.

Menehune had been there every night and had cautioned his mother not to let the girls be seen till the search was over. She was instructed to hide them in a cave with which the grass hut communicated. The dwarf had built the house for concealment. The end nearest the cliff was hung with *tapa*, over which were placed calabashes and cooking utensils. Near the ground, under the *tapa*, was a narrow entrance to a hollow in the rock, filled with rubbish. Creeping through this hollow, one came to a good sized cavern, where it was possible to build a fire, the smoke escaping by a number of the fissures in the rock.

The two girls, watching in the daytime for stragglers, retired into this cave when any one appeared, till they received a signal that the coast was clear. At night they made themselves comfortable on mats in the cavern. Thus, much of the day could be spent in the open air. They called it a *pilikia* (botheration), but made light of the discomfort.

After Menehune's warning they stayed nearly all the time in the cave, trying to amuse themselves in the best way they could. On the second day of this enforced confinement, Kelea, growing restless, and with her usual boldness and love of adventure, climbed into the clefts of the cavern and explored its recesses. She came upon streams of water, and slippery places where it was difficult to get a foothold, and where her candle-nut taper gave a fitful light. Persisting in her explorations she found, at last, an opening into the air under the blue sky. Standing outside, among tangled vines and piles of stones, she enjoyed the prospect which took in the whole of the Koolau district and the distant sea.

But attempting to return, she discovered that she had no more candle-nuts and no means of lighting one, even if she had it. Nothing

daunted, she determined to return on the outside and began the descent with much courage.
The sharp lava points cut her feet and she was
often stopped on the brink of a precipice over
which a cascade fell sheer down for hundreds
of feet. She twisted her *tapa* mantle more
closely about her and painfully toiled downwards, till she was conscious of having lost her
bearings, being shut in by high masses of rock.

The tired girl was almost ready to lie down
in despair, when she thought she heard a
sound like that of human voices. All around
her, nature was primeval, as if never invaded
by man, but she was more and more convinced
that she heard persons talking not far away.

The sound came from a fissure in the rock
against which she was leaning. Placing her
ear over the crevice, she heard distinctly the
words of several men in conversation. To
listen she crept lower down and took a position where she could hear better, although
entirely hidden from view among the rank
grasses and stunted shrubs.

To her amazement and horror, one voice,
louder than all the rest, was that of Paao, her
hated assailant in the vale of Iao. Still more
amazed she heard the company discussing
a diabolical plot against the king of Oahu
and his government. She could not see the

men, but from their language and tones she
knew they must be chiefs, because the difference between the *aliis* and the common natives
was very marked, not only in intelligence but
in voice and utterance.

A deep conspiracy against Kahahana's
authority was discussed in its details. The
number of warriors who could be relied upon
was given, and some of their names were mentioned in the course of the conversation. The
time for an attack on the royal house at Waikiki
was left undecided but all agreed that it should
be made very soon. Paao gave much information as to the King's forces and said that one
or two of the priests of the royal *heiau* were
in favor of the rebels. He also declared that
Kahekili, king of Maui, had promised him
aid.

Kelea's heart beat wildly, and she was
fearful lest some involuntary movement on
her part should betray her presence. Several
times she was obliged to take her ear from
the crevice and quiet herself. When the
council of conspirators broke up, she heard
them strike their daggers together and take a
solemn oath not to betray each other. Then
the chiefs, whose voices told Kelea that most
of them were young men, scattered in every
direction, over rocks and into ravines, adding

to the listening girl's terror lest they discover her.

Paao lingered a moment after the others had gone. Kelea heard him mutter : " So this revolt will give me revenge on more than one enemy. *Kà, hà, hà* ! I can choose my own fruit when I am made a priest." She shuddered at his words, as she thought of Pu' Aloha and her own fate, if the conspiracy succeeded with Paao for its leader.

When she heard this arch traitor leave the cavern, she felt impelled to get a glimpse of him as he went down the mountain. Clambering from her hiding place above the cave she hurried after his retreating footsteps, keeping at a safe distance. She longed to hurl a stone at him and fingered the dagger, which she always carried in her girdle.

Once, as a twig crackled under her foot, she thought she saw Paao turn his head ; instantly she dropped on the ground and to her great relief the man went on with quicker strides. Suddenly he stopped and seemed to listen. Then he searched the bushes on one side of the path.

These movements alarmed Kelea so much that, forgetful of everything but escape, she crept into the low shrubbery, slipped under the branches. climbed over rocks and, coming upon an abrupt declivity, slid down its side, regardless of the deep hollow into which she was plunging. Finding a place under a sheltering rock, where, lying prostrate, she could not be seen from above, she lay motionless for a long time.

At last, as all was silent, she began to scramble on, if possible to get back to the path which she had left in her fright. She feared nothing but an encounter with Paao, who might be in pursuit of her. She was a good climber and caught glimpses of the sun. Shaping her course towards the west, after more than an hour's painful effort, it was evident that she had lost her reckoning. The ravines became deeper and their sides steeper.

She determined to get on a high place where she could look off. She drank from a little pool and ate some *akala* berries, and began with fresh ardor to climb the rough side of a cliff.

Without looking down at the perilous way she had come, at last she arrived at a high point where a narrow ledge on the face of the crag offered a resting place. Panting, she sat down and for the first time saw that it would be impossible to ascend beyond the slight projection to which she was clinging.

Then, glancing downwards, she was amazed at the perils she had surmounted on her way up. The sheer wall above and the precipice below bewildered and appalled her.

Faint and giddy, she laid herself down as carefully as she could on the narrow ledge and clutched some large roots. She had been in this position some time, revolving the situation in her mind, when, suddenly, she thought she caught a glimpse of a moving figure far above her, appearing between the rocks and scrub trees on the top of the cliff. She was afraid it was Paao and dared not cry out for help.

She must keep her self-possession or she would roll off the ledge. She tried to think of other things, but when some loose stones and soil, dislodged from above, fell into the ravine, she knew that she was discovered and that somebody was trying to reach her. Getting on her feet she loosened the dagger that it might be ready at her hand.

There was a rustling of leaves and a crackling sound as if a branch had been broken. A point above the ledge shut off her view in the direction of the noise. Nearer and nearer came the sounds. If it were a rescuer, why did he keep so quiet? If it were Menehune, he would give at least a grunt to tell her he was coming. Only Paao, she thought, would come stealthily, and she clutched the handle of the dagger with a nervous grasp.

She had not long to wait in suspense. After a more portentous sound of some one descending on the other side of the jutting rock, out from the cliff swung a man clinging to a rope. Only a part of his back could be seen at intervals, as he tried to give his body the motion of a pendulum along the face of the precipice. Evidently he was endeavoring to get a foothold on the ledge.

A few seconds more and a successful thrust with his foot enabled him to catch the ledge. Then, feeling his way backwards, still holding the rope, he gained the footing that he sought, straightened himself up and, turning around, came face to face with Kelea.

There was hardly room for two persons on the ledge, but the man stood firmly, having the rope in his right hand, leaving the other hand free. Kelea trembled and turned pale as the stranger seized her with his left arm and held her fast.

CHAPTER XXVIII.

A SON OF A GOD.

WHEN Hookama left the region of the Lake of Fire on the side of Mauna Loa, he and his guide started for the heights of Mauna Kea, the twin-mountain by the side of Loa, where were gathered, at this season, the birds with the finest feathers known on the islands. It was a toilsome journey. Dead *koa* trees abounded, and after leaving the timber line, ledges were climbed, crevasses leaped, gullies traversed and clinkers of lava trodden under foot.

It was noon when they reached a mass of rocks where earthquakes had split the mountain, leaving immense caverns. Under the shadow of almost inaccessible crags, they prepared for their ingenious and arduous work of bird-catching. The constant rains kept the high lands below the summit of Mauna Kea,

green with foliage. *Ohia* and *lehua* trees,
ferns and tough grasses with long, spear-like
blades, covered the sides of the ravines and
grew high up on the cliffs, wherever enough
soil for their roots could be found. Only the
most expert climber could scale some of the
precipices, where the birds fluttered and gave
forth their peculiar notes.

. The *lehua* trees, which the *oo* and the *mamo*
loved, were beginning to blossom, and the
birds from the topmost branches were calling
to their mates. The *ohia-ai* (mountain apple)
was also in flower. From the lowlands the
feathery songsters had come to enjoy the
blooming season, and the *mamo* bird, having
the most precious of pure yellow feathers, one
beneath each of its wings, plumed itself and
twittered in joyful ecstasy. The spot chosen
by Lou, who was well acquainted with the
locality, was a picturesque dell, overhung
with crags and moist with numerous streams
and cascades.

The hunters built themselves a rude hut
under a shelving rock, thatching the roof with
long, tough leaves. In order to screen themselves from the rain and to conceal themselves
as much as possible from the keen eyes of the
little birds, they encased their bodies and
limbs in a flexible net-work, into the meshes

of which were looped strips of the *ti*-leaf, which hung, point downwards, on the outside,

The birds were wary, and only by the most adroit management could they be caught. The special bird the hunters sought was the *mamo*, shy and difficult to capture. It was the custom for bird-catchers to offer a prayer to the gods before beginning the sport ; then they made an offering of *ohelo* berries. At night they set up poles, long and slender. To these poles they affixed cross-pieces smeared with the sticky gum of the *papala* tree. They tied to the poles blossoms of the *lehua*, in imitation of the trees.

Each morning, hiding in a covert, with a fine line having a noose at the end, the snare being arranged on the pole, the bird-catcher imitated the peculiar whistle of the *mamo* and waited for the proud little bird to appear. Perched on a neighboring tree, prinking, pruning and displaying itself, it drove away other birds attempting to alight.

Now the hunter must use all his wits to capture it. After cocking its head warily from side to side, it advances to take the blossom, and the catcher, by a sudden jerk of the line as the bird sticks in the gum, secures his prize.

It astonished Lou, who was one of the most

skilful bird-catchers on Hawaii, to see how
adroitly Hookama snared his game and imitated
the whistle of the saucy *mamo*. He looked on
with wonder and admiration as the young *alii*
scaled the face of a *pali* (precipice) in following
up the flight of the elusive songsters. The result was that the two men captured more birds
and secured more feathers in three days than
many hunters obtained in six. It was the
element of danger, however, that made the
sport popular with the chiefs.

But as bird-catching was only a pretext for
the visit to Hawaii, Hookama reluctantly
abandoned the hunt and, to Lou's disgust, insisted on returning at once to Hilo. The guide
led the youth along a narrow trail, through an
immense belt of forest, till the two men
emerged on the bright, grassy uplands not far
from the picturesque village of Onomea, which
straggled along the shore by which they must
reach Hilo to the south.

Onomea, a populous village, five hundred
feet above the blue ocean, was like an enchanted place to the young *alii* after the toilsome tramp over the lava and the matted
grasslands of the higher regions. The air was
soft and delicious. Ravines, waterfalls, palms,
oheas and hibiscus decked the paths leading
down to patches of velvet green near the sea.

The surges, tossing spray over rocks and reefs, made the music that Hookama loved to hear, and his spirit was soothed by luxuriant Nature in her most enchanting forms.

The entire journey along the coast was a succession of delights. Even the deep and sometimes dangerous gulches which must be crossed, were nothing to the *palis* of Mauna Kea which had been climbed. The cascades, overhung by rainbows, gleamed in shining beauty as the eye followed up the many ravines; exquisite flowers and tropical plants filled the air with fragrance, and the young man, fresh as a lark and blithe as a bird, revelled in the joy of his young manhood, with the blue sky above him and the spangled earth beneath his feet. Life was a joy, and along the trail the villagers whom he met stopped and listened to the love songs which he chanted, as he bounded on his way.

Lou's bowlegs found it difficult to carry him at the same rapid pace. He liked the rough mountain better than the flowery coast. The only bird-song he cared for was the twitter of the *oo* and the *mamo*, when, trapped by his smeary gum, they fluttered their wings in vain attempts to escape the snare. He knew many of the people along the route and liked to stop and chat with the women, lying in the sun or bathing in the surf.

"His Islands lift their Fronded Palms in Air"

Hookama humored his whims and often waited for the little man, choosing some lofty point where he could look off at the distant sea-horizon and give play to his fancy. He was sitting one afternoon in a grove of cocoa-nut palms, with the sea at his feet and myriads of flowers, vines and fruit plants about him, when his eye caught sight of a hideous stone idol, half buried in a mass of bright yellow blossoms and amid a profusion of broad green leaves.

The misshapen image somehow suggested by contrast the magnificent sights he had witnessed at the volcano of Kilauea. As he re-called those appearances, it seemed as if Pele were after all the Goddess of Fire. At any rate such a goddess was worthy of worship, if she existed. He had felt her heated breath. Vol-canic clouds had covered him with her resplen-dent hair. Her voice was the thunder of ex-ploding rocks. Her caresses were flames and consuming fires. Terrible she might be, but she was grand.

"How near I came to being burnt to a cin-der when I was fascinated by her breath and Lou pulled me back from that awful chasm!" thought he. "If that grinning idol yonder had been in my place when the ledge broke off, it would have sunk like a stone in the fire. 'Son of a god ! ' I wonder what it means ? They call me so ; but what does it amount to, after all?"

What conclusion Hookama might have reached it is impossible to tell, for just at this uncertain and incomplete stage of his meditations, the head of Lou appeared down the trail, and, as he came nearer, Hookama saw that he carried in his arms a little sucking pig, a bunch of bananas and a wreath of flowers. Two fowls with their legs tied together were strung over the little man's shoulders, and from various parts of his person strips of *tapa* dangled and floated in the gentle breeze.

"I was getting hungry," Lou said. "Our stock of *kalo* gave out yesterday, so I told the people at the last village that you were the 'son of a god ; ' that the old prophetess of Pele said so ; and that you wanted a *hookupu* (gift-festival), such as they offer to high chiefs and *mois*. There they come," he called out, and soon Hookama was surrounded on all sides by a motley crowd which piled up fruit and cocoa-nuts at his feet and covered him with wreaths and flowers.

Then they all prostrated themselves in a circle around him and Lou joined in, floundering on the ground, with his head between the two chickens which cackled and fluttered in true fowl fashion.

"Well," thought the young *alii*, "son of a
god or not, they worship a decent looking fellow just as readily as they do that hideous
image," and, raising his right hand aloft with
his staff, he shouted, "Worship! worship!"
Then pushing aside an old crone with a ragged
skirt who tried to clasp his knees, he caught a
couple of the prettiest girls by the arms and
cried, "*Hula*; *hula*! (Dance; dance!)" All
the crowd joined in with glee, Hookama in the
midst of them, capering and jumping, wreaths
on his head and over his shoulders and arms.

It was the kind of a god the people liked, although they had never seen one of the sort
before. They were especially delighted when
Hookama, much to Lou's disgust, gave back
and distributed the gifts, retaining only those
attached to the guide's body. The people
were poor and Hookama knew it. "Too
many chiefs," as Lou said, "eat up the
people."

For the "son of a god" then, to lift off the
tabu, even for a half hour, was a very precious
boon, and since no priests were in sight and
no spy in the crowd, even the women dared to
eat bananas and cocoa-nuts, while the men and
boys gulped them down as if they had eaten
nothing for a week.

In due time, the two "bird-catchers" ar-

rived at Hilo Bay. Keawe welcomed Hookama, who said little or nothing to the
bigoted chief concerning his adventures, an
account of which the priestess of Pele had
spread broadcast. Lou kept his own counsel
also and was delighted when Hookama presented him with an entire bird-catcher's outfit.

The young *alii* spent his last night at
Cocoa-nut Island under the waving palms.
His warriors had been royally entertained
during his absence. They had engaged in
friendly games and contests with the chiefs of
Hawaii and had won their share of the prizes.
Other hospitalities, which civilization cannot
encourage, need not be mentioned. They had
witnessed, in awe-struck amazement, the spectacle of a burning river of lava, flowing down
the side of Mauna Loa till it reached the sea ;
they had been present at the *heiau*, where
human sacrifices were offered to Pele, to ward
off the anger of the offended deity, and they
would be glad to remain longer on the island,
which to them was a paradise of plenty and
pleasure.

But when, the morning after Hookama's arrival, the *alii* Keawe, surrounded by his warriors in helmets and cloaks, and with a swarming multitude of natives on the beach and in
the surf. shouted the last *Alohas* in honor of

the "son of a god" that had put out Pele's fires, it was a sight to stir the young man's blood and that of his followers too.

In the stern of his war-canoe and with his eight stout warriors at the paddles, the youth, covered with *leis*, heard the shouts of his admirers crowding a multitude of canoes as an escort, and repeated over and over his farewell words. But as he looked back from the open sea and saw a faint smoke from the distant mountain he rejoiced in every stroke of his men that carried him farther and farther from the realms of the fiery goddess.

Lou made the most sensible remark of this parting occasion, as he watched the war-canoe, headed for Oahu, far out on the blue sea.

"Idols! gods! What are they good for, when a 'son of a god' like *that* is more to my liking than a hundred Peles, and his legs are as straight as a palm?"

"*Paà, paà!*" said a dirty *Kanaka* standing near, who overheard the soliloquy. "Take care, or Pele's mankiller will give you a covering of ashes and a chunk of lava to mark the hole."

The only answer the bowlegged bird-catcher deigned to give was: "To *Milu* with Pele! It's where she belongs."

CHAPTER XXIX.

A DISCONSOLATE LOVER.

It happened to be the same morning on which Kelea lighted on the council of conspirators in the cave on the mountain, that Hookama in his war-canoe entered the inlet at Waikiki and landed once more on the shores of Oahu. He was received by the king and a retinue of warriors, who crowded about him and eagerly asked news from Hawaii.

Numuku, the chief of Nuuanu valley, was in the company, and though he touched noses with Hookama and treated him with a degree of courtesy, he showed no great delight over his return. He was too blunt wholly to disguise his real feelings, but he was too sagacious, knowing the king's friendship for the young man, to manifest any decided aversion. It was not good policy, under the circumstances, to treat Hookama otherwise than as his adopted son and a member of his household.

Hookama was too glad to be again in his native island to notice anything peculiar in Numuku's reception of him, and he was too eager to see Pu' Aloha, to think much about any thing or any body except the lovely maiden who had waved her red mantle to him when he departed (it seemed to him a long time ago,) on his adventurous journey.

Hookama's second in command and the other stout warriors who had manned his warcanoe, were loud in his praises as a leader, and had marvellous stories to tell of the enjoyments afforded them by the chiefs of Hawaii. Even the beautiful beach at Waikiki, with its fringe of tall cocoa-palms, was nothing, they averred, in comparison with the waving palms and soft breezes of Cocoa-nut Island, in the lovely bay of Hilo.

Hookama was not long in seeking and obtaining an audience in the royal house of Kahahana, and although he had not succeeded in arranging an alliance between the king of Hawaii and the king of Oahu, yet the good offices shown to him by the Hawaiian chiefs pleased the king, who accepted with evident delight some of the precious feathers of the *mamo* which the young *alii* had obtained. Besides, the king had received a message of good will from Kahekili of Maui, with a re-

quest for further aid, in case the king of
Hawaii should start out on another raid. As
usual, the treacherous Kahekili made great
promises, even going so far as to engage that
at his death, Kahahana should be appointed
his successor. If all the chiefs to whom the
same promise was made had come to the
throne, there would have been more kings at
loggerheads on Maui, than there were reign-
ing sovereigns on all the islands of the group.

The good-natured king only laughed when
Hookama told him of the old Hawaiian king's
prophecy and his agreement to meet him in
the land of ghosts. He felt of his stout arms
and smote his broad chest with his fists and
asked his young friend if the wizened old
warrior had been able to stand on his thin legs
without support, during his interview with
him. As for Kamehameha and the other
giant chief, the young king acknowledged
their warlike ability and congratulated Hookama on having escaped in his contest with the
"Lonely One," whose superiority was well
known throughout all the islands.

The king had no local information for
Hookama except the result of the Council of
Chiefs in favor of sustaining the present regime.
He was not very hopeful of securing the con-
tinuance of their support, but he was taking

measures to thwart any treacherous schemes which the malcontents might devise ; and he gave Hookama to understand that he should rely implicitly on his loyalty.

To this the young *alii* assented, and expressed the strongest desire that his friendship might be tested in any desperate enterprise by which he could serve the king.

As the king knew little concerning the private affairs of many of his chiefs, he could not give Hookama any news of Numuku's household, so that the youth hastened homeward, after the interview, full of excited expectation, as he thought of soon seeing Pu' Aloha. He had felt a strange diffidence on this subject, when he met Numuku at the landing, and so had asked no questions. The old chief quite naturally volunteered no information, especially as the continued absence of Pu' Aloha reflected upon his guardianship. Besides, he had no good reason to give for her flight, except that he had pressed her to marry him and Paao.

Blithely and joyfully, Hookama crossed the dry and dusty plains. Singing a merry song he skirted the sides of *Puu waina* (Punch Bowl). Almost out of breath, so rapidly did he ascend Nuuanu stream, he came nearer and nearer the enclosure, expecting every moment to catch sight of Pu' Aloha, who, he was sure, had seen his canoe in the offing and was waiting for him, although his eye had not discovered her in her lookout on the tree. "Perhaps," he said to himself, "the little flower is holding herself back, to make the welcome more delightful," and he entered the area where the chief's houses were grouped, as one would tread upon enchanted ground.

It was under the glare of the hot sun that he crossed the sward, and he attributed the stillness and the absence of moving objects to the heat. Under the shade in a distant corner was the little grass lodging-house of Pu' Aloha covered with flowering vines. The verandah was tenantless, and the opening was hung with *tapa*. "Perhaps," said he, "she takes her nap at noon; I ought not to disturb her." He gave a low whistle, as he used to do, and waited with palpitating heart for the answer. Even Menehune was not at his post.

Some women, in their houses near at hand, heard the well-known signal, and coming forth, greeted him with effusive welcome, but at once changed the greeting into a wailing chant, as he said eagerly, "Where is my flower? Is she sleeping?" "Alas!" they cried in a chorus of lamentation, "she has gone; many days;

no one knows where ; Numuku has beaten us many times."

Hookama pushed aside the *tapa* and went into the room, which was as Pu' Aloha left it the night of her flight. Evidences of her hasty departure were on every hand. The air of the room, usually fragrant with blossoms, was close, and a few *tapa* mantles were lying on the floor as if dropped in the hurry of her escape. The revulsion of feeling, in the young man's mind, left him in a bewildered state; he hardly believed his eyes and could scarcely restrain his tears. He caught up a red mantle of gauzy *tapa*, which he had often seen on Pu' Aloha's shoulders and rushing rapidly to his own hut on the other side of the enclosure, gathered together some of the things he used in bird-hunting—a long coil of stout cord, a strong staff, a calabash, a hatchet of stone, and a small gourd containing *awa*—and, without stopping to reflect, was on his way up the valley-path before the women could finish telling all they knew.

They had given him, however, unconnected scraps of information : She had gone *mauka* (towards the mountains) ; scouts had failed to find her ; Menehune went every day to search for her ; Numuku was cross ; the priests had killed a hog and found bad omens. All these

gossipy details made Hookama sick at heart,
and the whole world, so beautiful to him before,
was turned into a wilderness.

As he ran up the valley, the sombre cliffs in
shadow gave his heart a pang. " Perhaps her
body is lying in some deep, inaccessible gulch.
She has fallen into some narrow fissure." He
asked incoherent questions at the doors of the
huts along the way, and the women answered
softly as if they knew he was a disconsolate
lover. They could give him no information.
They had been questioned over and over again
by Numuku's scouts.

When he reached the opening, where the
valley is a mile in width, he struck off into the
forest on the right, climbing the mountain by
a well-known path. Every gully, stream, cliff
and peak was familiar to him; he passed up
among hollows, dark in shadow and silent as the
grave. In his agony he forgot all prudence and
was startled, after a headlong leap over a wide
seam in the rock, at the danger he had escaped.
Leaning on his staff to take breath, he listened
intently for the slightest sound. If a dead
branch fell at his feet he started as if he feared
a sad discovery.

For hours he wandered, not aimlessly, but
searching gulches and jungles; his feet were
bruised and sore, and the *tapas* which he carried

on his arm were torn in the dense thickets. He had cut his way through almost impassable underbrush and waded through morasses and streams. He had stood on lofty ridges and searched with eager eye the landscape. He had explored many a cave, for he knew that fugitives were often secreted there, fed by the natives who always sympathized with those who fled from either justice or cruelty. One of these hunted creatures he met in an obscure gully, grubbing for roots, who told him that the assassin of the priests had doomed him for sacrifice. To this poor *Kanaka*, who was scared almost out of his wits at the approach of Hookama, he gave a few drops of *awa* and a cake of baked *poi*.

He was almost disheartened as his search seemed fruitless and his limbs became weary. He was obliged to rest, in order to get strength to keep on. Seated on a high rock, looking up a deep ravine, wider than most of the gulches which he had crossed, he followed with his eye the desolate crags, fallen and decaying trees, lofty precipices and descending torrents. He wondered if by any possibility Pu' Aloha could have wandered into a place so forbidding.

Scanning the jagged walls of the opposite side of the stupendous chasm, he thought he saw a white spot, some distance up the precipitous slope. As he strained his eyes, for the distance was great, he fancied that the white object moved and became like an upright streak, an unusual color on the side of these lava *palis*. " Could it be a living being, at such a height and apparently clinging without support to the smooth crag? Was it Pu' Aloha?" The bare suggestion made him tremble. But soon the probability that the maiden was alive summoned back all his strength. Climbing in and out, around wide fissures and across fallen trees, he at last reached an opening where he could obtain a nearer view. Yes, it was a woman with a white tapa, but she had evidently fallen from either faintness or exhaustion, and, with her hand clutching something, a root or vine, she lay on what seemed at that distance a slight projection from the face of the cliff. He did not dare to call out, for fear that his voice might startle and perhaps dislodge her from her dangerous position. Moreover, he was so far off that probably his loudest shout would not reach her ears.

With incredible skill and great daring, he crossed the gulch and climbed the height, and finally gained a spot as near as he could estimate over the place where the white figure was lying. He had with his eye marked a tree, on the summit, and it served as a guide. If he could tie his rope to the roots and swing down he might reach the object of his pursuit. But he saw that the rope would not measure half the distance.

Nothing daunted, for he was in the habit of taking risks, he coiled the cord about his waist; swung himself over the cliff by a vine rooted securely in the rock; then made a bold move and, clinging to the vine, threw the rope, lasso-fashion, towards a tree which grew out of the cliff and drew the supple trunk within his reach. Disengaging the rope, he jumped and caught the tree which swayed and bent under his weight. It was a perilous descent, with the tree vibrating under him, but he gained the ledge from which the tree was growing and tied the rope fast to its roots which were larger than the trunk itself. We have seen how he then descended and gained a footing on the narrow ledge. No one but a skilled bird-catcher would have attempted or could have performed the feat, in the face of such difficulties.

CHAPTER XXX.

AN UNEXPECTED MEETING.

NEVER was there a more astonished couple than Kelea and Hookama, as they stood on that narrow projection half-way up the cliff on Kouahuanui mountain. Kelea had not thought of Hookama as a possible pursuer or rescuer. Hookama had no idea that Kelea was within a hundred miles of Oahu.

"Kelea! you here!" was Hookama's first exclamation, "I thought it was another—" he was about to say "another woman," but checked himself as he saw a strange look on her face. She grew pale and more agitated as he regarded her with an expression of surprise and disappointment. Her body shook in his grasp.

"Tell me," he cried, not knowing what else to say, "how did you get here?" Her only answer was an increasing pallor and a loosening of her hold on the rock. She hung heavily on the arm by which he held her, as if her strength were failing, and faintly murmured, "You swore there was no other; let me go; fling me down the *pali*. Oh, Hookama, Hookama!"

Her weight was becoming too heavy for him to support with his left arm, and his right hand which held the taut rope was cramped by the strain. If he let go, either of the rope or of the girl, there was great danger of a catastrophe.

Perceiving the imminent peril, the young man changed his tone: "Kelea! command yourself. Lie down and cling to that root, or we shall both fall into the chasm. This is no place for weakness." The girl obeyed and he assisted her to lie down. Then, with both hands on the rope, he cautiously looked about for means of escape.

They could not climb back by the way he had come down. He could not lower the girl, for the rope was fastened above. There was a chance for one person, leaving the other on the ledge, to swing off by the rope, the loose end of which, when let go, would reach several feet below the place where they stood, but would thus be swung around the point, and out of the reach of the one who was left.

One could then drop from the rope to a projecting rock a few feet lower and, by a comparatively easy descent, get down the rest of the way.

The person left on the ledge without the rope must take his chances of some other way out of the difficulty. He explained the method of escape to Kelea, but she flatly refused to go, if he must remain.

" What cares Kelea," she said in a tender voice, " how soon she finds her 'time to sleep,' now that Hookama has come back and is willing to save her life at the expense of his own! No, no, save thyself; thy life is far dearer to me than my own," and she looked up into his face with an expression that he had never seen on her countenance before.

He turned away as if to examine the means of escape more carefully, but his thought was, " Is then her love for me like that ? " After peering over the ledge, he pretended to have discovered another, although more difficult way down and, turning to Kelea, declared in a cheerful voice, " Now for the rope ; I can easily descend."

It was only after he assured her, over and over again, that he could go down the way she had come up, that he prevailed on her to leave the ledge. " I must be a poor bird-catcher if

I cannot climb down where a *wahine* has come up," he exclaimed as he put the rope into her hands. Her nerve was equal to the emergency, for she boldly made the plunge, descended hand over hand and landed in safety.

The next moment she called out joyously to Hookama to lower himself on the other side of the ledge, and climb down by a big root, from which a tough *koali* vine was hanging. Hookama lost no time in following the suggestion, and the two joined each other, after a hard scramble, at the bottom of the gulch.

The young *alii* broke the painful silence that fell upon them both as they stood together in the shadows of the valley, by saying, as he pointed to the narrow ledge, " The rope is there ; now let somebody else try to get a girl off that wrinkle of the cliff, if he can."

Kelea mechanically turned and looked up towards the ledge, but she was not looking at the rope. Her soul was quivering in the presence of the man for whom she had dared much and would dare more, even at the risk of losing everything but his love. She was burning with the desire to feel the thrill of his touch, the joy of his affection, or even the heart's ease of a single kindly word. The impulse came upon her, not with the recklessness of her previous passion but as a strong inclination, to throw her arms about him, lay her head upon his shoulder and cling to him as for her life.

Her eyes grew lustrous and her heart throbbed beneath the folds of *tapa* wrapped about her. Unconsciously, she loosened the cloth that concealed the charms of her neck and shoulders, and turned towards the object enshrined in her soul.

Hookama hardly noticed her movement, although his eyes were in that direction. His thoughts were wholly on Pu' Aloha. He was provoked, almost angry that he had rescued Kelea, when another and a dearer one was the object of his search. It was a most inopportune moment for any advances on the part of the girl. At this particular time she was an obstacle in his path, he must guide her out of the wild country and delay the pursuit on which his whole mind was bent. He was almost in despair lest his search should be fruitless.

As the girl turned towards him, her glowing face mocked his anxiety. With as calm a voice as he could command he asked where he should take her. He did not question her as to how she came to the island. He seemed indifferent and without curiosity.

Instantly, all the haughty manner of the

proud woman returned as she replied, "I need no guidance; as I came I can go. Leave me to myself, since you treat me as a slave!"

"But I cannot let you go alone; night is coming and the way is dangerous," rejoined the youth in a less irritated voice. "You may live in a cave or in the hollow of a tree, but I shall see you safe somewhere before I leave you. You are lost, and you know it. I am perfectly at home in these wild lands. Answer me then, where do you live?"

Kelea felt that it would be useless to resist and at once described the house on the cliff. Hookama knew it well and the way to it. He often went there in his expeditions. He and the old "mother" were excellent friends. With hasty steps he started off and Kelea followed.

After an hour's toil over the rough country, going in single file and without exchanging a word, Kelea demanded a halt. She was tired and must rest. She sat down on a fallen trunk by the wayside, and Hookama stood near by, with his back towards her, while he impatiently struck the ground with his staff.

Kelea looked about her at the wild flowers growing profusely at her side and finally after calling a number of them by their names, she plucked one of the loveliest, and, as if com-

muning with her own thoughts, said in a subdued tone of voice, " *Pua-aloha*, the fairest of
them all! " She was repeating the words and
holding the flower to her bosom, looking around
for more of the same kind, when Hookama, as
if startled from a reverie by the name, wheeled
around and faced her, exclaiming, " Pu' Aloha!
what do you know of her ? Tell me at once."

The flush on the young man's cheek revealed
the indignation he felt against the girl who
spoke so calmly, as he supposed, of one whose
very existence, so precious to him, might at
that moment be in deadly peril.

" Pu' Aloha ? Pu' Aloha ? " replied Kelea ;
" I was only looking at the flower called by
that name. Pu' Aloha!—" and firmly setting
her lips and teeth, she looked steadily at the
youth, who could not restrain his impatience
and, completely off his guard, fiercely ejacu-
lated, " Tell me where she is, if you know. I was
searching for her when I found you on the
cliff. If you think—" But Hookama was not
allowed to finish the sentence. Kelea, stung
by his tone as much as by his language, cried
out. " Aha, my *alii*, then she is 'the other.'
Had I only known it sooner ! Why did you
not tell me in the vale of Iao and save me this
long journey in search of you ? "

As if revolving something in her mind, she

continued, half speaking to herself : "Ah, yes ! I think Menehune said something about a girl of that name who ran away from a chief who wanted to marry her, and from a man called Paao, who was in league with the chief.

"Pu' Aloha; " she looked into the flashing eyes of Hookama as she lengthened out the torture; "Pu' Aloha ; the girl that was lost and came not back to the loving pair in Nuuanu valley, who sought her so tenderly. Pu' Aloha!" and she shot a keen glance at the *alii*, who was kept silent by the hope of hearing something that would give him a clue in his search for his loved one.

"Ah, yes ! You were looking for her when you found me. I see it now. You would cast me into that chasm "(pointing to a yawning riff in the rocks near by,) "for one glimpse of your 'flower of love'—you would kill me—do not speak yet—yes, kill me, if you might, by doing it, clasp this sweetheart to your breast.

"I see; I see!" and leaving this acting of a part, the excited and now angry girl spit forth words of scorn and wrath and fury at the man who waited with brain on fire to hear the end, if at the end he might learn where to find the treasure of his heart.

"I hate you, Hookama! As I loved you with all the ardor of a flaming torch, I hate

you now with the red fire of a Pele's wrath.
Go to your Flower of Love! She is at the
house on the cliff. I have been with her there
for weeks, and she has never so much as
breathed your name. Go and be happy with
your goddess, if she condescends to let you
touch the tip of one of her fingers ; but remember, if you dare tell her that I have made
love to you—or that I have even seen you—
I will devote you both to the infernal gods.
Go, and may the thought of Kelea poison your
life, till you sink into the pit of *Milu*, where
perhaps your other victims await you, to
torment you forever."

She hardly knew what she was saying.
Hookama became more and more angry. His
impulse was to spring at her and close her
mouth, lest she should revile Pu' Aloha as well
as himself. Kelea divined his purpose and,
before he could take a step to execute it,
swiftly and lightly bounded from the path
and was on the high rocks over the way, with a
heavy stone ready in her hands to hurl at him
if he attempted to follow. Her nostrils were
distended and her strong arms poised the missile above her head.

Hookama saw at once the folly of urging the
girl to further words or acts. It would be
madness to make her his enemy. What might

she not do to Pu' Aloha? His first thought was of that. He crossed his arms therefore over his breast.

"What foolishness, Kelea, to act like *la-e puni* (one marked in the forehead)! Think you I would hurt you? that I mean you any harm? I swear by all the gods to say nothing of this to any one. You will be safe with me. Come down and leave your wrath behind you. There is no need of—"

But Kelea, dashing the stone into the gulf, with a gesture of disdain and defiance turned her back and disappeared from his sight, as if she had sunk into the chasm, where she had hurled the heavy rock. Hookama made no attempt to follow her. He quickly pushed on to the house on the cliff, eager to meet his beloved, hoping to find her more of a woman than a goddess, notwithstanding the assertions of Kelea and his own fears.

CHAPTER XXXI.

BETROTHED.

THE moon, just rising over the *pali*, shed a flood of light upon the youth's approaching figure, as he came around the point of the cliff which jutted out at the turn of the path close by the house. On the *lanai* was the idol of his soul. He thought she was watching for his coming, for Pu' Aloha, hearing footsteps and awaiting the return of Kelea, involuntarily turned and was starting towards him.

With a cry of joy, for instantly she recognized his form, the eager girl hurried to meet him. The two lovers clasped each other in an ecstasy of delight and for a blissful season were in that paradise where young love finds mystic signs known only to the initiated.

For the first time in his life Hookama felt the thrill of intense, abounding and complete rapture, which comes but once yet remains an unwasted memory for all time. Nothing he had ever experienced could compare with the supreme moment, in which, all uncertainty vanished, he realized that Pu' Aloha's heart of hearts was his. If, till this hour, the maiden had been a goddess to be worshipped, a being far above him to be enshrined only in his heart, now, clasped in his arms and telling him with her own lips that she loved him with her whole soul, she became still more adorable but not so far off. He liked this better, and so did she.

The moon hid its face behind a fleecy cloud, and even the blind "mother," who came out as unusual sounds reached her ears, was oblivious of the mysteries into which pagan souls, as well as others, are guided by the god of love, a deity unknown among their mythological divinities.

But when the silver orb soared above the cloud like "a floating thought," the twain now made one, followed along its luminous pathway, shining across the threshold of the house, and having told the "mother" of their betrothal, called on her to consummate the customary usage. She threw over them the *marriage tapa ;* only a few formal words, and Pu' Aloha and Hookama became husband and wife, according to the approved manner of Hawaiian chiefs.

The absence of Kelea was noticed both by the "mother" and Pu' Aloha, but Hookama allayed their apprehensions by pointing to the sky, which had become wholly free from clouds, and to the moon, which filled all things with a radiance as bright as that within his heart. The ceremonial, such as it was, found its conclusion when Hookama partook of a well-seasoned calabash of *poi,* which he much needed after his long abstinence, and then in a tangle of vines at the side of the house, he and his bride screened themselves from the mists arising from the valley.

There was so much to tell each other, to say nothing of trifling interruptions between the sentences, that the newly wedded pair might have forgotten everything except their own confidences had not suddenly the grotesque body of the dwarf-giant intercepted the moonlight and created a most undesired diversion of their thoughts.

Menehune was very demonstrative in grunts and monosyllables over Hookama's return, and Hookama was unusually profuse in acknowledging his services to Pu' Aloha. The dwarf, however, regarded the occasion in a somewhat different light from that in which the lovers saw it, and his actions corresponded more with his point of view than with theirs.

He squatted down in front of the couple, as if impressed with the idea that a watchman was needed to keep off intruders, and gazed steadily at them, in silent endeavor to express his unqualified approbation. He had witnessed a few of their love passages, as he came around an angle of the rocks into the enchanted circle, and evidently wanted to see more, thinking, doubtless that nothing could be more natural and in keeping with the important occasion.

The eyes of her favorite dog, or a wistful look on its face, would not have disconcerted a woman of Pu' Aloha's strength of mind under similar conditions, even with Hookama's arm about her and her head nestling on his shoulder. But somehow, Menehune's interested look made her cheeks burn and her eyes seek the ground.

The soul of Menehune was certainly expanding; his narrow, darkened mind was catching some gleams of light, whether the lovers cared to be the medium of the new radiance or not. In fact, they were not just then in an altruistic mood and inwardly resented the dwarf's sympathetic approval. Their mutual caresses ceased and they began to talk about the weather. "It is too damp to stay longer out of doors." They also

shifted their relative positions and Hookama
adjusted the *tapa* mantle about Pu' Aloha's
shoulders.

The spell was broken. Menehune's face
gradually resumed its usual stolidity. His
mind wandered and his eyes stared into va-
cancy. He was less and less interested in taking observations. His head dropped forward
and he clasped it with his big hands. His ears
hung limp. It was not long before the falling
asleep of the squat figure at their feet was dem-
onstrated to the amiable lovers by sounds so
utterly at variance with the music in their
hearts, and the dissonance jarred so much on
their ears, that, quietly and without waking
the sleeper, they went into an eclipse beyond
the jutting rock.

When Menehune came to himself, a little
later, and found himself alone, he stood up
straight, pulled his ears, looked inadvertently
at the moon and went into the house. If he
had been gifted with a tail he would not have
wagged it, and the pitiless lovers lost a golden
opportunity of enlarging still more both the
mental and the emotional horizon of their
most devoted follower.

It had been only by chance in her wanderings that Kelea, soon after leaving Hookama in
the summary way we have described, crossed

the path of the dwarf-giant on his way to the house on the cliff. She managed to give him an idea of Paao's conspiracy and a description of the cave, which he knew well, having often explored the recesses of this lonely mountain for purposes of his own in connection with the house where his mother was living.

She made him understand that he must warn Numuku or the king, the very next day. She said she was going away on a visit for a few days, and when he offered to go with and guard her, she declared that she had no fear and that he could be of greater use to Pu' Aloha. The dwarf, whose intelligence in matters of war and wood-craft was singularly shrewd, comprehended the situation; and, delighted to know that his mistress needed him, made no further offer of his services to Kelea, but after a few grimaces and antics, in token of his joy at the prospect of capturing the traitor, strode off over crags and through the scrubby bushes making a bee-line for home, where he found Hookama as has been described.

The next day, he told the *alii* what Kelea said about Paao and was cautioned to tell nothing of it to the women, except that he had met Kelea who would be absent a few days. As for himself, Hookama was impatient to learn more of the conspiracy. He must over-

throw Paao's nefarious schemes, and he must
go to the king at once; Menehune might go
with him.

To Pu' Aloha he explained the situation as
a matter already known to him, and referred
casually to the fact that Menehune had met
the woman they called Kelea, and who said she
was going away for a few days. As he en-
larged on Paao's treacherous actions, Pu' Aloha
gave him an account of the traitor's odious
proposals to her. This made the young man
furious. It helped him tear himself away from
his bride, and, followed by the dwarf, he took
his way down the mountain. He obtained
more information from Menehune and gave
the dwarf orders which made him of great service as a spy on the movements of Paao, during the next day.

When the king heard Hookama's story he
sent at once for Numuku. The old chief was
thunderstruck at the story of Paao's treachery.
At first he would not believe it; he said it was
one of Hookama's tricks. But after learning
all the the details he became convinced that
the conspiracy was imminent and dangerous.

The two chiefs arranged at once for an expedition to capture the conspirators. Menehune had discovered that a meeting would be
held the next afternoon by the rebels, in the

cave. Numuku agreed to lead a dozen of his warriors and Hookama selected the same number from the king's bodyguard, among them Maili, who knew the paths over the mountain.

When this arrangement was completed, Hookama, in presence of the king, told Numuku that he had found Pu' Aloha and that she was now under his protection as his wife. The old chief fumed and raged at this announcement and the two chiefs would have come to blows then and there, had not the king sternly commanded them to refrain, reminding them of the necessity of friendship and prudence in the face of the conspiracy which threatened the very existence of his authority.

It was difficult to pacify Numuku, who cared less for Pu' Aloha than for his pride as the first chief in authority under the king. However, when the king promised him still greater privileges and said that thereafter Hookama would be under his own immediate command as a member of his bodyguard, the chief grudgingly consented to waive the matter in dispute and went off, after touching noses with Hookama in token of more or less amity.

CHAPTER XXXII.

HOOKAMA AND PAAO SETTLE A QUESTION.

HOOKAMA spent a restless night. In his waking vigils, thoughts came to him which aroused all the innate savagery of his nature. He brooded in the darkness over Paao's treatment of Pu' Aloha till his soul was wrought up to a high pitch of wrath. Hot passion made it impossible to close his eyes. His mind harbored the most fiendish means of torture. He would tear out his enemy's heart; pluck out his eyes.

It was the young *alii's* first experience of the passion of revenge. No object had presented itself before this time to call out this feeling. In the heat of battle there was no stimulus to excite this passion. He fought as a warrior bred to arms; partly under the excitement of the conflict and in part to win renown. If he felt the rising to white heat of his temper in actual conflict with a foe, it was without any personal hatred in his heart. He could see a vanquished enemy taken to the *heiau* as a sacrifice to the gods, without the least angry emotion, as he would have gone himself.

Now, wrought up to a frenzy by his hate, he looked on Paao as a monster to be throttled, a fiend on whom he would stamp and over whose mutilated body he could dance and sing. Under these new conditions, the underlying proclivity of his savage nature to revenge came uppermost.

During the morning, the warriors of Hookama's troops sauntered off one by one as if for a stroll in Manoa valley, having been ordered to meet near a waterfall at an appointed hour. Their heavy spears had been sent to the rendezvous before daydawn with men to guard them. Numuku and his band were to meet them there in the afternoon.

To pass away the time, not caring much whither he went, Hookama bent his steps toward the *heiau* near *Leahi* (Diamond Head.) It was a gloomy, walled enclosure of several acres in extent. The walls of dark brown stone, thick and high, were surmounted by hideous idols of various shapes and many degrees of ugliness. Over the entrance were the grinning heads of victims who had been sacrificed.

Ordinarily, the young chief would have passed by this forbidding structure with its ghastly symbols, and perhaps have given it no thought. Now, its dismal horrors met the conditions of his irritated mind. He folded his arms and surveyed the frightful array of heads as if affording himself relief from his own reflections. They were tangible emblems of what he would bring upon Paao. After sating his passion with vowing the same fate to his enemy, he retraced his steps, and, at the king's house, ate his noonday meal without betraying any emotion. He had now a visible picture before his eyes of the end and aim of his revenge. It gave him sufficient self-control to allow him to narrate to the king, in a lively and amusing manner, some of his adventures with Lou, at the volcano on Hawaii.

No sooner, however, was he with his troops of warriors on the mountain trail, than his passionate mood returned more violently than ever. The wild country teemed with suggestions of the evil things which Paao might have brought upon Pu' Aloha. His hand clutched his long, heavy spear, as he strode on in his wrath before his men. He was even ready to look on Numuku with favor, since he had become an ally in dealing out vengeance to the far more execrable object of his resentment.

When the two bands, under command of the old chief, approached the cave where the conspirators had been in council, it was evident that they were forewarned.   Instead of scattering to their homes, they awaited, like brave Hawaiian chiefs as they were, in battle array the coming of their pursuers.   All but one or two were young men, yet, with the single exception of Paao, who counselled flight, the fifteen nobles, conscious of no wrong in plotting to overthrow the weak government of the king, determined to win or die.   If they won, it would be the first step toward ultimate victory.

An open space around the cave afforded ample room for hand-to-hand encounters.   A barricade of stones had been hurriedly erected and the conspirators were massed behind it. A whoop and a yell gave the signal to the king's warriors.   The desperate rebels met the onset with a shower of javelins and the points of their long spears.   Two of Numuku's band fell to the earth.   Orders had been given to secure as many of the malcontents alive, as was possible.   The king's warriors therefore made strenuous efforts to disarm rather than slay their foes.

They wrested the spears from their hands. They clutched them around the body and held

up, by the wrist, hands that wielded the dagger
or the javelin. The ground became slippery
with the blood of the combatants. At the
close of the struggle eight of the conspirators
lay dead or mortally wounded on the sward
while six of the king's warriors never would
fight again. Two of the rebel chiefs escaped
but five were prisoners, more or less wounded,
and each was well bound with cords.

Hookama, early in the fight, singled out
Paao and rushed upon him furiously, uttering
the most exasperating taunts and carelessly
exposing himself to his adversary's thrusts.
Paao's blood was up, and seeing Hookama's
frenzy he hoped to win an easy victory. His
skill soon proved more than a match for the reckless fighting of his opponent, who was at last
forced back against the rocks near the cave's
mouth, where he was obliged to defend himself with his heavy stone-battle-axe from the
long dagger and javelins of Paao.

Menehune had been watching the combat
from a perch on the top of the cave. He was
not a trained fighter and carried no weapon,
but whenever he saw an advantage gained by
any conspirator, he jumped down and caught
the rebel by the legs, tripping him up. He
thereby contributed his share towards the
capture of a number of the enemy. The

crowning achievement of the dwarf was the part he took in settling the question between Hookama and Paao. The faithful fellow supposed that Hookama could take care of himself, but when he saw him hard pressed by Paao, he felt called upon to interfere, even at the risk of robbing his master of a share in the glory of victory.

The two combatants were by themselves near the entrance of the cave, with quite a space between them and the other fighters. Paao was lunging forward, with his javelin aimed at the exposed breast of Hookama, who stood against the rock. Before Paao could thrust the weapon, Menehune ran and hit him full in the back with his shoulder. The blow sent him head foremost towards Hookama, who caught Paao's head between his legs as he plunged forward. Then, as Paao grasped Hookama's legs which held him by the neck as in a vise, Hookama fell on his knees and pinned Paao under him to the ground. Before he had time to do more, Menehune improvised a scourge from pieces of a broken javelin, and, swinging it in his big right hand while his left pressed down his victim by the small of the back, he proceeded to belabor the right and left flanks of the enemy, thus revenging himself on Paao for numerous affronts in days gone by, and paying off old scores for Pu' Aloha and Hookama.

Having thus satisfied his sense of what was just and right under the circumstances, the dwarf sat on the prostrate body while Hookama twisted thongs around the legs and arms of the crestfallen descendant of many generations of the priestly line. The two men then tumbled Paao into the cave, and Menehune stood guard at the entrance with Paao's javelin in his hand, leaving Hookama free to engage other warriors more worthy of his prowess.

Two days after the capture of the conspirators by Numuku and Hookama, the inner area of the *heiau*, near Leahi, was the scene of unusual activity. Preparations were going on for the sacrifice of the five conspiring chiefs and Paao, who had been closely guarded in prison, awaiting the decision of the king and his counsellors. The priests made a vain attempt to save Paao ; two of them had secretly despatched the messenger that warned the *alii* at the cave on the mountain. The high-priest, Kaopulupulu, claimed exemption from the king's jurisdiction for Paao, because of his priestly lineage.

But Kahahana was firm. " Down face " was

all the reply he gave to those who pleaded for the traitor's life. In this, he was seconded by Hookama, whose chagrin at Paao's advantage over him, in their hand-to-hand fight at the cave, only served to quicken his desire for vengeance; he hoped that he might never see his enemy's face again except as a sacrificial victim. He had nursed the feeling of revenge till it controlled him and drove out every other thought from his mind. Numuku tried to save Paao, but finally yielded to the king's persistency and to the counsel of the royal chiefs, who felt that an example must be made to strike terror to disloyal hearts.

At twilight of the same day, the king gave the signal for the prisoners to be led into the *heiau.* They came with arms pinioned and escorted by a guard. No warrior among then showed signs of any fear of death. They carried themselves majestically, as if marching to a triumph.

After being placed in a row, in front of a platform of smooth stones, on which their lifeless bodies were soon to be laid, they were taken out one by one, to be despatched by the priests. It was a sacred offering to the gods.

Paao came last, wearing a look of bravado and with a step which betokened a fearless spirit. Hookama turned his head away, after a hasty glance at his enemy, who returned the look with an expression of the utmost scorn.

Further details of the barbarous and bloody rites, at the immolation of the five young chiefs, need not be given. The sixth victim was Paao. The ceremonies had been prolonged, by a pretended necessity on the part of the priests to consult the oracles. The tapers burned low in the hands of the attendants. In a dim and murky light befitting the tragedy, two naked priests bore the body of Paao to its place on the blood-stained platform and laid it with the other gory victims. The horrid marks of slaughter were on the face and shoulders. The king advanced alone and looked on the man who had kindled treason in his realm. No remorse for the traitor's death was felt in his heart. The sentence was just. It was the will of the gods.

During the part of the ceremony which related to Paao, Hookama did not look towards the altar, where the consummation of his vengeance was accomplished. He was satisfied because his foe was dead and would no more "cross his shadow." Besides, did not Paao, as the inciter to treason, richly deserve his fate?

As the king and the chiefs passed from the gloom of the *heiau*, (leaving the bodies of the slain on the altar for the elements to deal with, a little earth having been thrown upon them,) suddenly there appeared showers of flashing meteors in the sky. It was a grand spectacle which some of the warriors interpreted as a good omen. Numuku, with his usual grunt, said to Hookama, who happened to be near, "Another blunder of the king. Another chance lost to conciliate the rebels. These young chiefs ought to have been spared. Now, many of the old *aliis* will rise. Get ready for another outbreak, young man! See, the sky is warning us!" and he pointed to a new burst of stars.

But Hookama, who might have saved Paao, had he chosen, stood in gloomy silence looking at the brilliant display, saying to himself, "These stupid warriors! What do they know about omens? I've seen the sky like this a dozen times and nothing happened. Pele made a great fuss at the volcano, but nothing came of it. Those hypocrites, the priests, make the gods and give the omens. These dull chiefs are gulled; I'd rather have my bowlegged guide Lou, than a score of them; I hate the priests. They tried to get Paao off, the scoundrel! They are at the bottom of this conspiracy too. If I were king—." He checked himself, as if the thought were an ignoble one, and the image of his friend, the king, prevented any further ambitious dreams.

"I only wish he had a little more sense, with all his amiability," was the thought that concluded Hookama's soliloquy, as he found himself alone under the suddenly darkened sky.

CHAPTER XXXIII.

AN APPARITION.

THE king of Oahu found that he had stirred up rather than put out the spirit of rebellion by his summary execution of the captured rebels. He therefore determined to crush the insubordinate chiefs before they wholly undermined his authority. He could rely on a large part of the warriors that had followed him to Maui, and had fought with him at Wailuku. An expedition was forthwith planned against several of the disaffected *aliis*, beyond the pass, which guarded the *pali* at the end of Nuuanu Valley about six miles from the royal house at Waikiki.

The king also despatched a messenger, secretly, to the king of Maui, the treacherous Kahekili, asking again for reinforcements; a procedure about which he did not consult his loyal chiefs. not even Numuku or Hookama.

Taking the field with his army and leaving a small contingent at Waikiki, to guard against a hostile approach by sea, he made his headquarters at the *pali*, where the valley abruptly terminates in a precipice falling sheer down a thousand feet; a steep, rough path on the eastern side being the only passage to the plains where the insurrection had broken out.

This location of the royal army's base at the *pali* gave Hookama, who was captain of the king's bodyguard, many opportunities, in the intervals of forays against the rebels, to visit the house on the cliff. It was a hard climb up from the pass to the house, but this meant very little to the ardent young husband.

Nowhere on the island of Oahu do the showers clothe the mountain slopes with greener verdure and more luxuriant growths than in this region of the wonderful *pali*. The water-falls are fed from the mountain peaks and sunclouds float gently away, " tears of the trade-winds," to dissipate themselves in cooling mists.

Pu' Aloha, now that she no longer feared pursuit either from Numuku or Paao, was free to enjoy the marvellous eastward view of the sea, from the heights above the house on the cliff. She wandered, at her own sweet will, among the picturesque dells that beautified the upper ridges, although she never strayed far from the house. These little hill-valleys were all the more attractive, lying as they did between rocky walls and impenetrable thickets.

Hookama had built a small grass house for his bride and himself near the house of the "mother," and although Pu' Aloha missed the companionship of Kelea and longed for her return, she found abundant and agreeable occupation in simple household cares and in gathering *ilima* blossoms with which to adorn herself to please her lord when he climbed to her bower. If ever savage lovers enjoyed an idyllic honeymoon under most favorable conditions, it was beneath the spangled heavens and on that fragrant mountain's breast, where eternal summer dwelt and no conventionalities marred the golden hours.

Love was still hovering with its earliest and sweetest charms over the happy pair, when one day Hookama announced a distant expedition which would occupy at least a week, against an insurgent chief who had entrenched himself at Punaluu, on the northeastern coast. He cautioned Pu' Aloha not to extend her wanderings far from the cliff, because lawless bands were prowling about and desperadoes were hiding in the mountains. He promised to send Maili, who was in his band, to assure her

of his safety, as soon as the chief of the Punaluu district was subdued.

When Kelea disappeared after Hookama's
rescue of her from the ledge and her violent
denunciation of his rejection of her passion,
she started with a vague purpose of throwing
herself on the king's protection at the royal
house. The information she could give of the
conspirators' cave would make her welcome.
Had she not met Menehune and sent by him
the warning to the king she would have
carried out her intention.

But, with that burden off her mind, her
courage gave out when halfway down the
mountain, and, remembering the secluded
house of a native, who, with his wife, lived
back of a spur of the hills, above Manoa
Valley, she went there and claimed hospitality.
This was a claim that no Hawaiian, however
poor, ever refused. In this case, the astonished peasants gladly welcomed the queenly
woman who promised to pay them liberally
for secrecy and entertainment.

They gave her the whole of their rude grass
hut, which they cleaned up for her use, and
made for themselves a shelter of boughs not
far away.

Kelea spent the first night in this seques-

tered spot in alternate fits of hysterical weeping
and passionate anger. She thought she hated
Hookama, as she had told him, but her new
feeling of intense jealousy toward Pu' Aloha
proved the contrary. It was the lovely, artless girl who had been her closest friend, that
now became the object of her strange, unjust
and unreasoning aversion. She recoiled from
no vindictive suggestion of the evil spirit that
possessed her.

Every lovely trait in Pu' Aloha that had
attracted her—her artlessness, her confiding
nature, her loving ways—seemed but so many
artifices to win away her lover. Even her con-
fession of her passion for Hookama was an exhibition of her selfishness. Kelea's vengeful
feeling drove her hither and thither, from scorn
to pitiless wrath. For days the changed girl
gratified her envy and hatred by plotting
ways and means to outwit her rival. She
even went so far as to visit a *Kehuna* to learn
if it were possible to pray her enemy, as she
now conceived her, to death. This was a last
resort and sometimes proved effective, the
victim yielding to his fate when he learned
that he was singled out by the sorcerer.

Carried away by her jealousy, this surf-
rider of Maui in her frenzy would go after
dark to the shore and, swimming the breakers,

imitate the action in pantomime of smothering
her victim in the surge. She obtained the
powder of a poisonous herb and carried it
with her. Her distorted imagination caused
the gentle being, against whom her frenzy
arrayed her, to appear in her dreams as suppli-
cating for pardon which the relentless avenger
would not grant.

Kelea rambled over the hills, half bereft of
reason; she ventured to the heights over the
house on the cliff and, hiding herself, watched
for Pu' Aloha to come forth, that she might
even take her life. At lucid intervals she tried
to dispossess herself of this mania, since somehow she shrank from this extremity of active
vengeance.

When she thought of Hookama's joy in the
elysium of Pu' Aloha's smiles, she recalled the
days she had spent with him in the vale of
Iao and, though many of his words rankled in
her memory, she repeated them over and over,
as one might press sharp thorns into the flesh
to quicken morbid sensibilites. She treasured
the ivory dagger, with its poisoned point, as
a souvenir which suggested death as a last resort, if all her hopes should finally be lost.

A few days after Hookama's departure,
Pu' Aloha climbed the path behind the cliff,

to a spot a short distance away, from which she could see the promontory of Kualoa, beyond which lay the district where Hookama was fighting in the army of the king. It was her habit to visit this place, where she dreamed of her husband and tried to imagine his feats of valor.

On this occasion, she did not rest her eyes exclusively on the landscape, which stretched like an enchanted realm from the emerald sea to the lofty, buttressed hills, clad to their tops in luxuriant foliage. With a far-off, dreamy gaze she was looking at a little fleecy cloud, beyond the extreme point of the marvellous scene, thinking that perhaps it hung over the very spot where her lord might be resting after a day's hard struggle. She watched the shadows as they wrapped a portion of the lovely landscape in gloom, and was wholly absorbed in pleasing meditation, so that the approach of a stranger, coming towards her from behind, was unobserved. It was a man, who had passed around a heap of rocks at her back and now stood in the deepening dusk of the twilight looking down upon her and apparently waiting for her to turn her head towards him. As she did not turn, he came forward.

Startled at hearing the footsteps of a

stranger, Pu' Aloha sprang to her feet, and, turning towards him, saw, to her amazement and horror, what seemed to be an apparition from the dead. Without a word, for her tongue was paralyzed, she arose to flee by the path, when the figure darted forward and caught her about the waist, not roughly but firmly, and in answer to the frightened expression on her face, said in gentle tones: " Yes, Pu' Aloha, I am—Paao! By no means dead; but more alive than ever. The gods will that you shall yet be mine."

He said no more: it was useless to speak further; he held a lifeless form in his arms, which he laid on the matted grass. Then, rushing to a hollow rock near by, containing water, he scooped it in his hands and came again where the girl lay pale and motionless on the ground. He had placed her there most tenderly, for he meant to do her no harm. But the motion of his hands and arms, dashing the water in her face, was as if he were smiting the prostrate girl.

His body was bent over her, with his back towards the pile of rocks, when a slight noise behind him caused him to turn his head halfway over his shoulder. Before he could see clearly whence the sound came, or straighten himself up, a strong hand seized him by the neck and a sharp dagger was thrust with fearful force into his side.

Blood gushed in streams from the wound. He fell or was pushed over on his side, as Kelea, for it was she, quickly lifted Pu' Aloha, who, with half recovered consciousness, opened her eyes upon the ghastly sight. There lay Paao on the ground, weltering in his blood, the dagger still in the wound.

With life fast ebbing, the dying man, by a great effort, raised himself a little and turned his glazing eyes, first on Kelea with a look of utter astonishment (for he had not known of her presence on the island), then on Pu' Aloha, who covered her face with her *tapa*, while he tried to gasp a few words: "Ah, Flower of Love! I go to the gods, hated by you whom I have loved—yes—as my own soul—loved—I meant no harm"—and as his eyes fell on Kelea, he muttered, "Murderess!"

Then, pulling out from his side the dagger which he knew was poisoned, he made one more attempt to speak, and said: "I meant *that*," feebly lifting the weapon in his hand, "for the butcher—assassin—may the gods—" but he could only whisper the word "Hookama," as he fell back dead, with a look of intense contempt on his face which the last

agonies of death did not remove. He was
gone, but his dying words called for no pity.
The dead face awakened no regret for his
fate.

Kelea's strength almost failed her, but she
was able to lift Pu' Aloha, who was overcome
by the tragic scene and too weak to rise.
With great effort she carried the terrified and
helpless girl to a mossy bank away from the
ghastly spot, and tried to calm her by soothing words, although she herself was distracted
by contending emotions, now that the deed
was done.

She had set out that day from her temporary
home near Manoa Valley with the terrible de-
sign to confront Pu' Aloha, whose habit of
coming to her favorite lookout she had discovered after many days of espionage. If her
rival refused to surrender her lover, for Kelea
did not know of their marriage, she cared not
what happened ; but an evil voice in her heart
cried, " Kill her ! " and she might not have been
able to resist it. She was impelled along this
course of action, whatever the result.

Coming stealthily in sight of the spot where
she expected to behold the rapt face of the
girl, looking expectantly and longingly towards
Kualoa, as she had seen it on two previous
days from her place of concealment, to her

amazement she saw a man hanging over the prostrate body of her rival as if he had slain her.

The sight of the apparently lifeless form of one who had been so dear to her wrought an instantaneous change in her over-charged mind. The dead girl could no longer stand in her way. That was her first thought. Then followed the old feeling of endearment. To punish the murderer she rushed upon him and struck the fatal blow, not knowing, till the stroke was given, that the supposed assailant was her old enemy Paao.

With the warm body of Pu' Aloha in her arms all her love came back. As the rescued girl called her " dear " and " my own Kelea," she could not repress tears of gratitude that she was safe. But near by lay the dead Paao. What was now to be done? His own dagger in his hand, and his death-wound on the left side made suicide the natural theory if his body were found. Besides, was he not supposed to be sacrificed in the *heiau*? How did he appear alive after his body had been laid on the altar?

The poor girl in her arms could give Kelea no advice ; she could not even tell her yet the circumstances attending the assault upon her of Paao, if assault it was. Kelea's quick wit seized

at once upon the idea that if Paao were considered by the world as a dead man, why not
bury him, and so blot out his memory forever?
But who will undertake the task? She cannot do it. Her heart revolted at the thought
of ever looking on that hateful face again.

All her questionings and plans were put to
flight, when her ear caught the sound of
hurried steps, climbing over the rocks. The
heads, and soon the stalwart shoulders, of Maili
and Menehune appeared behind a slight ridge
which separated from the path the spot where
the two girls were sitting. If Kelea allowed
them to go on and find the body of Paao, she
and Pu' Aloha might slip down to the house
unobserved. Then the evidence of suicide
would shield them from all suspicion. She
must decide at once; but with her usual quick-
ness, she determined to call them and tell them
the whole story.

The men listened in utter astonishment and
remained as if paralyzed at the end of the recital. Kelea bade them go and see for themselves. They hesitated, and it required all
her persuasiveness to induce them to approach
the man who had been twice killed. He
might be alive again, for all they knew to the
contrary.

At last, having seen and been convinced,

they returned, and Kelea, swearing them to secrecy by all the gods, induced them to carry the body to the bottom of a lonely ravine, through which a circuitous stream ran with abundant water; there they would find a deep pool, in which to sink their burden, weighted with stones. Then they must roll all the loose rocks they could handle into the pool and let the traitor find his way as best he could to the hidden land of Kane.

Maili told Pu' Aloha that Hookama had sent him with the message that a battle, favorable in its result to the king, had been fought and that he would be at the house on the cliff the next day. "Then be in haste," said Kelea to the two men; for with an instinctive desire to save Hookama's feelings, she wanted to relieve him forever from the sight of his hated foe.

The men found the dark pool, underneath a shelving rock. It was almost stagnant and a green scum had settled on its surface. In the dim light, they flung the body in, then dropped into the circling ripples the largest stones they could move, and, having finished their disagreeable task, the two nervous functionaries lost no time in climbing out of the gulch into the more wholesome air of the heights.

"Say, comrade," asked Maili of Menehune,

"if Paao cheated the gods in the *heiau*, will they let him into *Milu*?"

"He'll have to 'swim round the cliff'* if they do;" grunted the dwarf in his usual laconic style."

"Or find a new 'gap in the ridge downwards,'"* added Maili, as he thought of the stones they had tumbled into the pool. "I wish I had kept that dagger," he murmured to himself. "Perhaps the rascal will fight his way out again. I wonder how many lives he's got."

It was discovered, a long time after Paao's final disappearance, that he escaped from the *heiau* by the connivance of the priests, who smeared his face and shoulders with blood instead of slaying him, and handed the eye of a large hog to the king, instead of the left eye of the supposed victim. Then, after the departure of the chiefs, they put another body in Paao's place on the platform and covered the six corpses with loose earth. There was no careful scrutiny after the execution of victims and few entered the *heiau* for many days, so foul were the odors.

Paao was advised by the insurgent chiefs, whom he joined the morning after his escape, to remain in hiding for the present, lest his

* Hawaiian expressions.

appearance in the rebel army should bring the priests under suspicion. He was roaming over the mountain, when he chanced to discover Pu' Aloha, and his passion for her brought him to a tragic end. The tarn into which his body was thrown is called *pepo-loko* (black pool) to this day.

When Maili and Menehune returned to the place, where Kelea was trying to arouse Pu' Aloha from her prostration, they found the latter in a state bordering on hysteria. And even Kelea's strong nerves were giving way, but the change from her period of jealous frenzy to her old affection for Pu' Aloha buoyed her up.

Maili attributed Pu' Aloha's condition to the ghost of Paao, which he believed still hovered near, according to the current superstition of the Hawaiians. He imagined that he heard the peculiar sound (*muki*), which a ghost produced, till after a time it ceased altogether. He had recognized in Kelea the woman who gave him the shells on the island of Maui, and his admiration for her robust beauty made him her willing servant. Menehune, however, hardly realized the gravity of the situation. His eyes twinkled as he chuckled to himself and thought of the dark pool.

But night was approaching, and at Kelea's

bidding Menehune took Pu' Aloha in his arms and carried her to her house. Kelea hesitated a moment but soon followed, with Maili, and it was not long before she and Pu' Aloha sought relief in each other's arms on the same couch.

CHAPTER XXXIV.

HOOKAMA DISCOVERS HIS ANCESTORS.

THE next morning, Pu' Aloha, prostrated by the tragic events of the previous day, could hardly lift her head. Kelea, suffering more in mind than body, was glad of the necessity of silence, since it relieved her from unpleasant questions. She noticed the signs in Pu' Aloha's new home of her changed relations with Hookama, but was able to suppress all jealous emotions. She determined, however, not to meet them together lest the old feelings should return.

Maili, who announced that Hookama would arrive early in the afternoon told the young women, who were lying on soft mats in the *lanai*, that there had been a fight near Punaluu, in which the rebels were defeated.

They paid little attention to his account of the battle. but when he narrated Hookama's part in it, both the girls sat up and listened with eagerness. He said the young *alii* had shown the greatest bravery. Towards the end of a bloody skirmish, the king, advancing at the head of his bodyguard, threw himself upon a band of warriors entrenched in a defile. The assault was furious but the defence was equally desperate. The king was in the midst of the foemen, swinging his powerful battle-axe, when a chief sprang forward and made a thrust with a spear which would have put an end to the king's career, had not Hookama parried the blow, receiving a severe flesh wound in his left arm. At the mention of the wound Pu' Aloha turned pale as death, but recovered when Maili assured her that it was a more painful than dangerous one.

Continuing, the warrior said that the *alii*, with his right hand, killed the assailant with a dagger and then led the attack which put the enemy to flight. An armistice had been agreed upon when Maili left the camp, and he thought there would be no more trouble with the rebels after such a defeat as they had met.

Pu' Aloha rallied a little, as she thought of the prowess of her lord, but she was too languid to notice the expression of Kelea's countenance which would have revealed to a more suspicious and more alert mind at least some hint of ardent tenderness and admiration for the hero.

Kelea watched the face of Pu' Aloha and was surprised at herself that all her own jealousy had disappeared. The younger girl's look was so ingenuous and she gave her every now and then such affectionate glances that Kelea's only wonder was that she had ever harbored any thought of her insincerity. Once when Pu' Aloha threw her arms around her friend and said: "My darling, I owe my life to you; I only wish you could be as happy as I am with my lord," Kelea's emotions so overcame her that Pu' Aloha again embraced her, exclaiming, "But you shall have nothing save *aloha* from me as long as you live, and I will make Hookama love you too." Kelea buried her face in the bosom of the affectionate girl and vowed to herself that she should never know what had passed between her and the man whose whole heart her friend most certainly possessed.

"Believe me," continued Pu' Aloha, "I only wish two women could drink at the same fountain—but in such matters you know this is impossible." Kelea knew this too well, and from any other lips the words would have been like a stab in her heart. But she found, as the sun approached the zenith, that she could not meet Hookama in her present state of mind. Therefore excusing her hasty departure to Pu' Aloha, by saying that she had left an important matter to be attended to at a friend's where she had been visiting, she slipped away to the hut over Manoa Valley; and she went none too soon, for passing beyond a place where two paths met, she saw Hookama going up and barely escaped his notice.

Great was Pu' Aloha's joy when her lord appeared. He was clad in magnificent array. A superb yellow cloak of priceless feathers reached to his knees; on his head was a lofty scarlet helmet; he held in his hand a richly carved spear and a dazzling *malo* was wound about his loins. He approached in very grand style, carrying himself majestically, but having a quizzical look on his face, as if to say : "Look at me! Did you ever see such a fine sight?" Pu' Aloha, weak as she was, started to meet him, only to be met by the point of his spear, levelled at her bosom.

"Keep off," he cried, as if in mockery, but, seeing her pallor, he threw back his cloak and showed his bandaged arm and other marks of wounds on his breast.

She came close to him full of sympathy and as he bent down she put her cheek to his and clung to him, partly for support and partly because of her anxiety on account of his wounds. With his unwounded arm about her, he replied to her tender inquiries, " Scratches, only skin-deep. How could I have marched all day, if they amounted to anything more? But, dear one. why so pale? Surely you are ill. What has befallen you? What has happened? You do not look like yourself. Tell me! you are as white as a sea-bird."

She led Hookama to a grassy mound and gave him a brief account of the tragedy of the preceding day, dwelling in glowing words on the defence of her honor by Kelea and the death of Paao at her hand. He tried to rise when she came to the point where Paao called Kelea " murderess " and Hookama an " assassin; " but she detained him and nestled closer to his side, as he contented himself with heaping imprecations on the traitor and uttering words of praise for the brave girl who had saved his darling's life, as he supposed.

Pu' Aloha's heart beat with emotion as he warmly commended Kelea's courage, and the excitement kept the maiden for a time from sinking back into the languor which had oppressed her. Hookama saw that she was becoming exhausted; pleading, therefore, his own weariness from the long march, he drew her towards the house and made her recline on the mats, saying that he too had a tale to tell that would cheer her up.

Laying aside his helmet and cloak, he told her that they were the trophies which he had taken from a rebel chief whom he had slain in battle. "A regular *alii-kapu* (sacred chief,)" he declared.

"Don't think for a moment," he continued in a bantering tone, "that I have worn that bushy wig all day in the hot sun. Oh no! but my troop, that came with me and are gone down to the camp at Waikiki, insisted on my appearing before my '*aloha*' in a style befitting my new rank. Wouldn't you like to know what it is, and what my new name is? Foolish girl! you would like to see me a real *alii-kapu*, wouldn't you? Well, lean on me and I will tell you something that will drive away all thoughts of the horrid day you have had."

Then, to cheer her up, he told her a surprising story, which seemed more like a dream than a reality. He spoke rather facetiously and made fun of the whole thing, so that, had it not been for the trophies, the helmet, spear, cloak and a rich ivory hook, worn only by the highest chiefs and which Pu' Aloha discovered hanging to his neck, she would not have believed a word he said.

"Well, you see," he began, squeezing Pu'

Aloha's hand in his own, "you, sweetheart, have always made me think that I am an uncommon personage. Then, that old, wizened, dried-up specimen of a king at Hawaii told me that I was the 'son of a god.' The hag at the volcano, priestess of Pele, fell down at my feet and worshipped me, followed by Lou, the apostate, who never before worshipped anything but his own paunch. After all *that*, and even from our first acquaintance, our king intimated to me several times, that I was the limb of a big tree, (on which I suppose many of my ancestors were hung by the heels); and he as much as told me that the natives would want my bones to make fish-hooks and spearheads, after I was dead, as you know they make them for luck from the relics of high chiefs.

"Then, think of his telling me in a private talk one day, that if I had my rights I would own a whole island; (I supposed he meant Molokini, that nasty little rock, off Maui). Another time, (I thought he was losing his mind), he wanted to change *malos* with me, which you know means a great mark of esteem. Once again when we were talking of the *Kiha Pu*, the magic shell which could call up the genii, he said, 'Why don't *you* blow it?' I replied, 'Why don't you?' to which he answered 'I cannot, though you can.'

"But the queerest thing of all was the day before yesterday. After I had got this cut on my arm,—it twinges now,—the king took me to his *hale*, the best one at Punaluu, once the home of the chief whose sacred helmet you have just touched with profane hands, and whose spirit I sent to *Milu* along with several other noble rebels.

"When we were comfortably settled on the luxurious dead chief's best mats, what did Kahahana do but call in an old, grisly *kilo* (prophet or bard,) who wanted to chant a *mele*; I supposed to help us go to sleep after the fighting of the day. I said, 'If he wants to chant, let him chant!' and so he began in a droning, monotonous way; soon he got excited and screamed so loud that I couldn't sleep if I wanted to. Then he wound up, after a long list of names, which bored me to listen to, with a perfect screech as he called out 'Hookamalii,' and rushed up to me, flinging himself down and kissing my feet.

"I had half a mind to kick the fellow, but he was an old man and my feet were bare, so I turned to the king and said, 'My *alii*, what's this man doing and what does he want, anyway?' To my surprise the king replied, 'He has been singing your *mele* (pedigree ;) didn't you understand it? He says the gods sent

him to another old bard on Kauai who taught
him this *mele*, and he has been searching for
you, all over the group.' 'Then he lies,' I said
to the king. 'Yes, he does, in part, for *I* found
your *mele* (pedigree) with the *inoa* (symbol of
rank); and why he claims to have discovered it
let him answer.'

"The miserable *kilo* confessed that he did
not find it as described, but declared that bards
always pretended to find such things, and, at all
events, the pedigree was true. Then I asked
him to chant it again and let me learn it. Perhaps there was something in it my *wahine*
(wife) would like to hear.

"He was very ready to go over the whole
thing again, and this time I listened. It began :—

> "*' He eleele kii na Maui,*
> *Kii aku ia Kane ma.'* *

but I'll not bother you with it all. The gist of
it was that many generations ago, there came
to the island of Kauai a big chief, Moikeha.
Well, this big fellow was the earliest ancestor of whom anything is known, of a bird-
catcher called Hookama."

Hookama drew Pu' Aloha nearer to him
with his right arm and went on with his story.

---

*A messenger sent by Maui, to bring,
To bring Kane and his company.

"Now, I'll tell you a bigger 'brownie' tale than that. This famous chief had three sons and one foster son. The eldest son's name was Hookamalii! That is where my name came from, so said the king, and I am not an 'adopted' at all. I am Hookamalii! That's my real name and I am the last lineal descendant of old Moikeha and the rightful heir to half the island of Kauai.

"Tumble down now, all ye natives, and make obeisance to my conspicuous figure! Put my helmet on that rock yonder and salute it! His *moi*ship feels too stiff to be getting up to be worshipped just now."

Hookama gave Pu' Aloha a squeeze as he proceeded. "And did not the great granddaughter of Hookamalii, *my* progenitor, the beautiful Maele, start the Kalona line on Oahu, by giving her husband another of my respected ancestors, — whom may the gods preserve! —and allow me in a similar fashion to see my honored line continued!"

"Why are you not king of Kauai, then?" asked Pu' Aloha, with a sly glance at Hookama.

"Didn't I say, you ambitious woman, that you would be content with nothing short of royalty? But you cannot be gratified this time, for the second son of old Moikeha be-

THE POOL OF KAPENA

came king of Kauai somehow, and the *moi*ship
has descended in that line to this day.
Isn't it enough to own half an island, without
the bother of a throne? Look at Kahahana!
who would want to be in his place?"

Pu' Aloha's eyes glistened as Hookama
clasped her to his breast and said, "But you
are my Love-Queen any way, and what more
do you want. King or no king, I warn all
persons not to invade your kingdom in my
heart—and—" (playfully) "I warn you, too, if
you do not pay due respect to my magnificence, I'll—but who is that?"

Both called out in the same breath. "It's
Kelea!" as, at that moment, the girl came,
in breathless haste, around the point of the
ledge and, with somewhat of confusion in her
manner, which Pu' Aloha attributed to her
hurried climb up the mountain, gave Hookama the startling news that a fleet of canoes
was between Koko Head and Leahi apparently
steering with all speed to Waikiki.

"They are warriors, and the chief at the
royal house says they are rebels. They yell
as if coming to attack, and the chief wants you
to make all haste and take command. Your
troop wants you and there are only fifty warriors at the camp. The canoes are full; at
least a hundred men. I met the messenger

and ran ahead of him, thinking Pu' Aloha
might want me to stay with her while you
were gone," and Kelea sank down exhausted,
with her eyes on the ground.

Hookama advanced towards her and took
both her hands. The girl blushed deeply
when he praised her for her rescue of Pu'
Aloha, and thanked her for coming with the
news of the fleet. Before he finished speaking
the messenger appeared and corroborated
Kelea's message, also relieving her from her
confusion and the necessity of replying to
Hookama's kind words; for instantly Pu'
Aloha, with the spirit of a heroine, rose up and
exclaimed, addressing her lord, "Go, go at
once ! A warrior can use his spear with one
hand free. It tears out my heart, *Alii-nui*,
but the gods will give you the victory."

The poor child nearly fell while uttering
these brave words, but, clinging to Hookama,
she added : " What is your half of an island,
if you cannot defend a whole one with fifty
men against a hundred rebels ! But promise
me to take care of yourself," (the woman's instinct got the better of her courage for a moment). "The spears of rebels are long, and
they have two hands to wield them. Only
promise me this, and go."

" I promise," said the *alii*, as he clasped her

to his heart, and calling for food and a gourd of *awa* for the messenger, he forgot his own need till Kelea brought him a portion also As she handed it to him she said in a low voice, " Thank you for all your kind words. My life for yours if needed. Let the messenger carry your spear and cloak."

The last words were spoken in a louder tone and the man took the weapon and garment, giving a look of admiration at the handsome woman as he exclaimed : "I too will guard the *alii* with my life." He had overheard her whispered words, and was rewarded for his loyalty with Kelea's most grateful look.

CHAPTER XXXV.

SURF-RIDING AT ITS CULMINATION.

No sooner were Hookama and the messenger out of sight than Pu' Aloha, having already coaxed her languid pulses to their utmost limit, fell face downward into the springing grass, murmuring in an agony, " He must not die; he must not die ! " She shed no tears, but a shiver ran through her frame as Kelea and the "mother" tenderly lifted and carried her into the house.

They rubbed her limbs gently and bathed her forehead, but it seemed almost as if she were slipping away from them into the darkness. Incoherent utterances came feebly from her lips. " My love ! my *alii* ! I flung him off —wounded. Oh! the black *tapa*; Aohe! aohe !" and the poor child tried to rise from her couch, grasping at something with her hands, but only clutching the air.

Applying every known restorative, the women, piteously weeping, saw a mystic beauty
all at once stealing over the sufferer's face, as
she opened her eyes and noticed them bending over her. For the first time since Hookama's departure, breathing naturally, she
reached out her arms and drew Kelea close to
her, saying in a most rational voice, "Dear!
you must go and watch over him; I have had
a vision. A shower of javelins like rain, but
you hid him in a cloud. Give me only one
clasp of your strong arms, that I may feel
your strength. If I only were able!—but you
can do it. Don't wait. The 'mother' will
care for me. I am better now." Seeing hesitation on Kelea's face, she added, "If you do
not go, I must. I cannot stay, after the
dream! You or I—now, dear!"

The mutual embrace was given and Kelea,
who had longed to go before Pu' Aloha spoke
of it, hurried away, after a loving look and
the cheery words, "I'll bring the color to
your cheek, darling, when I bring back your
Hookama."

From a high rock in the Manoa Valley
Kelea saw a sight that would cause a less
courageous woman to tremble with fear,
but careless of self, she studied the situation.
Behind a parapet of loose stones in front of

the royal house, two score of warriors stood at bay ; on the right was a large fish pond protecting that side; on the left, a thick undergrowth.

The conflict was raging at the wall ; the assailing warriors were leaping upon it only to disappear, falling inside or flung back by the defenders. Some bodies, wounded or dead, were lying within the barricade and a larger number were stretched outside on the ground. There were desperate rushes from without and fierce resistance from within. Kelea saw one man, standing in the rear of the defenders, as if directing their movements. He was the only warrior wearing a helmet, and a scarlet coat was wound about one of his arms. Every now and then he advanced and hurled a javelin, as a foeman tried to scale the wall. When, by numbers, the enemy gained an apparent advantage, this chief, whom Kelea at once recognized as Hookama, was in the thickest of the fight.

Kelea's first impulse was to rush towards the combatants and do what she could to shield Hookama, remembering Pu' Aloha's words. But she saw no women there and shrank from the conspicuous position of a solitary woman among the warriors.

Again her eye ranged over the whole scene,

taking a bird's-eye view of land and sea. The royal house, the struggle in front of it, the dry plain to the beach, a line of tall cocoa-palms along the shore, the white beach with the canoes of the rebels drawn up on the sand. Beyond, the huge rollers, the surf, the impassable reef and the quiet, blue ocean, stretching to the horizon. All this was taken in at a glance; but as her eye passed towards the east, her keen vision caught sight of a canoe, rounding the point of Leahi jutting into the sea. Then more canoes came in sight.

The paddlers were urging their boats onward with rapid strokes, as if to reach the one opening through the reef, opposite Waikiki. Were they friends or foes? She saw that the combatants at the royal house had become aware of the new-comers. There was a lull in the fighting, as both assailants and defenders looked towards the flotilla in the offing. They all appeared to be in doubt as to its character. If a reinforcement to the rebels, the case of Hookama and his band was not only desperate but hopeless. If it meant aid for the defenders, the defeat of the rebels was sure.

Suddenly there was a movement on the part of the rebels. A score of them rushed to the fish pond on the right, shouting and plunging into the water. It was a flank movement, a final *coup*, either in sheer desperation or in confidence of a victory because of help near at hand.

Kelea gazed steadily at the fleet, which rapidly skirted the reef in the open sea. To her great joy, she recognized the peculiar shaped canoes and the streamers of Maui, her own island ; Kahekili, the king of Maui, had for once kept his promise and sent a hundred warriors. Hope inspired the maiden's breast ; Hookama might yet be saved, if he and his band could hold out.

She started to go towards the scene of conflict. Possibly she might shield the young *alii* in the last deadly struggle. She heard the rebel warriors yell, as one after another gained the bank of the fish pond next the royal enclosure. Some of the defenders were rushing to meet them, leaving thinned ranks behind the barricade.

But a shout from the shore, raised by the few men in charge of the rebel canoes, came clearly to her ears. They were calling to their comrades to flee. They had discovered that the new arrival meant their own destruction.

The friendly fleet, however, paddled very slowly, until at length it stopped. Then it turned back. Obviously there was some cause for this doubling on its course. Kelea, accustomed to watch the movements of canoes at Waihee, her home, knew that the warriors in the canoes were looking for the passage through the rolling breakers. They were evidently in doubt as to the entrance, never before having visited these shores.

Her joy was turned into an agony of fear. Would they be balked, just on the eve of saving Hookama and his men? Must the aid, so near, prove unavailing? She felt that something must be done, and done quickly.

A crowd of natives, non-combatants, old men, women and children, stood on one side in the plain towards the sea, looking on from their safe position at the fight near the royal house. It was a chaotic, distracted throng, a wailing multitude, aimlessly running here and there, or throwing themselves on the earth in terror.

Divesting herself of her mantle, Kelea ran swiftly towards this motley crowd, and, speeding her way in and out among them, gained a large space, unobserved, on her way towards the canoes on the beach, and the men who guarded them. The natives, watching the conflict, paid no attention to her. But the men with the canoes soon discerned her flying figure coming towards them. At first they paid little heed, as she was alone and only a woman.

Straight as an arrow, she took her course towards them. Though they saw her as she ran, they paid more attention to the fleet and the fight than to her. Nearer and nearer came the girl, her long hair flying in the wind. She ran as if her life depended on her speed. The men at the beach, thinking her a messenger, awaited her approach now that her object seemed to be to communicate with them. It was a shrewd manœuvre of Kelea.

Within a hundred yards of the little group of warriors, she suddenly wheeled on her course and sped over the sands towards the breakers. Before the surprised watchers divined her real intention, or thought of pursuing her, she had gained a large space and was in the midst of the rolling surf. Even then, the men were bewildered and could not believe that a woman would dare to breast the high, combing waves. One started to follow her but soon lost sight of her among the breakers ; saying "She's gone crazy ; let her drown !" he turned back.

But the girl swam on. Now her muscular strength and skill in surf-riding came into full play. With strokes that sent her swiftly forward and skilfully diving to avoid the force of the larger, oncoming billows, while adroitly taking advantage of the receding waves, she swam for the inlet, which she had discovered on the day when she distanced all competitors in the surf-riding contest.

Cool enough, even in the excitement of the struggle, to turn her head as she rose to the crest of a high wave, she saw that the contest still raged at the royal house. With renewed resolution on she ploughed, lifting her arms to signal the war-fleet.

Fortunately, the surf-rider of Maui was in her element. Here was the consummate result of her life in the surf on the shores of her native isle. The waiting fleet outside the reef soon perceived her signals and steered in the direction to which she pointed. They espied the entrance before she reached it, and their swift paddles, shooting the canoes, one by one, into the curving waves at that point, passed inside the dangerous reef.

All eyes were on the swimmer, as she waited in the water resting her tired limbs, till the first canoe came near. In the stern of the large war-canoe stood a tall chief, and when Kelea flung back her hair from her face and looked up at him, a cry escaped her as she recognized *her father!*

Stout arms drew the girl into the canoe where she sank down at the feet of the chief,

waving her hand towards the shore and urging on the crew.

There was no time for explanations.

The stalwart warrior looked grimly down
at his daughter as he carefully steered the
craft according to her guidance, while the men,
recognizing the lost *wahine*, their famous surf-
rider and princess, the pride of Waihee, bent
to their task with redoubled enthusiasm.

The rebels, guarding the canoes on the
beach, fled into the thickets. The warriors
from Maui, beaching their canoes, seized their
weapons and, without a moment's delay,
rushed towards the scene of conflict. Their
movements had been seen by both parties of
the combatants, but the assailants still hoped
to beat down the warriors who were left behind the barricade, and so make a better de-
fense for themselves against their new foes.

As for flight, they knew that would be fatal.
Whither should they flee? The open plain
afforded no shelter, and their canoes were in
the hands of the enemy. Besides, Hawaiian
warriors knew how to die in battle but not to
flee. Therefore the fight continued with redoubled fury on both sides as the allies from
Maui ran to join in the fray. The issue
was no longer doubtful. The crowd of
natives, non-combatants, came nearer the

field of battle. Their shouts of cheer and encouragement were borne on the air to the ears of Hookama and his band. Women screamed in their exultation, and louder grew their voices as they saw, at the head of the swiftly approaching column of fresh warriors, a woman, carrying in her hand and waving a long spear with a blood-red pennon streaming at its tip.

With hair dishevelled and a loose *tapa* mantle, which she had snatched from one of the canoes, flying in the wind, she led the race. Her skirt was torn and her shoulders were bare, but the look of victorious resolution on her face, as she turned towards the warriors rushing after her like an avalanche, and her war-cry, " In the name of all the gods!" caused them to leap forward with a yell.

The rebel band, reduced to half its numbers, bravely wheeled their outer ranks to their new foes, while their warriors next the wall still fought those who tried to leap over and despatch them. Crushed was that stout-hearted phalanx, as between the upper and the nether millstone. Fighting to the last, no quarter given or received, they died where they stood, to the last man, and their bodies lay piled as high as the barricade itself, to attest their brave defiance of death.

It was a hard won victory for the warriors

of Oahu. Hookama's band had but a score
remaining after the fight. Several were
drowned in the fish pond, in hand-to-hand
wrestle with the flanking party of the rebels.
When the slaughter was over and the warriors
of Maui were attending to their wounded,
doing also what they could to assist Hookama
and his exhausted men, the disorderly crowd,
women in search of their husbands, old men
always getting in the way and eager for the
spoils of the enemy, swarmed into the field of
carnage, and indescribable confusion was the
result.

Searching among the wild and unrestrained
throngs, Hookama, who had watched the
movements of Kelea in the surf and as she led
the column to the attack, was suffering the
torture of anxiety as to her fate ; she was nowhere to be found. In the excitement of the
last struggle he had lost sight of her and feared
she might have been stricken down.

At last, meeting Maili, he asked, " Where is
Kelea ? " " Who *is* Kelea ? " called out one
of the women, carrying a calabash of water to a
wounded warrior. " She led the troop," was
Maili's hurried answer as he whispered to
Hookama that Menehune had carried her to
the royal house early in the final combat.

Instantly a mighty shout arose. It was

started by the woman to whom Maili had spoken. "Kelea! Kelea!" was roared and shouted and screamed by hundreds of voices, as if the excited multitude had found vent for the tumult of their agitated emotions in re-echoing the words. "Kelea, the Surf-Rider! Kelea the Conqueror! Where is she? Crown her; she has won the day!" and the boisterous people, rabble, warriors and the braves from Maui, all followed Menehune, who thought it was a fine thing to do, and led the way to the king's large house.

A few moments earlier, Hookama had discovered Kelea lying on a couch, resting but flushed with excitement. After she brought her father and his warriors into the conflict, knowing that the result was certain and that she could be of no further use; shrinking also from the sight of the slaughter, which had none of the elements of even-handed warfare in it, she found the dwarf, or he found her, and, under his protection, she entered the deserted royal house.

For the first time, the young *alii* knelt before the maiden and, taking her hand, pressed it to his forehead. "Oh, Kelea! I owe you my life: Brave girl! Glorious—"

"Crown Kelea!" came the echo of the shout from the multitude without. "Kelea

the Conqueror!" There was the noise of
tramping people. Hookama rose to his feet
and had only time to say—"Yes, my Kelea,
you *have* conquered—you have conquered *me*,"
when Menehune and the crowd burst into the
room, halting as they saw the young *alii*
standing in a dignified manner before the
young woman lying on the mats.

But even his presence could not repulse
their onslaught or quiet their shouts. They
insisted that Kelea should come out and be
crowned. Seeing that they persisted and were
full of loyal enthusiasm, Hookama assisted
Kelea to rise and, with her hand in his, the two
walked through the parted throng and stood
in the verandah in front of the royal house.

Then as if pandemonium was let loose, the
whole space was filled with a frantic multitude.
They waved pennons and spears; women
flung their *tapa* mantles in the air; warriors
shook aloft their battle-axes and javelins.
Flowers from the king's garden, branches from
the palm trees and hastily woven wreaths were
showered on the couple, till they were literally
covered up in the fragrant blossoms and stood
knee deep in aromatic *maile* vines. Shouts and
cries were lifted to the skies. Some cheered
Kelea, and some Hookama. Their names
were uttered in the same breath. It was an

ovation in which both shared, although the name of Kelea aroused the most enthusiasm and elicited the loudest utterances. Menehune was turning somersaults in front of the crowd.

" It is a betrothal (*hoopalau*)," said a *wahine* to Maili who stood in the crowd. It was Kamili, to whom he had given the shell. She had come in search of him to tend him if wounded, but he had escaped with slight hurts. " It looks like it, but I think there is another ahead of this one," he replied, with a sly wink at Kamili, remembering certain indications he had seen at the house on the cliff.

Menehune overheard the conversation and his ugly face had a grin across it, wider than the gashes which gave him the look of a ghoul. It was a gleam of his newly awakened consciousness that enabled him to get at the root of the matter as he pinched the girl's arm and grunted in her ear, " Pu' Aloha, one ; Kelea, two." She seemed to comprehend his meaning and gave him an answering smile, which confirmed his notion of the final result.

There was another spectator who took a personal interest in the scene. Kelea's father was standing with the commander of one of his war-canoes, narrowly watching his daughter and Hookama, as they stood on the verandah, the recipients of this impromptu ovation. He saw a look of intense happiness on her face and he thought the young *alii* looked proud and satisfied, with the handsome girl leaning on his arm. He also noticed that they exchanged glances, which he interpreted as an experienced father naturally would do.

"A fine pair, *alii-nui*!" said the warrior at his side. "I saw that young chief come near capturing the giant warrior of Hawaii, and he would have done it, if the Lonely One had not swooped down to the rescue. I have heard him called Bird-Catcher; perhaps he has snared the sea-bird already, eh?"

The chief made no reply, but in his heart he had already chosen the handsome youth for his daughter, if the gods so willed.

CHAPTER XXXVI.

ALOHA!

KELEA returned, under Menehune's escort, to the house on the cliff, after an interview with her father, the chief of Waihee. He asked her to go back to Maui with him, but as she begged to remain, that she might nurse a dear friend who had been kind to her in her exile, he finally consented. He exacted a promise from Hookama that Kelea should return to Waihee when he sent for her, after the recovery of her friend. The young *alii* gave the pledge with some reluctance, but finally concluded that her father's will was law, according to custom, and that he could not refuse.

The king of Oahu soon after returned from his victorious expedition against the rebels beyond the *Pali* and was prodigal in his praises of Kelea's courage. His return relieved

Hookama from duty at the royal house and enabled him to retire at once to the house on the cliff to recuperate his strength.

After receiving many hospitalities the chief of Waihee and his warriors, none of whom were slain in the battle with the rebels, set sail amid the shouts of the crowd assembled on the shore. His war-canoes were decorated with flowers and his men richly rewarded by the king for their services.

There was one thing that disturbed the mind of the chief of Waihee. He learned, just before he embarked, that Hookama had intimate relations with another woman, who was the "friend" whom Kelea wished to stay and nurse. This complicated matters, but it was too late to change the plan, and the king assured him that he himself would answer for his daughter's safety and welfare.

When Kelea returned to the cliff she found Pu' Aloha so ill and weak that all her sympathies were aroused and she gave little heed to her resolution not to witness the marital happiness of the newly wedded pair. Indeed, in Hookama's heart there was so much anxiety that he was glad to have Kelea near to nurse his bride. He forgot everything but the use of means for the recovery of the invalid.

For weeks Pu' Aloha made no progress towards recovery. The shock to her nerves had utterly prostrated her. The good "mother" was an adept in simple remedies. Menehune, full of sympathetic feeling, which he expressed in his peculiar style, gathered roots and herbs from the woods and streams. Kelea applied ointments and lotions. Hookama would have nothing to do with the *Kehunas*, and in this he was seconded by Kelea.

There were days of hope, and days that were hopeless ; days, when the beauty of the sick girl's face was like that of a thin alabaster vase, with the light shining from within. Her blue veins showed through her fair skin and the hectic color went and came. Her slender figure gradually lost its graceful curves. The hands, folded across the soft, white *tapa*, became thin and nerveless. Hookama suspended a netting, like a hammock, under the shade of the overhanging cliff, where the cool, upland breezes swayed the vines drooping from the rocks. It was a spot from which the shadows of the clouds, chasing each other over the mountain slopes, made the landscape a picture of beauty, and the sunsets, seen over the sea, were a dream of color in a mist of gold.

On the lovely afternoon of a day that had greatly encouraged the hope of Pu' Aloha's ultimate restoration to health, Hookama was

at the side of the hammock gently swinging its
occupant, whose spirits were unusually buoy-
ant. Kelea had gone away with Menehune
for flowers and fruit.

The conversation turned on the absent girl.
who had been treated by them both, since the
battle at the royal house, as one to whom they
owed the deepest gratitude and for whom they
felt the sincerest regard. Pu' Aloha, with a
tranquil and winning expression, had been re-
hearsing the story of their mutual affection,
when she suddenly looked into Hookama's
face and, in a tone of the most artless simplicity, placing her thin, white hand on his, exclaimed :—

" My dearest! I believe Kelea loves you.
She has never breathed such a thing to me, but
love's eyes you know are keen. Dear! Hasn't
she proved herself worthy of the best we can
give? Couldn't you love her, and keep on
loving me a little the best? "

This unexpected question, impossible under
conditions of a less primitive social code, was a
startling one to Hookama, but it was as natural
to the innocent maiden as if she had said to
her husband, " Which do you love best, your
mother or me? "

There was no hesitation in her voice and no
diffidence in her manner. She was a child of

nature, untrammelled by conventional ideas, knowing nothing of the law which makes one woman the complement of one man. She was not even swayed by what may be called the instinct of union between two alone, in the heart's holiest bonds. Filled with unselfish trust and love towards Hookama and Kelea ; trust in him as the noblest man and love for her as the dearest woman on the earth, she spoke from her inmost heart and really longed for an affirmative reply.

Turning on her a look of the fondest devotion, Hookama answered :—

" Do you mean, my beloved, that I might love Kelea in the way I love you? Are you not my only love-queen, my sweetest flower of love? Can any other be to me what you are? Will the *pua-aloha* yield its place as best of all the flowers in Hookama's garden? You cannot mean it," and he folded his bride to his breast with caresses which revealed to her that no other could possibly be to him what she was, no matter what relations he might sustain to another as a true friend, or in that still more intimate connection which the custom of his people allowed and indeed often made obligatory upon high chiefs.

Hookama's words not only disclosed to Pu' Aloha the depth of his affection for her, (and her heart beat faster as she realized that she was his only love), but they also taught her that no two women could possibly be equally beloved by one man, however noble and generous his nature.

Hookama knew too well Kelea's nature to think for a moment that she would consent to share his love with another, or be the second in his affections. She was more than ever a mystery to him. That she loved him with unchanging ardor was certain. Although a savage, he had already begun to comprehend how her first passion had become chastened and ennobled. Her robust beauty appealed to his admiration and he felt its captivating power. Her devotion to him and her willingness to give her life for him, he understood; but why she clung to the idea that he might give her the love which was centered wholly on Pu' Aloha he could not conceive.

Did she think that at some distant day, he would love them both alike? Was she under the delusion that by and by something might happen to transform him into a different being, so that he could satisfy her heart and still be true to his first love? He repudiated, as unworthy of the least consideration, the idea that possibly she hoped he would weary of the sweet child and turn to her for a more satisfying affection. He could give her marital rights, for all chiefs had as many wives as they could support, but he knew this was not now her desire.

The horrible thought was suggested to him by some evil spirit, that Kelea might hope to come nearer to him if Pu' Aloha should die; but this infernal suggestion was chased away instantly, as he remembered her profound love for his dear one and her unselfish conduct and tender care of her from the time she first knew and loved his " Flower."

It was all an enigma to him. He would let things go on. The gods (if there were gods), must straighten it all out. It was too much for him.

But Pu' Aloha's question and his answer brought one good result. It put out of Pu' Aloha's mind forever the thought of sharing with Kelea the heart of her husband. She saw how impossible a thing it was, and it made her more tender than ever towards her friend. She pitied her, and the affection she had felt before deepened into a yearning towards her, a desire to comfort her, which showed itself in most endearing forms.

As the weeks passed, Kelea was so completely wrapped about by the charmed atmosphere of Pu' Aloha's loving devotion that her thoughts centered more and more upon the lovely invalid. She was pleased with Hookama's courteous attentions, but she almost idolized the beloved friend, whose love satisfied her soul.

Hookama made every effort to cheer and encourage his bride with anticipations of bright joys to come when her health should return. He related to her and Kelea his adventures; he told of his experiences at the volcano and, in rather a jesting manner, of his challenge to Pele and the remarkable coincidence of the collapse of the lake of fire.

This incident made a deep impression upon Pu' Aloha and secretly she brooded over it, till at last, made more superstitious because of her physical condition, she felt a morbid dread of Pele's wrath. She remembered the legend in which vengeance was meted out by the enraged goddess to Kahawari, a chief who insulted her and whom she followed in a river of burning lava. Earthquakes and fiery phenomena were the visible evidences of her malignant spirit. It was the common belief that only by the sacrifice of human life could her anger ever be appeased.

The sweet maiden's spirits became more and more depressed and, after Hookama's persistent inquiries, she at last confessed the cause. "O, dearest! Pele must have a victim. She will follow thee till she is avenged. Her wrath will surely fall on thee or on one thou dost love. Either thou or I must be a sacrifice. Willingly give I my life for thine, if it will save thee." Hookama tried every expedient to rid her of the terrible idea. He laughed at her fears, and finding this of no avail showed her the impossibility of Pele's vengeance reaching from her far-off domain on Hawaii to Oahu.

In spite of all he could say or do, his lovely flower drooped, and, like one whom the priests "prayed to death," it seemed as if nothing would remove from her mind the fatal presentiment which possessed her. One afternoon the atmosphere suddenly became oppressive; clouds gathered and assumed a lurid hue; the little group on the cliff perceived a slight tremor of the earth; a more vibratory shock of earthquaking followed, such as Oahu sometimes felt when violent explosions were occurring at the volcano on Hawaii. Hookama was standing apart from the women, when, out of a cloud-burst, came a bolt of lightning, striking and detaching a mass of rock above him which nearly caught him as it hurtled with a loud crash into the ravine below.

"A warning from Pele!" cried the shrinking

girl, and she buried her face in her palms, shedding copious tears. Kelea threw her arms about her and supported her into the house. Hookama followed, wearing a look of weary hopelessness. Neither he nor Kelea could rally the affrighted girl from her despondent mood. She only moaned and whispered : " I am willing. O Pele ! take me as the offering and spare my beloved ! "

It was, however, soon perceived by the two watchers that Pu' Aloha's hold on life was becoming more and more feeble. Her smile was as sweet and her words as gentle as ever, but she smiled most sweetly when she said, " My time to sleep is coming soon," and after that she smiled and spoke less often. Even the fragrant wild flowers which she loved failed to receive from her more than a passing glance.

At last there came a day, when balmy odors were wafted in from the vines clambering about the house and beginning to put forth fresh blossoms. A magic light was upon the distant peaks. The clouds floated almost motionless in the sky and the air was so still that one could hear the breakers on the far-off shore.

Pu' Aloha was evidently sinking. Hookama hung over the form of his beloved as if it held a spirit from the land of dreams. Kelea's arms were about the fragile creature ; she raised

her a little from the couch that she might take
one more look at the sky and the hills. The
blind "mother" stood by, and Menehune was
leaning against the thatched wall; his heart was
learning the meaning of true love in death.

Here, surrounded by all the rank growths of
centuries of paganism, the Flower of Love
exhaled its sweetest fragrance in dying, as if
its roots had been nourished in another, more
congenial soil.

The perfect day was drawing to its close.
The twilight shadows crept along the landscape as the setting sun diffused its last, roseate
hue over the sky. A slight movement of Pu'
Aloha's lips suggested a desire on the part of
the dying girl to speak. Kelea drew her close
to her heart. With his hand, Hookama gently
smoothed her forehead, around which still
clustered the luxuriant locks. His sturdy
frame shook with irrepressible emotion.

Something like a prayer (to whom he knew
not) came to his mind. It was a wish for one
more word from his beloved, to interpret the
wistful look on the sweet face and the tender
meaning in her eyes.

The prayer was granted. As if the memory
of all the joyous days with those dearest to her
gave her a momentary strength, Pu' Aloha
took the hand that rested on her forehead and

placed it on the hand of Kelea who was supporting her. From the half-closed lips came whispers, inaudible save to the two for whom they were uttered—faint, feeble sounds—but articulate enough to reveal the last unselfish wish of the sweet Flower of Love:—

"My own—dearest—will of the gods." Then, turning an almost seraphic look upon Hookama and Kelea, her pure spirit took its flight, as she murmured:—

"Betrothed—Aloha!"

THE END.

AUTHOR'S NOTE.

WE introduce our readers to the Hawaiian savage at his best. The coarser side of him is only hinted at ; it would not be pleasant reading. Life was not wholly idyllic in pagan Hawaii during the latter part of the last century.

The Hawaiians were higher in the scale than most of the other Polynesians. Their chiefs as a class were far above the common natives. They seemed to belong to a superior race. Some of the chiefs—both men and women—were remarkable, if not for what civilization calls virtue, at least for virtue in the classic sense of valor. They were chivalrous in their fashion, and showed up well in some of the kindly as well as in warlike traits.

One of the characters mentioned in this story became a regenerating force in Christianizing her people, before she died at the age of sixty-four ; and one of this Queen Regent's consorts, the king of Kauai, is spoken of by a United States army chaplain as one of whom " he never knew a word or action unbecoming a prince." As for skepticism concerning the gods, the High Priest of Hawaii, introduced into this story, was the first to apply the torch to the temples, it is said from conviction, before the missionaries landed in 1820.

Poetry and a regard for beauty in nature, some say, are not found among savages. But the *meles* or legendary chants which the Hawaiian bards recited have both these elements. As an example, the Lament of Lo-lale, in the original legend of Kelea, of which only a fragment remains, is full of poetic pathos, and Nature is invoked to grieve with the royal husband over the loss of his wayward bride.

The idioms of the conversations in the romance are necessarily more English than Hawaiian, but the similes are caught from authentic Hawaiian sources. All the setting of the story,—customs, characteristics, battles, politics, kings, warriors,—is historic or traditional, from the best authorities. It must be added, that one exceptional character, *Pu' Aloha* (The Flower of Love), is presented by way of contrast, and exerts a refining influence impossible in wholly pagan life.

The illustrations are of localities in the story, more interesting than imaginary pictures of the actors in their various " situations."

The author is greatly indebted, for kindly revision and valuable suggestions, to the Hon. G. D. Gilman, Ex-Hawaiian Consul General at Boston, whose early and long residence in the islands constitutes him an authority.

NEWTON, MASS, 1900.